Mossy Creek's self-styled mystery maven, Peggy Caldwell, found my father's body in his barn, beside an overturned carriage.

"When he didn't answer, I got the strangest feeling," Peggy said. "Looked as if he'd been trying to worry the wheel off the axle and the jack had come loose just as the wheel fell right across his throat and cut it. I dropped onto my knees beside him and tried to move that blasted wheel, but I couldn't budge it."

"I understand," I said, voice breaking.

"Then I saw I was kneeling in a pool of blood still seeping into the dirt floor from under his head."

I nearly collapsed. Peggy Caldwell had now gone to the far side of 'Way Too Much Information.' Trying to steady my dizzy brain, I went to a very polite mental tearoom and found myself thinking, bizarrely, *Poor woman. Must have been terrible for her.*

Peggy looked me straight in the eyes. "That's when I knew he'd been murdered."

The Cart Before the Corpse

A Merry Abbott Carriage-Driving Mystery

by

Carolyn McSparren

BelleBooks, Inc.

BelleBooks
PO BOX 30921
Memphis, TN 38130
ISBN: 978-0-9841258-3-8

We at BelleBooks enjoy hearing from readers. You can contact us at the address above or at BelleBooks@BelleBooks.com

Visit our websites – www.BelleBooks.com and www.BellBridgeBooks.com.

10 9 8 7 6 5 4 3 2

Cover design: Debra Dixon
Interior design: Hank Smith
Photo credits: Skeleton:© Chris Harvey - Fotolia.com
                  Hat: © Brian Griffith
                  Gloves/cane: © James Steidl - Fotolia.com
                  Carriage: © Galló Gusztáv @ iStockphoto.com

:Lr:01:

Chapter 1

Sunday Afternoon, Chattanooga, Tennessee
Merry

I should learn to count chickens instead of eggs.

I'd already packed my computer and printer in my truck and checked out of my motel. The scores were posted on all the driving classes except the cross-country marathon. As show manager, I'd passed out ribbons and trophies. Once the marathon ended and the scores were tallied, I could drive away from the horseshow grounds with a happy grin and a fat check.

That's when I heard the screams. "Runaway!" I turned and raced across the field toward the start of the marathon course. When the screams continued, I knew this was more than a loose trace.

Please God some nervous horse had yanked his lead line from his groom and wandered off to graze, or decided he didn't feel like being harnessed to his carriage today and trotted away dragging his reins and harness behind him.

Just so long as he wasn't also dragging a carriage.

A runaway horse harnessed to a driverless carriage is a four-legged missile with no guidance system.

I was still fifty yards from the start of the marathon course when I saw Jethro, Pete and Tully Hull's Morgan stallion, kick out with both hind feet and connect with the steel dashboard of their heavy marathon cart with a God-awful clang. Terrified, Jethro reared straight up in his traces and tossed both Pete and Tully off the carriage and into the dirt.

"He's going over backwards!" somebody screamed.

Amy Hull, Pete and Tully's thirteen-year-old daughter, clung to the back of the carriage. Her normal job was as counterbalance around fast turns. Now, she was trying to keep both Jethro and the carriage from landing on top of her.

"Jump and roll, Amy!" I shouted. "Get out of the way!"

She jumped, landed on her feet and rolled away from the carriage. With less weight to overbalance him, Jethro came down solidly on all fours, Thank God.

But then he took off at a dead run across the field, with the carriage careening wildly after him.

Still screaming warnings, some people ran to help the Hulls. Competitors stamped on their carriage brakes and reined their own horses in hard to keep the course from erupting into a re-run of the chariot race in *Ben Hur*. Poor Jethro was terrified. With the eighteen-foot reins flying behind him, the carriage had become his personal banshee. He had to escape it if it killed him.

It might. As well some of the rest of us, horses, competitors, trainers and spectators alike, if we didn't stop him. And nobody else was trying. Everybody not rushing to help the Hulls dove out of the way, cowered behind trucks and horse vans, huddled in the tents with the food and the vendors and prayed that Jethro wouldn't decide to charge them.

Jethro weighed three quarters of a ton. The steel marathon carriage weighed only slightly less. The horse had become a runaway eighteen-wheeler with four legs and a terrified brain.

He craved sanctuary. He was desperate to find his people so they could get the monster off his tail. He didn't know he'd left them behind in the dirt. Somehow I had to focus his attention on *me*, let him know that one human being wanted to save him from the monster that chased him.

He swerved past a four-wheeled spider phaeton pulled by a huge black Friesian gelding. Friesians were originally bred to carry Lancelot in full knightly armor, so they're graceful but massive. The axles passed one another with barely room for a single piece of blotting paper between them. Anne Crawford, on the Friesian's reins, stood up and screamed. Her Queen Mary hat with its pheasant tail and orange tulle flew off her head and landed on the Friesian's broad rump. The Friesian kicked at it.

The hat fell in the dirt and the Friesian relaxed, thank the Lord.

Jethro spun through a ninety-degree corner around the stables. The carriage rocked dangerously but righted itself. Then he headed straight for the parking area where over forty trailers and trucks were closely aligned in rows.

I ran to cut Jethro off, waved my arms and yelled to get his attention in hopes he'd be so startled he'd pull up or swerve away before he reached the narrow lanes between the vehicles.

He knew how wide *his* body was, and that he could fit between the trailers and trucks. He didn't have a clue how wide the carriage behind him was. If it stuck hard, he'd be yanked up on a dime. The steel carriage might disintegrate.

Jethro could break his neck. Carriages are replaceable. Jethro was not.

Jethro galloped straight at me. Behind him the carriage caromed from side to side and clanged as it side-swiped trailers and trucks like the steel ball in a pinball machine.

At the last minute, I dove between a silver *dually* and a bright red Ford Two-Fifty truck as Jethro thundered by, still pursued by his invisible banshee. If he even noticed me, he darned well didn't care. I wasn't one of *his* people. He headed for the access road, the only paved road on the farm the road that cars and trucks drove on—cars and trucks that might collide head-on with Jethro.

I sprinted across the field in front of the stable. If I could get ahead of him . . . He came out from between the final pair of horse trailers and swerved onto the road as I reached it.

Without warning, his aluminum shoes slipped on the paving, and all four feet flew out from under him. He crashed onto his side and tipped the carriage. His sharp hooves flailed the air.

I knew he'd start struggling to his feet in about ten seconds. I did the only thing I could do. I yanked off my jacket, tossed it over his head, sat on his neck and leaned both hands on his shoulder.

The minute I covered his eyes and he felt my weight, Jethro relaxed. He was drenched with sweat, his sides heaved, and every muscle trembled, but in his mind the banshee wasn't after him any longer, although I could still hear the wheels spinning behind him. I didn't dare turn to look.

"Somebody undo the girth! Unhook the tugs and the traces!" I shouted over my shoulder. "Get this carriage off him!" He shivered and struggled, but quieted when I spoke to him gently and caressed his sweaty neck.

"You're okay, sweetie," I whispered. I could recite nursery rhymes so long as my voice stayed calm and my hands caressed his neck. He trusted that I could free him of the banshee. Behind me, I heard people shouting, calling for knives to cut the harness free. Careful to keep his eyes covered, I rocked Jethro up on his shoulder just far enough to allow the steel shaft under him to be pulled free, then pressed his head down once more onto the pavement. A minute later, both shafts slid backward away from the horse. I couldn't take my eyes off him, but I could hear people grunting as they shifted the weight of the carriage. I kept stroking and talking.

After what seemed like an eternity I felt a hand on my shoulder. "Merry, we've got the carriage up and the harness free. Time to get him up." My heart lurched. So long as Jethro stayed quiet under me, so long as he didn't scramble to his feet and try to walk, we didn't have to assess his injuries.

I didn't want to know. If he'd broken a leg . . .

The first thing you learn around horses is how fragile they are in mind and body. You protect them and care for them as well as you can. Sometimes that's not enough, but it's the job we sign on for. They can't take care of themselves. I'd tried to help Jethro, but I had no idea whether I'd been successful.

"Merry, I'm going to haul you back away from him on your butt. Don't want you catching a hoof in the head when he tries to stand." I felt strong hands under my armpits. I knew the voice. Jack, the Johnsons' groom. Probably strong enough to lift *Jethro* if he had to. He swung me away and to my feet as though I weighed about as much as a little Jack Russell Terrier, then dropped a heavy brown arm across my shoulders and turned me against his chest. Behind me I heard Jethro's hooves scrabbling. "He's up, Merry. You can look."

I felt Jethro's warm breath against my neck as I faced him and leaned my shoulder against his. "Please be okay," I whispered. Jack hooked a hand on his bridle, but Jethro was too worn out to go anywhere. The stallion took a tentative step, snorted once to frighten any residue of banshee away, then took two more steps. He walked 'dead sound,' meaning without injury, in civilian terms. He was bleeding from a couple of shallow cuts on his shoulder, probably from collisions with the fenders of trailers. He'd scraped himself a bit from the asphalt on the road, but the damage was minor. A few stitches, a little Betadine antiseptic, and he'd be fine. Amazing that he hadn't ripped a leg tendon on the fender of a truck or gashed himself to the bone on a trailer door.

"Merry, honey," Jack said, "Idn't that your good leather jacket?"

I looked down. It was the only thing I'd had to toss over Jethro's head. He now stood with his front hooves squarely in the middle of four hundred bucks worth of tan suede.

"It's okay," I said and laid my cheek against Jethro's dark brown neck. "What on earth happened?"

Jack pointed toward the railroad tracks that ran along the far side of the fence by the road. "You know how you told 'em not to set the first leg of the marathon so close to the train track?"

I nodded. "But thirty or forty trains have rattled by in the last two days. The horses couldn't have cared less. The show committee said I was crazy to worry."

"Uh-huh," Jack continued. I watched his enormous hands flex into fists. "The dumbass engineer on that last freight must-a decided it'd be cute to blow his whistle as long and loud as he could just when he got even with Jethro. Shoot, like to scared *me* half to death. No wonder Jethro spooked. If I ever find out that devil's name . . . "

Looking at Jack's face, I prayed for the engineer's sake that Jack never would find out his name. Jack was the kindest, gentlest man I knew until you messed with his horses. Then it was a thermonuclear explosion. I once saw him pick up an incompetent fill-in farrier at a horse show up by the scruff of his neck and toss him halfway down the barn aisle. The farrier had driven a nail straight into the quick of a mare's hoof, then went right on shoeing her after she thrashed and squealed. Frankly, I thought Jack had been extremely forbearing. I'd probably have cracked the man over the head with his hammer.

"Are the Hulls okay?" I asked. I'd been so busy worrying about Jethro, I hadn't given his drivers a thought.

"Tully's got a broken wrist and Amy's got a scraped chin. Other than maybe fifty thousand dollars worth of damage to vehicles and trailers, everybody's just fine, including Jethro. Thanks to you," Jack said.

Jethro still stood in the middle of my jacket, but there wasn't much point in moving him now. I doubted Pete Hull's insurance would include a new one. "I haven't run that hard since I was in high school." I leaned over and put my hands on my knees to steady my breathing. I'm well past thirty, although

I don't generally let on just *how* well. I do have a daughter out of college, however, and though I'm in good shape, jogging in the park hadn't prepared me for running flat-out over a rutted hay field. It's a miracle I didn't trip, fall flat on my face and break my ankle. "Thank the Lord I didn't have to run any farther. Like to have killed me. Pure luck I caught him."

"And guts," Jack said and shook his head. "The insurance companies are going to have a field day on this one."

"Hey, girl, you're a hero!" Pete Hull trotted up and smacked me on the shoulder.

"Just lucky, Pete. Y'all okay?"

"Gonna be. I told those idiots on the show committee we were asking for trouble to run the first leg of the marathon that close to the railroad track."

Still, it was easier to blame me, only a hired hand, after all, as the show manager, than to blame the show committee or the paying customers. Somehow I'd wind up carrying the can for the accident. Although it's a rule that drivers wear hard hats during the marathon, a number of the old guard still grumbled.

They all refused to wear hard hats during the other classes, although the rules say that no one can ever be penalized for choosing to wear one. The ladies preferred their summer straw hats festooned with feathers and ribbons. The men wanted their top hats and bowlers. Elegant, but those wouldn't protect their skulls in case of a runaway like Jethro's. The show committee would be after me to talk and talk and talk about whose fault Jethro's escapade was. If I hadn't needed my check, I would have run for my truck and ducked them. But I needed the money, even if I didn't get the accompanying smile and pat on the back for a job well done.

"Will you go with me to see the head of the show committee?" I asked Pete.

Before he could answer, my cell phone rang. I dragged it out of the pocket of my jeans and answered it, grateful for the interruption.

"Ms Abbott? Merideth Lackland Abbott?" an unfamiliar voice said. Male, heavy southern accent.

"Yes?"

"No easy way to say this, Mrs. Abbott. I'm afraid your father has met with an accident."

I grabbed Jack's arm. "Hiram? What happened? Is he all right?"

"Um, I'm sorry, but I'm afraid he's dead."

The next thing I knew I was sitting on the ground while Jack shoved my head down between my knees. That was when I threw up.

Chapter 2

Sunday Afternoon
Merry

Pete Hull took the cell phone out of my hand and held it to his ear. "Give her a minute. Who is speaking, please?" I looked up at him as he listened, and I saw his face go slack. "Hiram? He's dead?" The buzz started at once among the people who were gathered around us. "How? . . . right." He listened some more, then handed the phone back to me. "Merry, honey, I'm so sorry."

I took the phone and stared at it as though it was a copperhead. Finally I put it to my ear. "This is Merideth Abbott again. Who did you say you were?" Must be a joke. Men like Hiram Lackland didn't just up and die.

"This is Sheriff Campbell of Bigelow County, Georgia."

"Oh, God, did he have an automobile accident? Was anybody else hurt?" Hiram had sworn he'd been sober for ten years, but Hiram had always been a good liar.

I stuck my finger in my ear to try to cut the noise around me and turned away from the crowd. I felt like an idiot still sitting on the grass, but I wasn't certain I could get up on my own. My father had been pushing seventy, but these days, that's practically middle-aged. There had to be some mistake. Hiram Lackland was indestructible. Lord knows he'd tried to kill himself often enough. He was like Jethro. He left a path of destruction behind him, but always walked away sound.

"No, ma'am. Not an automobile accident."

"Don't tell me he turned over a carriage. He wasn't supposed to be driving alone."

"I'm afraid it was a freak accident. Look, Ms Abbott, it's kind of complicated to discuss over the phone. Where are you, exactly?"

Everyone except Pete had backed away. Jack was walking Jethro back to the barn. The others, I assumed, wanted to give me some privacy. Actually, I guess they really wanted to gossip about the whole Jethro incident. I reached up a hand so that Pete could pull me up. "I'm sitting on the ground in a pasture about fifty miles north of Chattanooga."

"You're not that far from Bigelow. We're in north Georgia."

"He emailed he was living in some little town called something-or-other Creek. What was he doing in Bigelow?"

"Um, Bigelow's the county seat. That's where the morgue is."

The morgue. That image hit me hard. Of course that's where they'd take him. He wouldn't care, but I did. I hunched my shoulders and said, "I can get on the road right now. How long is the drive to Bigelow?"

"Probably three hours or so. But, ma'am, he was living in Mossy Creek. That's where his place was."

"*Mossy* Creek. Now I remember. He said he had a studio apartment there in some woman's house."

"Yeah. Peggy Caldwell. She's the one who found him."

"*Found* him?

"She said you could stay with her as long as you need to. I'll call her and tell her to expect you tonight. You're going to be pretty worn out by the time you get here. It's not an easy drive. Not much Interstate. You got somebody with you? May not be a good idea you driving all this way alone right now."

"I'll be fine. I'm used to long-distance driving. But shouldn't I come to Bigelow instead? Do I have to identify—I mean . . . "

"No, ma'am. Mrs. Caldwell already identified him. No reason you should have to go through that. Anyway, it's Sunday afternoon. Took us a while to track you down."

"I'm a horse show manager. I travel." I made scribbling motions with my hand. Pete scrounged a credit card receipt and pen out of his pockets.

"Ms. Abbott, nothin's going to change between now and tomorrow morning. You get you a good night's sleep and come in late morning. Bigelow's only about twenty minutes from Mossy Creek. We need to talk, and there's some paperwork we got to finish. And don't you worry. Mrs. Caldwell knows everybody. She can help you make whatever arrangements you need. I'll have somebody call her to tell her you'll be there this evening."

He gave me the number of the sheriff's department, and his

private cell phone, which I thought was nice of him. Then he gave me Hiram's landlady's number and the address of Hiram's apartment in Mossy Creek, although Hiram had included it in his last email to me.

By the time I hung up, I felt utterly calm. That's the way I always handle disaster. It's what makes me a good show manager. After I solve the problem and calm everybody else down, that's when I go to pieces.

Even I couldn't solve this.

I started when I realized Pete still stood by with a look of concern on his face. "Oh, Pete, shouldn't you be with Tully and Amy?"

"They're in the EMT trailer getting patched up. Tully shooed me off to check on Jethro and you. I'm headed her way now. But Merry. Hiram. Dead? Is Hiram really dead?"

"That's what the man said. Some kind of accident, but he didn't go into details."

"I can't believe it. I thought he'd outlive us all." He shook his head. "Irascible old bastard. Sorry, Merry."

I started to giggle, then clapped my hand over my mouth. If I started, I'd have hysterics. Once my mouth was shut, I felt tears ooze down my cheeks. "Good epitaph. He would have liked it." I squeezed Pete's shoulder. He winced. "Oh, I'm sorry."

"Bruises on my bruises. Probably won't be able to get out of bed in the morning. This whole thing is going to cost my insurance company a bundle." He took my arm and walked with me up toward the parking area. "I am seriously considering putting out a hit on the engineer runnin' that train. Damn fool."

Pete was rich and powerful enough to make life extremely unpleasant for the man. "Don't you kill him, and whatever you do, don't tell Jack who he is or where to find him or he'll do the killin' for you. Tully would be angry if either one of you went to jail for manslaughter."

"Justifiable homicide." We stopped by my truck. "I'd hug you, but I'd probably scream in pain. You leaving now?"

"The show committee's bound to want to talk to me, but I can't deal with them right now."

"Don't you worry, I'll handle the show committee," Pete said. His face looked grim. He ran a multi-million dollar company. The show committee should be a piece of cake for him.

"And they owe me a check."

"You got a deposit slip in your purse? Give it to me. I'll pick up your check and deposit it tomorrow morning for you."

"Thanks Pete." I dug a deposit slip out of the satchel I use as a handbag and gave it to him. "I've already checked out of my motel. If they go on with the marathon, the show president can give out the awards anyway, so I was good to go right after the marathon until this happened."

"You get on the road. I'll do the explaining. "

I hesitated, half in and half out of the truck. "Pete, I didn't set that course close to the railroad track."

"Shoot, I know that. I won't let 'em use you as a scapegoat."

"If I leave now, it'll look like I'm running away," I said.

"Merry, your daddy just died! Git."

Jack walked up behind Pete. "Tully's hollering for you, Pete."

Pete nodded, patted my arm and limped toward the van the EMTs were using for their first aid station.

Jack stood at the door of my truck, waited for me to climb in and shut the door with a resounding smack. Mercifully, I had parked on the far side and away from Jethro's path of destruction, so my truck hadn't sustained even a *fresh* dent—at least. "Hiram was a fine horseman and a great trainer, Merry," Jack said. "Email us and let us know what's going on. If you have a memorial service, I know some of us would like to come."

"Jack, it's to hell and gone in No-where, Georgia, but I'll let you know."

I could see him in my rear view mirror as I pulled out onto the road and turned toward the big wrought iron entrance gates of The Meadows, the farm that had hosted the show. As I drove over the railroad tracks to the road, I considered turning around. I did not want to face three hours of solitary driving with nothing to think about except the father I would never see again.

I made it as far as a Wal-Mart parking lot before I pulled over, stopped, put my head down on the steering wheel, and bawled. We were so close to reaching some sort of meeting of minds, my father and I. Now we'd never have the chance.

Eventually I gulped myself into silence. Then I got angry. "How dare you die on me, Hiram Lackland? I loved you. Now I can't tell you." I smacked the steering wheel so hard I yelped, took a deep breath and calmed down.

What was I supposed to do now? Any death involves protocols and rituals, Southern deaths more than most. Even in retirement Hiram Lackland was a large fish in the small pond of international carriage driving. A great many people would have to be notified.

I couldn't face all that this afternoon. Still, a couple of people had to know right now. I dialed my cell phone and listened to it ring. Just as I was about to hang up—this was not the sort of thing one left on voice mail—it was answered.

"Hello?" She sounded breathless. She'd probably been out in the garden. She usually was in the spring.

"Mom?"

"Merry? What's wrong? Oh, Lordy, is it Allie?"

I hadn't heard the emotion in my voice, but she had and she'd jumped right to worrying about her granddaughter. "She's fine."

"You?"

"Not so good. Mom, Hiram's dead."

She caught her breath. "Hiram? What on earth? How? When?" I heard the creak of a wooden chair in the background as she sat down.

I choked back more tears. My mother was five hundred miles away in St. Louis. No sense in upsetting her more by letting her hear how upset *I* was.

"I always said one of these days he'd keel over dead with a heart attack," she said.

"It was an accident. I don't know the details. The sheriff of that place where he bought his new farm finally tracked me down at a show this afternoon."

"Where are you?"

I told her and reiterated everything the Bigelow County sheriff had said to me. "The crazy thing is that we'd been emailing and talking on the phone lately. Dad sounded happy. Wanted me to see his new place, spend some time. I think he had a crazy idea I might come work with him."

"Like that would have worked," my mother said.

"I was maybe considering driving down. I don't have another job for a couple of weeks. And now this. I can't believe it."

My mother's voice sounded quiet and a bit distant suddenly. "He'd been emailing me too. You know your father would never apologize, but he acted as though he wanted to make things right between us."

"Mom . . . "

"I've long since forgiven him for what he did to me. I'm not so certain I could let him off the hook for what he did to *you*."

"Don't forget Allie."

"She barely knows him. She thinks of Steve as her grandfather, not her step-grandfather. Have you called her?"

I shook my head, although my mother couldn't see the gesture. "I called you first. I figured you'd know what I'm supposed to do. You've always been the one to handle the deaths in the family."

"Each generation of women eventually hands over the death reins to the next, Merry."

"But when Gram and Granddad and Aunt Phil died, they had plenty of friends within shouting distance. You had help."

"Your father was kind of famous in a small way. . ."

"And lived on a new farm surrounded by strangers in a village in the boondocks of North Georgia. He didn't have anybody else. I am it."

My mother instantly switched to head-of-the-family mode. "Unless he changed his will, which I doubt since I had the devil's own time getting him to make one at the time of the divorce, you are his sole heir and executrix of his estate. Since he died in an accident, there will no doubt be a delay in releasing the body. You know we always like to have the funeral within three days of the death, impossible in this case. I would suggest a memorial service as soon as possible after you know what's what. Then either cremation or a graveside service at some later date. Do you have enough money?"

"For the moment. I'm due to start at The Meadows in a month breaking two-year-olds for Fergus Williams, and I'm running a carriage show in Southern Pines next month." If they still wanted me after today's debacle.

"I doubt he had much capital left after buying the new place and doing all that work to it, but he did have some life insurance, assuming he hadn't let it lapse or borrowed against it. That should come to you. It won't be much, but it should pay for the funeral and tide you over."

"Mom . . . " I hesitated, but I had to ask the question I'd never asked. "Do you ever regret . . . "

"Divorcing him? Not for a single minute, even if I'd never met Steve, nor built a stable life for us. They say first love never dies, but he made our lives hell, Merry. I had to get us away before he destroyed us." I could hear her breathing. "You may have reporters calling, although he's been out of the international limelight for some time. He will no doubt rate an obituary in *The Whip* and *Driving Digest*. Maybe a couple of other horse magazines. You know the sort of thing 'former driving champion dies, etc., etc.' Say nothing personal. Don't give them Allie's address or telephone number, and whatever you do, don't sic them onto Vic. God only knows what your ex would say to them."

"Mostly something along the line of 'that bastard wrecked my marriage'. Assuming he's sober enough to be coherent."

"We Lackland women don't have good luck with men, do we, darling? At least not the first time."

"No second time for me." As always after a conversation with my mother, I felt calmer and surer of myself. We talked some more, but nothing substantive, and finally broke the connection. I tried my daughter Allie's cell phone in New York, but on a beautiful April Sunday afternoon, I knew there was little chance I could get her. I left a message for her to call me, but didn't tell her why. She might get around to it, or she might blow me off.

I went into Wal-Mart for a couple of six packs of diet soda, a bag of ice and a couple of packets of peanut butter crackers, filled the ice chest, and got on the road.

My mother was only partly right about my father almost killing us.

Actually, *I* was the reason my mother walked with a cane.

Chapter 3

Sunday evening
Merry

By the time I found Mossy Creek, I'd gotten lost on hilly back roads twice and asked where to locate Mossy Creek at three convenience stores.

Since I did not have directions to my father's apartment, I called this Peggy Caldwell from my cell phone to find how to get there once I finally found Mossy Creek.

It was dusk before I pulled into the driveway at her address and simply sat. As long as I didn't get out, meet the woman, talk to her about Hiram, I could almost pretend Hiram was alive somewhere and would come home to his new apartment.

I could see why he'd liked the town and Caldwell's place, although he generally didn't pay all that much attention to where he lived. He seemed as happy sleeping on hay bales in a cold barn waiting for a mare to foal as he did in a state bedroom in some baron's castle in Bavaria. That's one trait he passed down to me. My daughter Allie, who is settling into her first apartment in New York with three other girls, haunts flea markets, IKEA, and Crate and Barrel. Once she makes her first million—any day now at the rate she's going—she'll switch to Mario Buatta and move into the Dakota.

Since I never knew how long we'd be staying in any one location when I was growing up, I learned never to invest my heart in making friends I might have to leave tomorrow, or my money in my surroundings and possessions. Good thing, since Vic took most of what we owned in the divorce. He might have taken Allie as well, except that she was already a junior at the University of Kentucky and interning at Goldman Sachs in the summers.

Who needed human friends when I had the horses? Although a horse may try to kill you occasionally, it's almost never out of meanness, and he won't betray you. No matter how miserable my life has been from time to time, I could always count on a gentle nuzzle from a velvet nose to lift my spirits.

Maybe I wouldn't feel so lost and miserable if there had been a handy horse to love on.

I was glad Hiram had found a place to call home. Looking out the window of the truck I could see that the house was a 1930s Tudor, but well maintained.

Hiram's landlady apparently liked to garden. Masses of azaleas in different shades ranging from coral to pale pink budded in her front yard, and the driveway dropped off sharply in back of the house to what looked like several acres of lawn with big trees and lush plantings.

Hiram said his apartment had been created on the lower level out of part of the garage. He could walk out the French doors from his small living room onto a patio under the main house's deck and into the back yard. He loved spring, and would have enjoyed the quickening life he saw from his patio.

He'd actually sounded enthusiastic about the place, which surprised me. The apartment came furnished, which didn't surprise me one bit. Most of the guest houses and above-the-stable trainer's apartments he'd lived in came furnished. I doubted he owned a stick of furniture.

Hiram did accumulate harness, tack, carriages, horse blankets and horse coolers, a million items he needed to look after his four-footed charges. Since I didn't see either a big diesel truck or a humongous horse trailer, I assumed both were parked at his new farm. His personal possessions probably fit into a couple of suitcases and maybe a garbage bag or two.

Personal possessions I'd be forced to go through. God, how I dreaded that. I doubted he kept old love letters from his lady friends on the carriage circuit, but if he had, I didn't want to read them.

I seldom managed shows in Hiram's part of the country or at the high levels at which he competed. Even on the few occasions I did, I generally managed to avoid coming face-to-face with him.

Maybe he thought he deserved the cold shoulder I gave him. Judging from his emails, after he retired and had time to look back, he finally began to *get* how badly he'd hurt Mother and me. And I had grown up enough to cut him some slack. He had never planned to hurt us, after all.

He always considered us a parallel universe. What he did in

his professional and personal life away from us shouldn't affect us. When he told my mother, "Honey, none of those women has anything to do with you and Merry," he believed himself. When he didn't come home on my birthday after he'd promised he would, he couldn't understand why I was upset. After all, he was *driving*.

I ran into his current and former mistresses at shows regularly. I was studiously polite, whatever turmoil I felt inside. After all, he was no longer married to my mother, so he wasn't committing adultery, although in some cases *they* were. I simply didn't want to know more about his personal life than I already knew. I think most kids feel that way about their parents. I know Allie feels that way about me. I'd no more discuss a new boyfriend (assuming I had one) with her than I'd fly to the moon. Even at his age Hiram was still a handsome man and a charmer. No doubt he'd charmed his landlady. I sincerely hoped he'd found someone he cared about who cared about him. She had found his body. Where? This apartment? Out at his new farm?

I don't know how long I had been sucking back the tears in her driveway when the front door of the house opened and light spilled out.

"Ms Abbott?" A female voice called. Strong. Not an old lady quaver.

I took a deep breath and climbed out of the truck. "Ms. Caldwell?" I went to her and offered my hand. "People call me Merry. Big joke."

"Why?"

"I'm not."

Her grip was firm. She was slim, nearly as tall as my five-ten and straight as a stick. No sign of a dowager's hump. "Please come in. If I leave the door open for long the cats get curious and wander outside. If they manage to make the front porch they have hysterics trying to get back in. I'll take you downstairs to Hiram's apartment in a little while. I assume you're hungry. Come in and have a drink and a sandwich. And please call me Peggy."

I had the feeling I'd be expected to eat even if I'd stopped at a fast food joint twenty minutes earlier and scarfed up double cheeseburgers, and that she wanted to talk. So did I, but not necessarily tonight. My stomach rumbled. I *was* hungry. My peanut butter crackers had worn off a while back.

I followed her into an entrance foyer. Not much furniture, but the Oriental rug on the floor looked like a valuable antique. So did the one that covered the floor of the living room, the one I could glimpse in the dining room, and finally, the one in what I assumed was the library, since every wall held floor-to-ceiling bookcases stuffed with books. Even at a glance I could tell the books weren't fancy by-the-yard editions, but well-worn paperbacks and hard covers. I could see the brightly colored spines of mysteries and detective stories. One of the larger books read *Murderers, Inc.*

"Hope you don't mind eating in the kitchen," she said. "I don't use the dining room except at Thanksgiving and Christmas."

I felt something warm around my feet and looked down to see a gigantic tabby cat the color of butter, oozing figure eights around my ankles. When I reached down to scratch his head, he rolled over on his back and offered a rotund belly. As I raised my head, I saw a big gray tabby on top of a leather recliner by the fireplace, while a small black cat crouched on the windowsill and a gray cat sat neatly curled on a cushion on the hearth. They all watched me intently. I wondered how many others were lurking out of sight.

"Just the four," Peggy said.

I was startled.

"I'm not reading your mind. People always wonder."

"I like cats."

"I'm glad. They own the place and generously allow me to have company if it's willing to pet them. The one making amorous overtures to your paddock boots is Sherlock. He's dumb but sweet. The old guy on the chair is Dashiell. He runs the joint. That's Marple on the windowsill and Watson on the hearth."

"Do they actually detect?"

"You'd be surprised. Now, what would you like to drink? Beer? Wine? Bourbon?"

"Actually, I'd prefer iced tea."

"Sweet or unsweet?"

"Unsweet with lemon and artificial sweetener if you have it.

These hips do not require sugar to spread."

"Woman after my own heart. Sit."

The kitchen cabinets had been redone at some time, but retained a dark patina. The appliances, however, were brand new steel jobs.

In less than five minutes we were drinking iced tea and eating thick home cured ham and extra sharp cheddar sandwiches while the cats regarded us solemnly from the archway into the library.

"I'm so sorry about Hiram. He's only been living here eight months, but I was fond of him," she said.

"I'm sure he was fond of you too. When that sheriff finally got hold of me, he said he'd tell me the details tomorrow when I see him, but he did say you'd found him and that it was a freak accident."

She set her iced tea glass down so fast it splashed on the butcher-block table. "That man is an idiot. I *found* him all right. But it was no accident, freak or otherwise. I'm afraid, my dear, your father was murdered, and very nastily, too."

Chapter 4

Sunday evening
Merry

Ooookay. People I know don't get murdered. Certainly not my father. He could drive anybody up the wall, but not to the extent that they'd kill him.

"I'm not crazy," Peggy Caldwell said. "I do not have Alzheimer's. I saw what I saw and know what I know. Somebody killed your father, Merry. The sheriff doesn't want to deal with it because this county is supposed to be an All-American, crime-free, real-life Mayberry, at least in the press releases and the political speeches. That's the way the governor likes it. Ham Bigelow. From one of this county's founding families. Born and raised in the county seat. He still keeps a home in Bigelow, and a lot of his relatives live there."

"My father was killed in a break-in? Burglary gone bad?" That, at least, was feasible.

"Not at all. Not in the way you mean."

"An addict looking for something to sell?"

As a horse show manager and horse trainer I'm not unfamiliar with drugs. In some rural communities, cooking shake-and-bake crystal meth is easier, cheaper, and nets more profit than moonshine. Of course, it's also a whole bunch more dangerous to cook, but I guess if you're hooked on the stuff and can't get an honest job, you'll risk it.

There's also cocaine, marijuana, and crystal meth in the horse show world. The drug of choice generally follows the socio-economic level of the user. The rich and their progeny use cocaine and smoke pot. The grooms and stable hands tend toward crack and crystal meth. Of course the real drug of choice, at least in the south, is good ole demon bourbon.

"I doubt even a hard-core addict would have thought to find drugs in Hiram's barn," Peggy said.

"So . . . his . . . body wasn't in his apartment downstairs?" It stabbed me in the gut to say it that way.

"I found him on the floor of his workshop out at the farm."

"He must have had a heart attack or a stroke."

She took a deep breath. "You're too tired to deal with what I'm trying to tell you, tonight. I'll show you downstairs and let you get some sleep."

"I'm not going to sleep until I know what this is about. Please, just tell me all of it and get it over with."

"If you're sure." She took another deep breath. "I have to tell you a little about the farm so you'll understand why I went out there. When you drive up to Hiram's place, you'll see that the gravel road up from the main road twists around enough hairpins to put up pin curls on a giantess. When it's mucky, even a careful driver can slide off the hillside and roll up in a ball at the bottom of the hollow. Friday night we had a frog-strangler of a storm with tornado and flash flood watches. Bad winds and rain all night long."

"Hiram said he owns . . . owned . . . " I hesitated, my throat working.

"It's all right to speak of him in any tense that makes you comfortable," Peggy said gently.

"He said he had some woods and thirty acres of flat pasture, with room for a driven dressage arena that's eighty meters by forty."

"That's right. I don't know whether you've ever been to Cade's Cove, up in the Smokey Mountains of Tennessee, but Hiram's farm was a smaller version. You wind up about three quarters of a mile of twisty gravel road clinging to the side of the hill, then suddenly at the top it opens up into a small plateau. Open pasture with woods around the edges. Like a giant hand squashed it down. The people who owned it before raised cattle and sheep."

I nodded.

"I wasn't surprised when Hiram didn't come home Friday night. Nobody in his right mind would drive down that road in the dark in a driving rainstorm. I assumed he'd bedded down in his workshop or the stable. I didn't worry when I couldn't get him on his cell either. Reception's iffy up there in bad weather. But after the rain cleared out on Saturday morning, I expected him home for breakfast, even if he still couldn't call me. We were planning to drive to Bigelow to hit some estate sales and antique shops. When he didn't come by ten, I got worried and drove up there. When you're our age, you learn to check on your friends when you don't hear from them regularly."

She sniffed and turned her head away. Interesting that she'd said she was expecting him 'home.' My father had a way with women. I wondered if he'd had his way with Peggy. "I found him in his workshop," she repeated.

Chapter 5

Sunday evening
Merry

"When Hiram first bought the place, the only structures still standing were a decrepit old house trailer not fit to live in, sitting across the pasture from the main road, and a big old barn that needed cleaning out, shoring up, and some paint, but was still structurally sound." Peggy lifted her shoulders. "We build stout barns in this part of the world."

"He turned it into his stable?"

Peggy shook her head. "Actually, as soon as possible he built a nice new stable behind it, and fixed up that old barn to use for storage and a workshop for the carriages."

I nodded. Hiram could fix anything on a carriage or harness that rusted or broke or rotted, and loved doing it. Most fathers teach their children to hunt or fish. Mine taught me to hammer brass tacks into leather upholstery. I felt my eyes tear and coughed, but Peggy saw what was happening and laid her hand over mine.

"Are you sure you wouldn't rather do this tomorrow morning?"

I shook my head. "I need to know."

Peggy nodded. "As long as you're certain. You must be completely worn out."

"Better worn out than worried sick."

"Very well. The old barn is impossible to light properly, but Hiram put in a bank of fluorescents over his work bench against the right wall and suspended another bunch of fluorescents down the center over the area he used to work on the carriages. He always had two or three in various states of repair, and whatever he was working on at the time in the center where he could see what he was doing."

I wanted to scream, *Get on with it!*

"He had one of those great big fancy carriages under the lights you know, the kind they use in downtown carriage rides in Atlanta or to carry the bride and groom after the ceremony?"

I nodded. "A *vis-à-vis*."

"That's it! That's what Hiram called it. Because the people sit face to face. "

Come on, lady.

"It was leaning over on its left side, like a car that falls off the jack when you're trying to change a tire?" She looked at me to see if I understood. I gritted my teeth and clenched my fists under the table, but simply nodded.

"I called out to Hiram, and when he didn't answer, I got the strangest feeling." She looked away from me and brought her fist up to her mouth. "I knew. I just knew. That's when I saw him." She took a deep breath and met my eyes. "I wasn't far wrong about the car and the jack. He was on the left side of the carriage by the front wheel. It's nearly as tall as I am and forged of iron and steel. Weighs a ton. Looked as if he'd been trying to worry the wheel off the axle and the jack had come loose just as the wheel fell right across his throat and cut it."

I was afraid that ham sandwich Peggy had fed me was going to come back up, so I took a big swig of iced tea and gulped. Peggy didn't notice. I suspected she was seeing that scene over again in her mind. Her eyes were full of unshed tears. I was way beyond tears and into plain numb.

"I dropped onto my knees beside him and tried to move that blasted wheel, but I couldn't budge it. I shoved and shoved and . . . even though I knew it didn't matter anyway. His face . . . " She raised her eyes. "My Ben died of a heart attack out in the garden. I found him too. I knew then just like I did with Hiram. I've always hated it when people say somebody's *gone*. But that's what it's like, you know? The spirit, the person that was there inside that body is just . . . " she spread her hands. "Gone."

"I understand," I said, voice breaking.

"Cell phone reception was back up to normal outside the barn by then," Peggy continued. "Nine-one-one promised to send a state trooper right away. In this part of the county that means half an hour easy. I told them the ambulance could take its time, but they probably didn't believe me. I went back in to sit with Hiram while I waited." She glanced away as though embarrassed to look me in the eye. "I'm afraid I called the blasted man everything except a child of God for getting himself killed in a stupid accident that way. He was strong and healthy and had plenty of good years ahead of him. Then I saw I was kneeling in a pool of blood still seeping into the dirt floor from under his head."

I nearly collapsed. Peggy Caldwell had now gone to the far side of 'Way Too Much Information.' Trying to steady my dizzy brain, I went to a very polite mental tearoom and found myself thinking, bizarrely, *Poor woman. Must have been terrible for her.*

Peggy looked me straight in the eyes. "That's when I knew he'd been murdered."

Chapter 6

Sunday evening
Merry

"It was just a stupid accident," I told her. "You said yourself the jack had slipped out from under the carriage and the wheel had fallen across his neck. Of course there was blood." My father's blood. I prayed he'd been unconscious from the moment the wheel fell, hadn't struggled against that terrible pressure against his throat. I dropped my face in my hands.

"But it wasn't, don't you see?" Peggy said. "There was blood from the wound in his throat, but not a great deal. It hadn't severed any veins or arteries. There shouldn't have been blood from under his head too."

"He hit his head when he fell back, obviously."

Again she shook her head. "That floor's packed dirt. He didn't fall far, and there was nothing sharp to cause bleeding." She reached for my hands and held them so hard I gasped. "That's not all. His body was all wrong."

I was definitely coming to the conclusion that she was a whack job.

"Stand up, Merry." I stood. Best to humor her. "Now, kneel down beside the table the way you would if you were trying to remove a tire."

I hoped she wasn't planning to bean me over the head or push the table over on me while I was down there, but I did as she asked.

"Lean over against the edge of the table. Where does it hit you?"

I could prop my chin on the edge. As I did I noticed four cats sitting side by side in the doorway watching intently as though they understood every word we said.

Without warning, she shoved my shoulder. "Hey!" I toppled backwards onto my butt with my legs folded under me. She reached down to pull me to my feet.

"Sorry, but I had to show you. Are you all right?"

I rubbed my rear end. "Uh-huh." I backed up a couple of

steps.

"Have some more tea." She poured my glass full and shoved the lemon dish to me. She turned in her chair, picked up a stack of papers from the kitchen counter, shuffled through them and handed one to me. "I'm sorry to show you this, Merry. It's Hiram. Don't look at the face. Look at the position of his body."

Of course I looked at his face. He didn't look dead to me. He looked like my father, stretched full length on the dirt and not quite asleep. The wheel didn't look like an instrument of death either. "What am I supposed to be seeing?" I asked. I touched his face as though I expected it to be warm.

"When you fell over just now, what happened to your legs?"

"I didn't fall over, you pushed me over, and they folded up under my butt, of course."

"So why didn't his?"

I stared at the photo. He lay on his back, full-length, arms at his side, legs straight with his toes within an inch of the axle where it dug into the dirt. "I don't know. Maybe he was standing up when the wheel fell off."

She made a sound in her throat. "If he'd been standing up and conscious, he'd have jumped out of the way. If he'd been kneeling the way you were, he'd have been holding the spokes of the wheel to lift it off and his knees would have folded under him when he fell backwards. If he'd fallen the way you did, that wheel was tall enough to land across his *forehead*, not his throat."

"You're saying someone laid him out," I said. I could feel my heart racing. I did not want to believe this woman, this stranger. An accident I could handle. Barely. A murder? No way.

"I'm saying someone came up behind him and hit him on the back of his head, which bled the way scalp wounds do, then laid him out on the floor and dropped that wheel on his throat to make it look like an accident."

"What do the police say?" I stared down at the photo on the table in front of me. "And how did you get this picture?" She handed me the stack of photos from her lap. "I always carry my digital camera with me in the car. I'm a bird watcher of sorts, and occasionally I see a new bird. Nobody ever believes me, so I've learned to carry my camera for proof. I did have thirty minutes to wait before the state police showed up, so I had time to fill the water trough and to take pictures of every bit of that scene. I watch CSI. I know how to photograph a crime scene."

"Weren't the police upset?"

The big yellow cat landed splat on top of the table in the center of the photos and sent them sliding in all directions. "Sherlock! Bad cat!" Peggy shoved him off and reached down to pick them up. "Actually, I didn't tell Chief Royden I took the pictures."

"Isn't that illegal?"

"Why? I didn't touch a thing, and it's not as though I plan to post the photos on Facebook, for pity's sake! I was afraid Amos wouldn't take me seriously about the murder and mess up the crime scene. And the next thing I knew, here came a state patrol trooper. Word had gotten down to the county seat—Bigelow— and the county sheriff called in the state. That rookie trooper they sent treated me like a total idiot and wanted me to call my daughter Marilee to come get me. Said I might go into shock driving down the hill. As if. He said Hiram's death was either an accident or a terrible way to commit suicide. And our own Chief Royden gave me a metaphorical pat on the head and told me to let the state handle the investigation, since it's out of the Mossy Creek city limits."

"Suicide?" I yelped. "Hiram was too darned pig-headed to commit suicide, not when I was coming to see him after all these years."

"Well, according to that child from the state police, it was either suicide or a terrible accident because the governor won't admit the people in his home county occasionally kill each other. As if it looks bad on his personal law-and-order record."

"Say what?"

"I told you we were crime free on paper. Nobody gets officially murdered in Bigelow Country, Georgia, except the occasional drug dealer or gang-banger. The governor keeps a country house in Bigelow and half his relatives live in the county. He likes to pretend his presence cuts the crime rate, and the sheriff plays up to his fantasy."

"But won't the county medical examiner recognize a murder?"

"I hope so, but don't count on it. Tomorrow morning first

thing I'm calling Ida Walker, the mayor of Mossy Creek, to get her to call in Amos Royden, our Mossy Creek chief of police, to stick his nose into the investigation if there is one. She can make a big enough fuss to bring in the Georgia Bureau of Investigation, governor or not. The governor hates Ida, who happens to be his aunt, and the sheriff hates Amos, so it should be interesting."

She pushed away from the kitchen table. "That's enough for you to take in tonight, young lady," Peggy said, as though I were fifteen instead of forty. "Come on downstairs and let me show you the apartment. Unless you'd prefer to stay up here with me?"

"Better get it over with."

"Fine. We can get your bags out of your truck on the way."

I trundled after her as though I really was fifteen. She might not have been in shock, but I sure was. My day had started at five this morning and gone steadily to hell ever since. I'd driven two hundred miles through the mountains on two lane roads, and now to be hit with murder! Assuming the nice lady wasn't the actual killer or completely insane—neither of which was a given—I was simply too exhausted to feel much of anything. Even my grief was on hold.

Peggy took my suitcase and my duffel bag out of my truck. I probably would have dropped them from sheer exhaustion. We walked down the driveway to the freshly painted door beside the bottom of her kitchen steps. "I wasn't certain the sheriff would locate you, or that you could get down here tonight, but I straightened up the apartment and changed the sheets and towels before I went to my daughter Marilee's for Sunday dinner, just in case," she said as she inserted a shiny key in the lock, opened the door and clicked on the lights.

Tonight I would sleep in my father's home, in my father's bed, but I would never see him, hear his voice, his laugh, see his grin, feel his hands grown rough from handling reins. Bad enough to lose him through a stupid accident, but if some human agency took him away from me, they'd better pray I never found them.

I dragged my bags past her and dropped them in the tiny entrance area, then spun to look at her. Obviously I was a darned sight more exhausted than I thought if it had taken me this long to remember what she'd said. "You filled the *water trough*? Hiram's already got *horses* out at his farm? I didn't know he'd actually started training. Who's feeding them and looking after them?"

"Don't worry about them. I'll just come in and show you where things are. You need a good night's sleep."

"You're looking after them? I can't ask . . . "

"Oh, no. Not me. Hiram's handyman, Jacob Yoder, is caring for the place and feeding the animals until you decide what to do."

Peggy moved past me, flicked on a light switch beside the door and stopped dead. "Sweet Patience on a monument! What on earth . . . "

I peered around her. If this was what she considered straightening up, she could use a maid service. Or a dump truck. Hiram had never been known for excessive neatness except with his horses and carriages, but he'd hit a new low.

"Look at this place!" Peggy flew into the room.

I turned in a circle, taking in the books lying broken-spined under the small bookcase, sofa cushions tossed around, pictures lying face down, mail strewn everywhere, and leather harness and reins crawling all over the floor like that snake scene in *Raiders of the Lost Ark.*

Peggy pulled a cell phone out of the pocket of her jeans and dialed. "Sandy? Peggy here. Somebody broke into Hiram Lackland's apartment while I was at Marilee's." She listened. "Well, of course I want you to send somebody over here. What?" She shut her mouth. "No, I don't think there's anybody still here." Her eyes widened. "No, I haven't checked . . . "

She grabbed my arm and yanked me through the door onto the driveway. "Come on, Merry." She kicked the door shut behind her. "All right, Sandy. We're outside. We'll wait for Mutt." She clicked the phone shut. "Sandy is the police dispatcher. She said she'd come herself, but she's due to go off duty right now." Peggy grimaced." Probably a good thing. She'd have her gun out before she climbed out of her car and wind up shooting one of the cats."

Some police dispatcher.

"She says there may be somebody still inside and wanted us out until Mutt gets here and checks it out."

"Who's Mutt?"

"One of our real policemen. Works for Amos, the police chief." She'd barely spoken the words when a squad car squealed to the curb and a large man climbed out and came toward us.

"Obviously, someone knew Hiram was dead and I was away at Marilee's," Peggy said. "I've heard about burglars hitting houses during funerals, but this is ridiculous."

She introduced me and stood aside while Mutt went over Hiram's apartment. When he came back, he shook his head. "Nobody there. What's missing?"

"We haven't checked, but who could tell?" Peggy said.

"Computer, electronic equipment?"

"The TV and VCR are there."

"Computer?"

"His laptop's upstairs on my library table. I've got DSL." She glanced at me. "He enjoyed having company while he worked."

"Uh-huh. Maybe looking for cash, judging from the mess. Would he have found any?" He turned to me.

"No clue," I said. "But I'd say no. He liked plastic. Said it made doing his taxes easier."

"Looks like somebody didn't find anything worthwhile, got royally PO'd, and trashed the place," Mutt said. "How about the door?" He shown his light against the door jamb and knelt down to peer at the lock. "Not a scratch. Who had keys?"

"Me and Hiram," Peggy said, then caught her breath. "Did they find them in his truck or on him?"

"Don't know, but it would be in the sheriff's report."

I shivered. For the first time, the idea that my father might actually have been killed got through to me. Why would anybody want him dead? He was never a rich man, although he lived and worked among the richest of the rich.

Apparently, he had enough money to buy his farm, build a new stable, and do the place up, but that probably used up his available capital and left him with a hefty mortgage besides. Had he done something illegal to make money to buy his farm? Hiram never used banned substances on his horses, and so far as I know had never even smoked weed in the sixties.

But would he have gotten involved with *people* drugs? I

didn't know him well enough any longer to say yes or no. He would definitely have been able to hook up with a drug connection. I couldn't see him actually selling dope, but he wouldn't be the first trainer to use his rig to transport drugs across country.

And people did get killed over drugs.

If someone took his keys and drove to Mossy Creek to search his apartment while Peggy was out, then the two events had to be connected. But if they wanted to rob Hiram's apartment, why drive out to his farm and assault him just to get his keys? It would have been easy to break in while neither Hiram's truck nor Peggy's car was here. Were they searching for money or something else? Did they force him to tell them where they were before they killed him? I sank back against front fender of my truck and closed my eyes against the very thought that he might have been tortured.

A moment later Peggy took my arm and said, "You are certainly not going to spend the night downstairs while someone's wandering around with a set of Hiram's keys. I'll have the locks changed tomorrow, and you can move downstairs then."

"She's right, ma'am," Mutt said, "I'll make a report on this. Tomorrow morning Amos can lean on the sheriff in Bigelow and get him to cough up a copy of the report on Mr. Lackland's death. Oh, and I'm sorry for your loss. I didn't know Mr. Lackland all that well, but he seemed like a real nice guy. He was going to drive a carriage around town on Easter Sunday afternoon and give folks rides like they do in New Orleans. Most around here never have ridden in a carriage."

My eyes stung. Typical Hiram. He did love showing off his carriages. He was probably planning to use the vis-à-vis. That might well be why he was working on it when he died. He must have at least a couple of new carriages in his stable area if he was actually training the horses on the farm, but they probably wouldn't hold enough passengers at one time to give Easter carriage rides.

I didn't know how many horses he had, what kind, or whether any of them actually belonged to him. They might all belong to owners who had sent them to him for training.

In that case I'd have to send them home as quickly as

possible. I sure couldn't drive them. I hadn't touched a set of carriage reins since my mother's accident and didn't plan to start now.

Chapter 7

Monday morning
Peggy

Before she climbed out of bed Monday morning, Peggy called Ida Hamilton Walker, mayor of Mossy Creek.

"Peggy, I'm so sorry about Hiram," Ida said. She sounded wide-awake. As the owner of an estate that included a working dairy farm, she'd probably been up for hours.

Peggy should have realized she'd already know. In private, she probably wore one of those aluminum foil hats that received direct input about everything happening in Mossy Creek from her command post on Alpha Centauri.

"I want you to ask Amos to investigate."

"I can't do that. Hiram's farm isn't in the Mossy Creek city limits. It's Sheriff Campbell's jurisdiction."

"Since when has anybody around here given a hoot about jurisdiction when one of our own is in trouble? He may have died in the county, but he *lived* in Mossy Creek. That ought to count for something."

"I know you liked him, Peggy, and I know he lived in your apartment, but he wasn't actually a Mossy Creekite."

"I'm an incomer too, in case you've forgotten." She considered offering a veiled threat about being a voter, but since nobody ever ran against Ida, that wouldn't cut any ice and would probably get her back up. "At least ask Amos to find out what's happening with Hiram's body. I'm afraid they won't even do an autopsy. They'll just put it down to an accident, bung him into his coffin and the ground in that order. If they do, somebody's going to get away with murder."

"Who said anything about murder?"

"I did, dammit," Peggy said. "I'm headed down to the police station after breakfast, and I plan to convince Amos that I know what I'm talking about. Sheriff Campbell would call the massacre at the Little Big Horn a terrible accident to keep the governor happy. We need an investigation from somebody who can't be bought or intimidated."

Ida laughed. "That's Amos all right." She thought for a long minute. Just as Peggy opened her mouth to interrupt, Ida said, "I seem to remember a few years ago we ear-marked that area of Bigelow County to take into the city limits of Mossy Creek at some future time."

"We did?"

"I have no idea, but I'm sure I can turn up a memo to that effect if I look hard enough." Ida chuckled. "Thank God for laser printers. That should give Amos enough clout to ask questions and poke his nose into Campbell's business."

Peggy let out a breath. "I knew you could fix this. Thank you."

"Tell Amos to call me after you talk to him."

"Will do."

*

Merry

I waited in the small reception area of the Mossy Creek police station while Peggy tried to convince the police chief that my father was murdered. I attempted to read an aged copy of *Golf Digest,* the only reading material available, while Sandy, the gung-ho dispatcher, snuck glances at me around the edge of her computer. She must have known who I was, but we hadn't actually been introduced. I decided she didn't know how to speak to me about my father, so she ignored me. I couldn't hear a thing that was going on in Chief Royden's office, but after twenty minutes, Peggy came out with a smile on her face and gave me a thumbs up.

A tall, attractive man in a beautifully tailored police uniform followed her out of the office and shook my hand. "Ms Abbott, I'm Amos Royden. I liked your father. I'm sorry for your loss." He nodded at Peggy, went back inside and shut his door.

Peggy gave a sharp glance at the dispatcher and whispered, "Come on, we'll talk outside," Once we were on the sidewalk, she said, "Bless Sandy's heart, but she does love to gossip."

"What happened?"

"He promised he'd talk to Sheriff Campbell and the medical examiner. That will make them aware that they won't get away with sloughing off. Depending on what he discovers, he'll call in a favor from the Georgia Bureau of Investigation."

Chapter 8

Monday morning
Geoff Wheeler, Georgia Bureau of Investigation

"I can't come up there to be your tame investigator," Geoff Wheeler said into the phone. "It's Monday morning and I haven't even checked what's happened over the weekend, much less finished my second cup of coffee."

"Sure you can," Amos Royden said. "The governor ought to be ordering half a dozen of you guys up here just to protect his mother and the rest of his kith and kin."

"You know darned well the GBI has to be invited into an investigation. Sheriff Campbell is not about to let an Atlanta agent into his quiet little county without a fight. Not to mention the governor would have a fit."

Geoff cradled the phone under his cheek, shucked his coat and hung it up. His extra-large mug of coffee steamed on his desk blotter where it wouldn't make a mark on the top. He wanted that coffee badly. He did *not* want Amos Royden trying to embroil him in Georgia police politics. "If he brought us in, he'd be admitting his presence didn't awe the criminal element into total submission."

"Governor Bigelow does not think that way. A few years back, he let his momma, Ardalene, bring in a bunch of convicts to landscape her garden."

Geoff leaned back in his chair and ran his hand down the back of his head. His coffee looked cool enough to drink without causing major damage to the roof of his mouth. One sip told him he'd been wrong, so he set it down again. He'd never courted pain. "I heard about that. Didn't they plant a bunch of opium poppies in the side yard?"

"Pretty things. Big orange red blooms. Pity the Governor's security detail had to pull them all out and dispose of them." Amos hesitated. "I've always wondered just how they did that. If they burned 'em in the incinerator at the dump they'd have turned Bigelow into one giant opium den. Whole county would have been stoned. Vast improvement, come to think of it."

"Bet there wasn't a dry eye in the prison when they heard they got caught," Geoff said. "Actually, it might have quieted down the hard cases for a while if they'd gotten away with it." He hesitated and tried the coffee again. Good to go. "I still can't come up there and butt into the Sheriff Campbell's investigation."

"What investigation? I just spent half an hour on the phone with him and twenty minutes talking to the medical examiner in Bigelow. The sheriff's ignoring the medical examiner's preliminary findings that the man was knocked out first and then had his throat crushed by a carriage wheel."

"Hell of a way to die if it actually was murder and not a crazy accident."

"Oh, it was murder all right," Amos said. Then he chuckled. "Peggy Caldwell, one of our leading citizens, who has read entirely too many Agatha Christie's, came into my office this morning before I had my *first* cup of coffee to show me a bunch of what she called 'crime scene photos.'"

Geoff choked on his coffee. "Say what? The last thing we need is some dotty Miss Marple turning an accident into a killing to amuse her bridge club. Where the heck did she get the photos?"

"Took 'em on her digital camera before the cops arrived. Darn good, too. Shot everything I would have shot. Thing is, Geoff, after talking to her and the medical examiner and going over those photos, I'm as certain as I can be without seeing what happened first hand that something's not right about Hiram's Lackland's death." He took a long breath. "If you can't investigate the death, then come up here and investigate the break-in at Lackland's apartment that happened last night. Got to be connected."

"Could have been one of your local felons who figured the pickins were good and the coast was clear. What was taken?"

"At first glance, not a thing, but whoever did it made one hell of a mess."

Geoff leaned back in his chair and ran his hand over his head. "C'mon, Amos. The Georgia Bureau of Investigation also does not send officers at my level to penny-ante break-ins where nothing was taken in burgs like Mossy Creek that have their own estimable police forces led by police chiefs of exemplary character."

"*Riiigght*. Look, Geoff, the guy was murdered. He was a nice guy, and he chose Mossy Creek to start up his retirement business. I don't give a hoot whether he was actually offed in Mossy Creek proper. I feel personally responsible and really pissed off. The mayor's placing Hiram's place in the Mossy Creek reserve zone, so we can say it's technically under our jurisdiction. Ida loves doing sneaky, underhanded things to Bigelow. She'll make it happen, but maybe not right away, and right away is when I need you. Consider it a personal favor."

"It's not by the book."

"The heck with the book, Geoff. For God's sake unbutton your damned starched collar before you choke yourself. You can be the most hidebound, ornery, stuff-shirted, stiff-necked pencil-pushing . . . "

"That's because doing it by the book wins cases against defense lawyers, my friend. My cases do not get thrown out of court on technicalities, nor do the people I arrest get off because some tech screwed up. Or I did, which is worse."

"So don't screw up. Find the right killer, make the case and get the SOB out of Mossy Creek."

"Amos, you do not need me. You are a fine officer."

"I am not an investigator. I'm a keep-the-peace policeman. I'm the kind of cop that when somebody says, 'round up the usual suspects,' I know who they are, where they are, and what they probably did. Not this time. I'm out of my depth and out of my league. Damn it, Geoff, I want this guy. You can get him." He paused. "Besides, you owe me."

Wheeler leaned back in his desk chair and propped his shoes on the edge of his metal wastebasket. "I knew you'd bring that up sooner or later. How long before we're even? Blackmail is a crime."

"What blackmail?"

Silence. Finally, Wheeler said, "All right. I'll give it ten days max. *If* I can get my superiors to agree, and if you'll promise me that your mayor will cover my ass."

"I'll call her this minute. I can almost guarantee she'll call the powers that be at the GBI herself. Wait a couple of hours before you bring this up to your superiors. Thanks, Geoff."

"Up yours, old friend," Wheeler said and hung up the

phone.

He swiveled in his chair and aligned his telephone carefully with the edge of his desk blotter. A cluttered desk meant a cluttered mind, and a cluttered mind missed things. His colleagues called him a fuss-budget. They also said he had a ramrod up his back. They could call him anything they liked so long as he made cases that stood up in court.

Amos's case should be relatively simple. Chances were the man had been killed either by a friend, family member, or employee. From the crime scene Amos had described, an opportunistic killing seemed a remote possibility.

Normal people really did want to confess if given the chance. He was a genius at convincing them he truly understood why they had done what they had done.

He didn't.

Most killers fell into a kind of no-man's land, where the inability to control a sudden rage led to a bloody corpse on the floor. Those people were generally appalled at what they had done. They tried to hide, of course. Nobody ever really wanted to pay for crimes committed, but sooner or later they broke and confessed.

He hoped the killer of this man in Mossy Creek would be one of those.

His gut told him otherwise.

Chapter 9

Monday Morning
Merry

"I've got time to drive out to Hiram's place and check on those horses before I meet Sheriff Campbell in Bigelow," I said to Peggy. "Just tell me how to find it.

"I'll drive you. You won't find it yourself," she said. "Not without MapQuest, a GPS and the triple A."

"You don't want to get stuck with me," I said. "I have to meet Sheriff Campbell, but I'll probably spend the rest of the day at the farm."

"Then I'll drive my own car and you can follow me in your truck. That way I can turn you over to Jacob Yoder and come home to wait for the locksmith to change the locks on Hiram's your apartment."

"May I take you to dinner tonight? Give me a chance to see some of Mossy Creek."

I expected her to hem and haw, but she accepted readily. "I'd be delighted. We have a good restaurant in Mossy Creek that doesn't cost a fortune or serve tall food."

"I beg your pardon?"

"Those stacks of puff pastry, one sixth of a zucchini and an ounce of steak drenched with brown goo in the center of a big white plate. Always makes me want to stop at Wendy's on the way home. No tall food at Mama's. You'll like it."

Sounded like my kind of place. We climbed into our respective vehicles and drove out of town to see where my father had died.

Fog still lay in the hollows as we left Mossy Creek and drove along a two-lane back road between thick woods. This high the trees were not yet fully leafed—two weeks behind where they had been in Tennessee—but gave off a green glow.

This was pretty country. Property around Aiken and Southern Pines is so expensive that only the rich-rich can afford land, but this looked like a reasonable alternative, especially if Hiram had found flat land on top of his hill. It was on a general line from Southern Pines down to Ocala and Wellington, Florida, where most of the full-time horse people spent a couple of months each winter. Easy to drop off and pick up horses for training and carriages for repair or restoration.

Easy, as well, to pick up a load of drugs in south Florida and drop it off in Atlanta. I shook my head. I refused to think of Hiram as a drug mule until I was forced to.

The curvy back road was impossible to drive fast. Good thing, since deer bounded across in front of Peggy's car twice. Once, a half dozen good-sized does bounced from the bank on one side and disappeared instantly on the other down a narrow trail between the trees. Then a doe with a pair of dappled fawns sprinted across and into a fog bank on the downhill slope. I even saw a cock pheasant strolling along the grass verge with his tail dragging in the gravel. He barely turned his head as we passed.

For the last few years, I've lived in fastidiously groomed flat country in Kentucky. This place with its wild woodlands, hills and dells called to me. I could feel my shoulders relax, even though I was going to the site of my father's death.

"You did good, Hiram," I whispered. I was happy he'd been able to enjoy his farm for a few months. He should have had years. If things had worked out between us, we might have shared those years. "Whoever did this, I hate you!" I snarled and hit the steering wheel.

Ahead of me Peggy's right turn signal came on, and she slowed. At first I couldn't see where she planned to turn, then I saw a pair of thigh high boulders marking either side of a gravel drive that curved up and seemed to disappear into the forest. Peggy was right. I'd have driven right by if she hadn't showed me where to turn.

The drive followed the twists and turns at the edge of the hillside. On the right, the trees and underbrush walked straight up out of sight. On the left—without a sign of a guardrail, mind you—I could stare down into a shallow valley. We drove over a drainage pipe laid under the road that allowed water to cascade from a small waterfall and down into a stream that I could barely glimpse through the trees at the bottom. If that causeway ever gave way, the road would give way as well, marooning anyone at the top of the hill.

Surely there must be another way down.

Just when I had decided we were driving up Mt. Everest, Peggy turned a final curve, and the road flattened out into a large gravel parking area in front of a big old barn, freshly painted red and sporting a new metal roof. This must be the barn where Peggy found Hiram.

I pulled in alongside her car. On the left edge of the parking area a white diesel crew cab four-by-four truck was parked, and past the truck, nose facing out, stood a thirty-foot extra tall, extra wide, aluminum gooseneck stock trailer. Neither truck nor trailer was new, but looked well tended. The trailer had a wide side door that could be used to load carriages. Hiram's truck, Hiram's trailer. He always took good care of his trucks and trailers.

Where were the horses? Where was this Jacob Yoder?

As I climbed out of my truck to join Peggy, a scream of pure rage rent the air, and I jumped a foot. Took me a second to realize what I'd heard. A donkey bray is like nothing else in the universe. Some of them start off with a series of grunts like a lion gearing up to roar, then they let fly. Some, like this one, started off at top decibel level and kept on. And on.

"That's Don Quixote, known as Don Qui," Peggy said as she disappeared around the left side of the barn. "That's his 'where in Sam Hill is my breakfast' bray."

An instant later he was joined by the whinnies of several horses.

"I thought you said this Jacob Yoder was looking after them," I said.

"He was certainly supposed to. Hiram will kill him . . . Sorry, I keep forgetting."

Beyond the original barn, which, from the height of its eaves, looked as though it might at one time have been used to dry tobacco, I saw Hiram's new stable across a track that ran at right angles behind the old barn. The stable was gleaming tan metal with a brass ventilation cupola on top.

Standing in the paddock beside it, five equines stared at us with baleful dark eyes. The smallest and obviously the most annoyed was Don Qui, three feet of miniature donkey with ears nearly as long as his face. He cut off in mid-bray when he saw us and glared, certain he'd gotten his point across.

Next to him stood a tubby Halflinger pony, gold with a

flowing flaxen mane and tail. Then came a pair of dark bays approximately sixteen hands high. Morgan, maybe, or Standard bred off the trotting track, or even some sort of European warmblood. The final horse dwarfed the others. Solid black with flowing mane, and probably feathered hooves hidden in the dewy grass, he stood at least seventeen hands and undoubtedly tipped the scales around a ton. His back was as broad as the average loveseat. Had to be a Friesian.

"They should have been fed hours ago," I said. "They swear they haven't been, but horses lie like rugs when it comes to food. Where is this Jacob person, anyway?"

"I am coming, blast you," said a gravelly male voice. A moment later a man I assumed was Jacob Yoder stepped out of the new stable. Since he stopped dead when he saw Peggy and me, he'd been damning his charges and not us.

He had several halters and lead ropes over his shoulder. I couldn't see his face because of the long-billed baseball cap he wore, but Central Casting would have hired him to play Ichabod Crane in a heartbeat. I probably weighed more than he did, and he stood at least six four. His bib overalls hung on him like faded blue elephant skin.

"Morning," I said and walked to him with my hand outstretched. "Could you use a hand getting them in?"

I had assumed he'd shake my hand, but he swung a couple of halters at me instead. "You are her."

"Yep. I'm her." I said cheerfully with a sardonic glance over my shoulder at Peggy. Jacob Yoder was obviously not one of life's great gentlemen. Close up I could see two day's growth of gray stubble along his jaw. His face was deeply lined and leathery from the sun, and his eyes were as red as pickled beets.

The hand holding the halters shook. Unless I was very much mistaken, Jacob Yoder was the poor equivalent of the rich alcoholics I saw around the show grounds. He was just getting around to feeding the horses because he had the grandfather of all hangovers and probably had used the hair of the dog to get him going. An alcoholic, ill-tempered, aging stable-hand wasn't what I'd been hoping for.

I *did*, however, need him badly right now. So I smiled my most cheerful smile (always a reach for me), took a couple of the halters and followed him to the five-bar gate that closed off the pasture from the barn. He'd passed me the largest and the smallest halters. Don Qui and the Friesian. The Friesian was a piece of cake. He lowered his massive head and stuck his nose into the halter. I followed Yoder across to the barn and inside where the first stall doors on either side of the center aisle stood open.

"Heinzie is in that one," he said, pointing to the second stall on the left. The stable lay in shadows, so I couldn't tell much about it, but it looked well constructed if not posh. I took care of Heinzie, who dove happily into his morning grain, while I went back for Don Qui.

"The jackass comes in with Heinzie," Jacob said. "Does not like to wait."

Now he tells me. I've had some experience with miniature donkeys. They are classified in carriage driving among the VSE's 'very small equines,' miniature horses and the like. They are generally driven in teams of two, because the only way to train a young donkey to drive is to hitch him up with an experienced donkey. The minute I walked up to him, Don Qui stuck his nose into the dirt so that I had to bend double to get the halter down to him. Just as I pulled it over his nose, he swung his head straight into my gut hard enough to knock the wind out of me, whirled past me, trotted out of the pasture and into the barn. I ran after him but needn't have bothered. He knew which stall he was supposed to be in and went directly into it.

"Knucklehead," Jacob said as he shut the stall door.

I bit my tongue, although I suspected 'knucklehead' was intended for me rather than the donkey.

As a show manager, I've learned to make snap judgments about people. I'm usually right. I need to know at once who's going to be a pain in the ass. I did not like Jacob Yoder.

"We must speak," he said with a glower. It would seem he didn't like me either. I started running down a list of stable hands I knew who might be free to come work down here until I could get things organized and know where I stood.

I wondered if Peggy had already driven away, but she was leaning on the pasture gate looking out over the property.

"Are those all the horses, Mr. Yoder?" I asked.

He nodded. "One is not a horse."

"Really? I hadn't noticed."

He dropped his eyes first. I'd seen plenty of Jacob Yoders. He'd take every advantage and be as rude as he thought he could get away with, right up to the point where he might get fired. If reprimanded, he'd go all innocent and work very hard for a day or a week until he thought he was flying under the radar again.

Hiram would have pegged him faster than I did. So why had he hired the man?

"Would you show me around the place after we put the horses back out?" I asked. That gave me forty minutes or so to check out Hiram's workshop in the old barn. Although I wasn't looking forward to it, I had to see where he was found, and I wanted to do it with Peggy. I couldn't in good conscience keep her hanging around while I went exploring the land with Jacob.

He nodded and walked back into the stable with his hands in the pockets of his overalls.

Peggy came to me, and we walked around to the parking area. "What a charmer," I whispered.

"I asked Hiram once why he hired the man. He said he felt an obligation to him and that he was an excellent worker when he put his mind to it."

"Yeah. I'll bet he is."

"No, I mean it. Except for hiring a contractor to erect the outside of the new stable, he and Hiram did most of the work on this place themselves in less than six months. I suspect he'd work fine so long as Hiram worked right beside him."

"But the minute he was alone, he'd go sit under a tree and drink his moonshine, or whatever I smelled on his breath."

We had reached the broad double doors of the barn that stood facing the parking area. A padlock had been locked through the hasp that closed the double doors.

"Do you have the key?" I asked Peggy.

"Hiram kept the extra keys on peg boards at the back of the workshop," Peggy said and pulled a padlock key from the pocket of her jeans. "Since the police didn't see fit to declare this a crime scene, I made it my business to take them before I left."

"Did he have a spare apartment key?" I asked, remembering that someone had used a key to get in to burgle the place.

She shook her head. "Not an extra one. I assume the police didn't find his key ring either on him or in the truck, and I don't think he kept anything but his truck and house key with him. He was amazingly neat for a man."

My eyebrows went up.

Peggy unlocked the padlock and moved it to hang off one side of the door. "Can you handle this?"

"I don't have much choice." I took a deep breath and stepped into the dark interior. Peggy followed and turned on banks of fluorescent lights hung from the heavy roof rafters.

Because of moisture, woodworm, termites and encroaching vegetation, very few old barns survive in *my* part of the south without constant maintenance. Either this one had been maintained well over the hundred or so years since it had been built, or Hiram had done a great restoration job.

The floor was dirt, but swept and raked clean. Tools hung from pegboard along the right wall over a worktable built of plywood on sawhorses. Along the left wall hung a half dozen sets of harness that looked clean and freshly oiled.

I carefully kept my eyes away from the four-wheeled vis-à-vis carriage that leaned on one axle in the center of the room. Beyond it stood two carriages in various states of repair. Unrepair, actually. Both looked like antiques. One was a dogcart, built high up above a wicker area that could be used to carry dogs. From here I could see the wicker was a mess. The other looked like an aged doctor's carriage, the sort country doctors drove to house calls.

Extra shafts, wheels, seats and other pieces lay or stood in ranks against the rest of the walls.

I saw no cobwebs and little dust. All the electric and hand tools were clean. Those that hadn't been hung on the pegs lay in neat rows on the worktable.

I had moved slowly around the walls of the workshop and now had no option but to look at the vis-à-vis in the center. I started with the side that still had both its wheels. It needed paint. The leather upholstery needed cleaning and conditioning at the very least. Since it was cracked with age, it really should be replaced, but Hiram could certainly have driven it as it was.

So what had he been doing with the wheel? If I wanted to believe the cops about it being an accident, the only thing I could think of was that he must have been repacking the bearings.

Yoder might know. Hiram must have just gotten started, unless someone had removed the container of axle grease he would have used.

I took a deep breath and walked around the side that canted.

The EMTs had leaned the iron wheel against the side of the carriage after they'd moved it off Hiram's chest, and the entire area was scuffed by multiple footprints and knee prints. I suspected Peggy had been the one to place the shop towel over the area where Hiram's head would have lain.

She was watching me. I pointed to the towel. "You?"

She nodded. "I came back in after they moved him to the ambulance. I could still see . . . the stain. I didn't want to."

"I don't want to either." I dropped to my knees. I don't pray much, but I did say a silent prayer that wherever Hiram had wound up, he'd have horses to drive and ride. For Hiram and me there could be no paradise without horses.

Like father, like daughter. I wanted to cry, but my eyes stayed hot and dry. "I promise I'll fix this," I whispered.

Peggy's fingers clutched my shoulder. "No, we'll fix this."

*

After Peggy drove away, I found Jacob Yoder lounging on a bale of hay outside the new stable. He'd already let the animals back into the pasture, but I saw no sign that he'd mucked their stalls. Maybe he was expecting me to do it.

When he saw me, he stood up with a sigh that started somewhere around his dirty work boots.

"I'm meeting the sheriff in Bigelow shortly," I said. "I'll be back after that. I'll pick up a couple of cheeseburgers and fries on my way. We can eat and talk. Okay with you?"

"Triple cheeseburger. Big fries, big Coke," he said. No 'thank you' or 'nice of you to think of me' and certainly no offer to pay his share.

"Fine." I turned away.

"Hey," he called after me.

"Yes?"

"You keeping me on or what?"

I longed to tell him to get his mangy ass off the property, but that would be counter-productive. Besides, there was a chance he either had killed my father himself or knew who did. I didn't want him disappearing on me. I could at least give him a chance to prove Hiram was right about him.

"Do you live on the place?" I asked as I turned back to him.

"Yonder across the pasture in the trees. Hiram and me did up an old trailer so it's just about fit to live in. It's over there where it is not so hot."

"What do you do for water and plumbing?"

"Bathroom and shower in the stable. Reservoir on the trailer for water. Drive it across the pasture in the back of my truck."

"I see. That means Hiram used you as a caretaker as well as a . . . " What? Groom? Handyman? Stockman? I had a suspicion that whatever I called him wouldn't sit well with him.

"Yes. We have worked long and hard to fence, build the arena and complete the inside of the stable. Then Hiram goes and gets . . . dies. Not a right thing." He narrowed his eyes at me. "Will you sell or stay?"

"I haven't had time to give any thought to what will happen, but for the moment, consider that nothing will change. Probating wills takes a long time." That was assuming that I was Hiram's heir and executrix. Maybe his will was what the burglar had been after last night. If so, he hadn't found it. I knew from a couple of Hiram's emails to me that his will was with his lawyer unless he'd moved it recently.

Unless he'd changed his mind and left everything to Peggy or Jacob, the whole shebang (and the entire headache) was mine. Including the bills and mortgage payment.

"I am paid every other Friday. I do not stay Friday night or Saturday here. I return late Sunday," Jacob said.

I nodded. I'd check to see if Peggy agreed with that, but for the moment, I had to accept what he said.

As I walked off again, he said to my back, "That woman she locked the workshop back when she left?"

Actually, I had padlocked it behind Peggy and me and kept the key. No sense in letting him know I had the means to open it, so I simply nodded.

"I might need tools."

"I see all the equipment you'll need to muck stalls and sweep the aisle. I should be back before you do much more." If he did that.

I left him grumbling. There had to be a very good reason for Hiram to hire this man as his only helper and to put up with him for six months. I wondered if Peggy knew any of the background of that 'obligation' Hiram had talked about.

Thirty minutes later I walked into the sheriff's office in Bigelow.

Sheriff Campbell was nothing like the cliché southern small town sheriff. He was shorter than I am, thinner than I am, shaven bald and as smartly tailored as a South American dictator. He wouldn't need pepper spray. All he had to do was aim the reflection from that shiny badge in a perp's eyes to blind him for life.

I had fed horses a couple of hours ago, but I was cleaner than most working farmers. When I walked into his office, he stood, wrinkled his nose almost imperceptibly, and shook my hand. I don't know what he'd been expecting, but I wasn't it.

"I am sorry for your loss, little lady," he said.

Nobody's called me that since my mother entered me in a pony lead line class when I was three. I wore a pink tutu, howled my head off and won sixth place. I liked the pony. It was the tutu I couldn't stand.

I managed a weak smile. "You said you wanted to talk to me? Have me sign some paperwork?"

"First off, you got any identification? Purely a formality."

I pulled out my Kentucky driver's license. I did not show him the carry permit for the pistol I keep in the center console of my truck. I drive horse vans long distances by myself. Even if I didn't need protection, I have to be able to put a horse out of its misery if it's hurt in an accident on the highway. I know that's an unpalatable thing to think about, but it's a fact of life. Part of the unspoken contract we have with the animals in our charge is not to allow them to suffer needlessly. So far I've never had to do it and I pray I never do.

"All right, Ms Abbott. Seems you're who you say you are. Terrible accident."

"I'd like copies of the police and medical examiner's reports, please."

He blinked and humphed. "Now, you don't want to do that. You need to remember your daddy the way he was."

"I need to know what happened to him more."

"Old man out there on a Saturday morning working all alone. Tire fell on him. Iron, antique thing. Heavy. Freak accident."

"In Kentucky the reports of accidental deaths are public records. I assume that's true in Georgia. So may I have copies please? I'll be happy to wait while someone runs them off for me."

His ears had turned an amazing shade of puce, but he was still playing nice with me. "Ordinarily, takes a week or so for the records to be available for request."

I put on my most charming and helpless smile. I can do charming when I set my mind to it. "But computers can do it much faster, can't they? I'm sure you realize I need to take care of things here to get back to my job." Which I'd probably been fired from after the accident on Sunday, but he didn't need to know that either. I think it was the prospect of getting rid of me that clinched it.

He picked up his desk phone and requested copies of all the reports. "The desk'll have some paperwork for you to sign so we can release the body. You decided which funeral home you want to pick it up?"

Peggy had prepared me for this and had already called the Mossy Creek Funeral Home, the mortuary she recommended. I still didn't know what I would do about a memorial service, but I wanted my father's body out of that morgue as soon as possible.

"She's already alerted the funeral home. Thank you so much, Sheriff," I simpered. "I'll wait for the papers outside. I know you're just overwhelmed with fighting crime." I shook his hand and left while he was still wondering whether I'd just given him a shot or not.

*

The staple food of horse show people is cold cheeseburgers with soggy French Fries. These looked better than most. I found Jacob leaning against the hood of Hiram's truck waiting for me. In the pasture, I could see the horses grazing, but had no idea whether he'd mucked their stalls or not. He might have wanted to eat before I chewed him out.

I handed him his lunch bag and a soda and walked past him into the shadowy stable out of the sun and sat on a bale of hay.

Jacob followed and sat on the bale two down. Didn't want to sit too close to me, no doubt.

I could hear the click of false teeth as he munched. He didn't look that old, but he also didn't look like a man for whom good dental hygiene had been a priority.

"So, Jacob, tell me about you," I said.

He cut his eyes at me. "Who talked to you?"

"I beg your pardon?"

"Hiram write you about me?"

"He mentioned he had only one man working with him full time until he got more business. I assume that was you."

"That all?" His shoulders visibly relaxed. Mine tightened.

"What should he have told me?"

Chomp, click, chomp, click, chomp, click went his teeth for more than a full minute, then he slurped his soda and burped. A significant burp. "I have no reason not to say. I have been inside the last few years."

"Inside what?"

"*Inside*. Prison."

"Oh." So I was dining al fresco with a felon.

"I am on parole. Must have a job and place to live before they parole you. I wrote Hiram. He hired me and put me up in the trailer. It was here when he bought this place." He made an unpleasant noise in his throat. I held my breath. I don't like to watch people spit. "We cleaned it up. Still not much."

"That was nice of him."

He spun so fast his soda slopped out of the can and onto the bale of hay. "Nice? No nice about it. He owed me. Owed me more than working me like a field hand and letting me live in that rusted trailer." Those rheumy, hung-over beet eyes blazed like lasers.

I shoved my back against the side of the stall. No need to look any further for someone who wanted to kill Hiram. I dug my hands into the pocket of my jeans and shoved my truck keys between my knuckles. If he came at me, I'd go for his eyes and run like hell back to my truck and my pistol. "Why did he owe you?" I said as quietly as I could. I used the same gentle tone I'd used on Jethro the stallion and for much the same reason.

His lips drew back from those shiny teeth. Then his whole body let go, and suddenly he was a thin old drunk with a hangover again. "Never you mind." He stood up, crushed the can, dropped it into the sack I'd given him, and walked off. "You wish to see this place?"

We spent the next hour and a half going over the stable. Inside the shiny new metal building, everything was utilitarian, but not fancy. Four sets of harness hung in the tack room and feed room beside cabinets for grooming and medicating supplies. A washer, dryer and water heater took up the far side.

A wash rack took up twelve feet in the center of the left aisle across from the tack room. At the back stood four carriages: a metal breaking cart, two Meadowbrook carts, one for a big horse, the other for a large pony or medium horse, and finally a four-wheeled Phaeton set up with a singletree to hitch a pair.

No cart small enough for Don Qui, so obviously he hadn't yet been taught to drive. Or ever would be, if it were up to me.

Jacob opened a door across from the feed room and stood back for me to go first. "Hiram called this the clients' lounge," Jacob said. "Said you could fix it up."

The room was twenty feet square with wood tongue and groove oak paneling on the walls and scored and dark stained concrete on the floor. No furniture, no curtains at the wide windows, no pictures on the walls, but a couple of stacks of framed photos leaning against the wall beside the door. I began to paw through them, but the first one stopped me. Hiram sat on the box of an elegant park drag behind a pair of beautifully turned-out bay geldings. He was waving a blue ribbon and laughing.

He looked so happy. And so old.

I set that picture aside and looked through the others. Hiram and his clients driving their horses in competition. Hiram driving hell-for-leather around marathon courses behind a four-in-hand or pair. Hiram as navigator or groom beside rich owners in top hats, or in the case of the lady clients, elaborate hats and fancy jackets. With each succeeding year, his hair grew grayer, the creases on his leathery face deeper, his eyes a paler blue. But that grin of exultation when he won never dimmed.

During all those years before he retired, did he ever wish that I were on the box beside him spurring him on? In the long nights he slept in motels and other people's houses, did he wish he still had a wife and daughter to come home to?

Or had he only grown lonesome after he retired and left the limelight to move down here?

"Hiram said you could hang the pictures," Jacob said. "Maybe find some used furniture cheap."

I turned away so he wouldn't see me gulp and choke back tears. Such a little thing, but something he'd been looking forward to sharing with me, the daughter he'd not been around to raise. The daughter who had returned the favor once I got old enough not to be around *him*.

The timing, as usual in my life, sucked. God must have taken Irony 101 in some celestial college and indulged Himself in it whenever He needed a break from running the universe.

"Where are his trophies?" I asked. His trophies were like most people's photo albums. I could trace his life in the names and dates of driving events etched on them. Hiram had managed to spend his life doing what he loved to do, and well enough to make not only a living, but a reputation. Of course, he'd also enjoyed another sort of reputation. He did like the ladies as much as they liked him.

The only ladies he hadn't paid enough attention to were my mother and me. But I'd never stopped loving him, although he probably thought I had. Maybe if I had forgiven Hiram sooner for his failures as a husband and father, I might have forgiven Vic for his. Eventually, I might even have forgiven myself.

Maybe, just maybe, I wouldn't have turned into a woman who couldn't trust any creature that walked on two legs.

"I have never seen trophies here. Are they at his place in town?" Jacob asked.

I hadn't seen them. Surely Peggy would have noticed if they'd been stolen in the burglary. Could he have taken a storage locker somewhere? Hiram had enough silver cups, bowls and trays to outfit a banquet at Buckingham Palace. Plus medals, bronze statues of carriage horses and plaques. A narrow shelf ran around the entire perimeter of the room two feet under the ceiling. Perfect for displaying awards. He said they impressed the clients. He must have expected me to set those out as well.

No sense in wasting time staring at an empty room. Let whoever took over the place from me furnish it, display his own trophies and pictures. "Come on," I said. Jacob followed me down the aisle and into the spring sunshine.

"Twelve stalls," Jacob said. "Planned to have them filled before full summer, maybe build another section next year if the economy gets better."

"Do any of the horses actually belong to him?"

"The Halflinger is all. The Dutch warmbloods belong to some millionaire in Southern Pines. Hiram says the owner is frightened to drive them. Sent them down here to make them bomb proof. Huh. No horse is bomb proof."

"Who owns the Friesian?"

"Hiram has him from a man in Aiken. He and the jackass were raised together. Can't stand to be apart. Can't show a horse with a donkey running around the dressage arena around with him." He frowned down at me. "He has other issues."

"What else? That sounds like plenty."

"You plan to keep training? Hiram said you are a good teacher. Said you used to be a good driver."

Actually, I planned to return the horses to their owners as soon as possible, but I didn't necessarily want to say that to Jacob. "I have no idea."

"Heinzie needs ground driving and long lining to get him used to being alone. A calm hand on the reins. Broken trace in the arena a while back scared him some. He is also lazy and loses his focus. Hiram had to correct him often. Needs confidence to drive without the jackass."

I enjoy ground driving. It requires only walking behind the horse far enough back to be out of range of a kick and teaching the horse to answer the reins and the whip. I wouldn't have to climb into a cart and pick up the reins.

"Dressage arena is back there behind the stable on the right," Jacob said. "So the clients can look out the windows and watch their horses work." He said 'clients' with a sneer. Obviously the rich and famous did not impress him. Or he envied them so much he hated them.

"Do you drive?" I asked Jacob.

He hesitated as though this was a trick question, then he said, "Got back into it after I moved in down here. Driving with Hiram when we were not building and fencing and cleaning."

So he could help on the reins.

He added, "I was in raised in Pennsylvania. I drove every day one way and another."

With a name like Jacob Yoder I should have guessed he was Amish. Yoder is practically the equivalent of Smith in some Amish communities. That slightly stilted manner of speaking should have clued me in. No real accent, no 'thee's' and 'thou's,' but he seldom used contractions or southern colloquialisms. If he'd been in prison, his speech patterns would have changed for the worse, not the better. He hadn't entirely lost the way of speaking he'd learned as a child.

Mother said Hiram had spent a year in Intercourse with an Amish family before he and my mother met and married. He said he learned everything from shoeing horses to sewing harness to plowing fields with a team of six Belgians across. To carpentry, repairing, restoring and building carriages. That's where he learned the woodworking skills he taught me.

The Amish are not only peaceable folks, they generally wash their own dirty linen. So how had Jacob Yoder wound up in prison? For what? And how could I find out? Surely the police would find out about his record. He would be the obvious suspect. That must have been why he told me about his stint in jail. If he really did have an alibi for the time of Hiram's death, he had nothing to worry about.

If not, however, he might take off for parts unknown.

Except that would really make him look guilty.

We spent the next hour walking over the dressage arena and the land. It was truly beautiful. Even this early, the pastures were lush green, mostly lespedeza, although I saw some timothy and Bermuda. They'd need cutting in less than a month if we had normal spring rainfall.

The peak of the hill I'd driven up did indeed look as though it had at some point been flattened by a giant's palm. Hiram's land undulated gently into old growth trees and tall pines along the edges. "What's over there?" I asked, pointing beyond the arena toward a thick stand of hardwoods.

"Mostly woods. Hiram did not own but to the second tree line. Past that tree line is another hundred or so acres. More hills. Many more trees. A couple of streams in the valley. Pretty, but not for a horse farm."

By the time we'd finished exploring, the horses were ready

for dinner, so I helped Jacob bring them in and feed them. Except for the bales in the aisles ready to be fed, most of the hay was stored in a lean-to shed behind the old barn, and the manure pile, always necessary in any horse operation, was on the far side of the barn away from the path and out of the way.

Jacob had indeed cleaned the stalls and filled the water buckets. He had not, however, swept the center clay aisle free of bits of hay. Hiram liked his aisles swept twice a day. I could hear him in my head as clear as though he were standing beside me with a rake in his hand. "Unmade bed, a clean house looks messy. Unswept aisle, a clean stable looks dirty." I turned away so that Jacob couldn't see me blink back tears.

The heck with the aisle. I'd make certain Hiram swept it tomorrow morning. I couldn't take much more today.

"Where did Hiram keep the records and his log books?" I asked as I dropped the last flake of hay into Heinzie's stall. "I haven't seen any filing cabinets. Not even a desk."

"Not in the workshop?"

"I'll check tomorrow." If there were any file cabinets or boxes for papers in the old barn, I hadn't noticed them, but then, I'd been concentrating on the area around the vis-à-vis. I didn't have time to open the barn again now. I was worn out and dirty, and I was taking Peggy to dinner in Mossy Creek. I started to ask Jacob what he'd be doing for dinner, but thought better of it.

"I go to Bigelow," he said as he followed me to my truck. "After I am washed." He pointed across the horse pasture to the trees where I could glimpse the corner of what must be his trailer. "I do not cook." Then he leered.

Obviously, *somebody* cooked. Female for sure. Probably where he went on the weekends to get drunk.

"Do you check the horses at night?"

"I let them out after they eat."

"Good." Hiram had taught me that the more time horses spent out in pasture, the healthier they stayed. I climbed into my truck and reached for the ignition.

"Hey," Jacob said.

I let my hand drop.

"You are not so stupid about horses." He stalked away.

Had I just received a compliment? Probably as close as Jacob Yoder ever came to giving one. The Amish are not noted for bitterness and bad temper. What had happened to turn him into a curmudgeon? A felonious curmudgeon at that.

Chapter 10

Monday evening
Geoff Wheeler

Geoff Wheeler clicked his briefcase shut and locked his desk. He was more than ready to go home. He hated Monday paperwork days when he seldom left his office. He'd even brought his lunch from home.

When he rotated his skull, the muscles of his neck popped like old silk tearing. He needed an hour in the gym but didn't have the energy. All he wanted was a thick steak, a big salad and a glass of good red wine, all of which waited for him at his apartment. As he rounded the desk, his phone rang.

He didn't even bother to swear. "Wheeler," he said when he picked up.

"Got your back," Amos said. "Ida went through our state senator, the sheriff and the lieutenant governor, but you're good to go. Come on up. You want to stay with me or at the local inn?"

Geoff closed his eyes. "The inn. I don't share living space with anyone, much less another cop. You're paying my expenses, right?"

"Hey, the GBI works for the public, right?"

"When we have to."

"So the State of Georgia should pay for this investigation. That's why the legislature gives you the big bucks."

"Uh-huh."

"I'll make you a guaranteed reservation for whenever you get here. Probably be late."

"It will be *not*, Amos. I'm tired, hungry, and have no intention of driving up to Mossy Creek until I've had a good night's sleep. I'll see you mid-morning tomorrow. You can buy me lunch."

"I'll ask Ida if she'd like to join us. She wants to meet you. For your information, I intend to marry the woman, so don't be flashing those baby blues of yours at her, got that?"

"As a favor to you, I'll keep my male magnetism under

wraps."

Amos snorted and. "Keep your Viagra in the bottle is more like it."

He rang off. Geoff sighed deeply and left fast before anyone else could talk to him.

Traffic in Atlanta sucked, but it gave him time to decompress and to think about what he was getting into. If the old guy in Mossy Creek actually had been killed, the sheriff and the state cops had destroyed the crime scene and compromised any evidence.

He preferred to have forensic evidence to back up every conclusion. That might not be possible in this case. He'd have to go on straight interviews and interrogation. What he called 'comparison shopping.' Ask questions until something didn't add up. The old fashioned way. He hated that.

He wound up fixing himself a couple of bacon and egg sandwiches and tossing his sirloin into the freezer. He cleaned up the kitchen and turned on the dishwasher, then loaded the washing machine.

He would have preferred to leave the kitchen in a mess and the underwear in his hamper, but he drove himself to keep his apartment straight. He hated facing mess when he climbed out of bed in the morning. Too many memories of waking to the aftermath of one of Brit's parties.

He set his clock early enough so that he could spend an hour at the gym on his way out of town, and collapsed naked and catty-cornered in his king-sized bed so his feet didn't hang off the end. Why not? He hadn't shared his bed with so much as a cat since his divorce.

He wondered as he drifted into sleep what sort of woman this Ida was if Amos had an eye on her. Amos had been one of his groomsmen when he married Brittany, and had said during the reception that he felt certain Geoff would never have to return the favor. This Ida was mayor of Mossy Creek, so she couldn't be a twenty-something popsy, but he'd be willing to bet she was eye candy.

Brittany had been eye candy too. Pity he'd taken ten years to realize the sugar coating surrounded a rotten center.

Chapter 11

Monday evening
Merry

Peggy gave me a shiny key for the new lock on Hiram's apartment door while we made plans to get together for dinner, then I dragged down the driveway to clean myself up.

I expected to find the same mess we'd left last night, but Peggy had apparently spent the time while the locksmith was changing the locks putting the books back into their shelves and straightening the mail and magazines. I really hadn't looked at the place last night before Sandy, the dispatcher, had sent us out to wait for Mutt, the cop. I should go over the mail to check for bills, but they'd have to wait.

Peggy had furnished the little apartment with comfortable overstuffed furniture, the sort a man likes to relax in. A decent sized flat screen TV hung on the end wall, and the small galley kitchen looked adequate for a man who didn't cook much.

Actually, if I knew Hiram, he probably had invitations for dinner almost every evening, and the ones where he wasn't invited *out*, the local ladies brought casseroles *in*. He was the perfect extra man. He played bridge, danced well, and looked extremely presentable. He liked women, and like most men who are famous in their own small ponds, he generally had to beat them off with a stick.

Not that he did. He tried to convince my mother that he really loved only her, and that his one-night stands were not germane.

Oh, sure. Maybe there's a woman somewhere who believes that, but if so, I've never met one. Vic never convinced me either.

The single bedroom had a king-sized bed covered with a handsome wedding ring quilt. The small bathroom backed up to the kitchen. I had been comfortable in much less palatial surroundings.

No trophies. No file cabinet. No desk. So where did he keep his logs and records? He must have paper backups even if he kept most of his files on his computer. Coggins tests for Equine Infectious Anemia came on paper, so did construction bills, information about worming and vaccination schedules, hay bills, feed bills, Jacob's salary. Like most careful horsemen, Hiram would have kept copies of everything.

Not only that, he always kept a running handwritten log like a ship's captain. If a horse came up lame, Hiram wrote it down and what he'd done to correct it. If he dosed a horse with Bute or Banamine, he noted it. If a horse acted up at the breaking cart, he wrote it down. I should be able to reconstruct everything that had happened in his life with horses. He generally used gray school exercise books, but I hadn't seen hide nor hair of anything that looked remotely like his logs.

And how about a record of the money he was taking in? Granted, it wouldn't match the outlay at this stage, but with boarding the pair of bays and the Friesian and the carriage repair work, he had some income. Bank statements?

There had to be a repository of some sort. Most likely a rented storage room. Peggy might know where. But surely he'd have kept his current log where he could get at it easily. Had whoever killed him found and stolen it?

Why?

Because it held evidence incriminating the killer, obviously.

I had brought my own laptop up to Peggy's last night, but locked it in my truck when I left for the farm. I didn't feel comfortable leaving it lying around where whoever had burgled the apartment could come hunting for it. I'd simply have to tote it back and forth with me. It would be loaded with emails about Hiram and requests for information from the driving magazines.

I'd have to organize the memorial service tomorrow. I needed to meet Hiram's lawyer to get the will probated and find out where I stood financially.

None of this dealt with the most important part of Hiram's death. Who had killed him? Who on earth hated him that much?

Chapter 12

Monday evening
Merry

Mama's All You Can Eat Cafe didn't look precisely like The Four Seasons in Manhattan, but Peggy assured me the food was nearly as good, if not as fancy. And much less expensive. I'm up for anything remotely resembling *haute*, or even *demi-haute* cuisine, and it seems Mama's fried chicken and chocolate meringue pie are legendary. I could eat my weight in either one, and suddenly that cheeseburger seemed a million miles away.

Peggy introduced me to our waitress Ellen Stencil, and told me that Mama's is family style. If there are no free tables, people sit where there are empty seats the way they do in Germany.

"I'm so sorry about Hiram," Ellen said as she leaned down to give Peggy a near-cheek peck.

Before our salads arrived, I was holding court. First to come by was a lady named Trisha Cecil with her husband Pruitt. She said in a near whisper, "Such a sweet man, and such a good bridge player." She smiled down at me. "Do you play?"

"Not since college, I'm afraid," I said. I didn't tell her that Hiram was a much better poker player than he was a bridge player. He taught me the difference between a straight and a flush when I was six, but the gambling bug never bit me. My allowance was much too precious to me to risk it on anything I couldn't stuff into my mouth. Preferably chocolate.

He gave up playing because he always won. If he was playing against the rich patrons who could afford to lose the money, they didn't like losing bragging rights. If he was playing against the grooms and other professionals, he didn't like taking their hard-earned cash. That same ability to assess the odds and play them consistently kept him in the winner's circle with his carriage horses. He didn't win every class, but he won often and well. He knew instinctively which chances to take and which to avoid.

"Oh, bridge comes back like riding a bicycle," Mrs. Cecil

said in that soft voice. "I know it's too early for you to be thinking of these things, but I do want to keep up my driving lessons. I'll call to schedule the next one." She left trailed by her husband who had not said a single word.

"What lessons?" I whispered.

"Didn't Jacob tell you?" Peggy leaned toward me and lowered her voice.

I shook my head.

"Hiram was teaching us to drive."

I gaped at her. "Us? As in you?"

She looked down at her plate and actually blushed. "I was his first lesson after he put in the dressage arena, and before that, we were driving the Halflinger in the pasture." Then she met my eyes and her chin jutted as though I had threatened her. "I've even driven Heinzie to the big Meadowbrook. We were talking about my buying a horse and carriage to show. We have several driving shows in this area, you know."

I gulped my iced tea and composed my face as though this was the first time I'd heard of them. "I know. Several." I managed a couple of them.

"I was his star pupil." Peggy waved a hand at the woman who had told me my bridge skills would come back. "She's got a husband, but the others are widows. Hiram was an attractive man."

"You think they might want to continue taking lessons now that Hiram's . . . not available? Surely they're not interested in seducing Jacob."

Peggy choked on her iced tea. "There's not a widow in Mossy Creek that is *that* desperate. Let's face it, after you mulch the azaleas and cover the roses, there's not much to do in a garden in the winter except read seed catalogs and plan for next spring."

"Gardeners?"

"I don't think Ida tried driving. She's the mayor and has her own beau, so she didn't hit on Hiram. Amos wouldn't like it."

"Amos Royden? The police chief would have been jealous of Hiram?" Oh, boy, that was all I needed. First I ran afoul of Sheriff Campbell in Bigelow, a considerably bigger jackass than Don Qui and unlikely to do anything to rock the boat about Hiram's death. Now I found that the Mossy Creek chief of police would have reacted badly if this Ida person came on to Hiram. Knowing Hiram, he *would* have, unless she looked like the Goodyear blimp or the Wicked Witch of whichever direction she came from. Even then, he might have reconsidered it if she was funny and rich. "What's Ida like?"

"Rich as Croesus, clever as a mongoose, and tough as pig iron."

"How old? And how thin?"

"Thin enough. Early fifties. She was the most beautiful woman in Mossy Creek, and would still give our Miss Georgia a run for her money."

Just Hiram's type. If I'd been able to cadge a sports' agent's fifteen per cent of all the money Hiram had talked women out of, I could buy my own horse farm and sit on my tush while illegal immigrants did all the work.

"So what's for dinner, ladies?" Ellen asked. I turned the menu over to Peggy.

"Evening, Peggy, Ms Abbott. I'm Amos Royden. We met this morning."

We shook hands across the iced tea glasses. He looked even better out of uniform. What a pity he was already taken, although not actually married. He was also a possible suspect in my father's murder if Ida had eyes for Hiram. He pulled up a chair and sat across from me. Without being asked, Ellen set a glass of iced tea in front of him.

"Did you talk to Sheriff Campbell?" Peggy asked.

Amos laughed. "He is not happy. He is uncomfortable around formidable women," he said to me.

"Moi? Formidable? I was sweet, but assertive."

"The worst kind. He did send me a copy of the autopsy report. He'd give his eye teeth to put Hiram's death down to some weird accident."

"But not you." Peggy said. "You believe me."

He put up his hands. "Give us a chance. I just got the ME's report this afternoon. I've barely looked at it. Maybe Sheriff Campbell's right."

"Don't be ridiculous," Peggy said.

The look he shot Peggy had her suddenly fiddling with her napkin. Then he looked back at me. "Okay. So come around to my office first thing tomorrow morning, Ms Abbott. We need to talk." He smiled and walked away.

"Oops," Peggy said.

During the entire dinner, Mossy Creekites whose names I could not possibly remember stopped by our table to meet me, offer condolences, tell me what a great guy Hiram was, ask when we were having the funeral, and what they could do to help.

Four asked how quickly I'd be back offering driving lessons. As if, but I didn't tell them that. Besides, I might have to figure out some way to continue teaching and training for the income. The horses needed to be fed and Jacob had to be paid, etc., etc., etc. After my less than glorious exit from the Meadows show, I might not have another show manager's job for a while. I might not even have that job breaking two-year-olds I'd been expecting.

I had not planned to have dessert, but by the time I had worked my way through my dinner with all the interruptions, my stomach was in knots, so I went for the chocolate pie. Chocolate will never let you down.

"Sorry," Peggy whispered. "We should have stayed home and ordered pizza."

"Not on your life," I said as I dug into meringue.

"So, when and how can I help?"

"When what?" I could have fallen into that pie and never surfaced.

"When are you going to do the memorial service and how can I help figure out who killed Hiram? And incidentally, when can we all take more driving lessons? Easter's only a week away, and Hiram promised he'd give carriage rides in the afternoon. I guess you'll have to do it."

"No way. Not happening." So much for the meringue.

"Why ever not?"

Mentally, I smacked myself on the forehead. Idiot. Why could I never learn to keep my mouth shut? I'd have to tell her something. I took a deep breath and folded my napkin beside the oversized dish holding the remains of the pie. "I haven't driven a horse in twenty years."

I expected her to jump on it. Instead, she took a deep breath and leaned back in her chair.

I reached for the check and laid my American Express card

on it. Ellen Stencil picked it up and carried it off.

"Want to tell me about it?" Peggy asked.

"Not here and not now."

"Fine. Over a brandy when we get home and don't have to drive afterwards. Mutt keeps a close eye out for DUIs."

"Look, I'm exhausted."

"No doubt," Peggy said. "But you can't just drop a remark like that and not elucidate." She laid her hand on mine. "I'm sorry."

"No, *I'm* sorry." I signed the bill and pushed my chair back. "Let's go home. Give me that brandy and I'll tell you."

Chapter 13

Monday evening
Merry

Peggy's brandy was Courvoisier and the snifters were crystal. The instant I sank into the club chair across from her chair by the library fireplace, Dashiell settled across the back of Peggy's chair and wrapped his tail across her throat like a feather boa.

Marple jumped onto my lap, kneaded my knee a couple of times, and curled into a ball. Watson took his position across the back of my chair.

Just as I figured we were finally settled and I couldn't drag out my story any longer, twenty pounds of ginger Tom landed splat in the middle of my chest, knocked the air out of me and decanted Marple onto the floor. She stalked away behind Peggy's chair and glared, not at Sherlock, but at me. Cats can always find a human to blame. Sherlock gave me a goofy grin, stretched out from my crotch to my clavicle and went to sleep.

"He does that to everyone," Peggy said, swirling her brandy. "So, why can't you drive Easter weekend?"

I took a deep breath and prepared to give her the edited version. "I had a bad accident a number of years ago, driving a feisty horse Hiram had forbidden me to exercise. He was only three years old, and way over my head."

"Why on earth didn't you listen to your father?"

"He was off at some top-level show in Virginia, although he'd promised me faithfully he'd be home for my birthday party that evening. He didn't even bother to call to say he wouldn't be there. It wasn't the first time he'd missed my birthday, but he'd always called. I was so mad and hurt I decided I'd show him I didn't need his help to be as good a driver as he was." I shrugged. "I wasn't."

"Oh, dear. Were you badly hurt?"

I shook my head. "My mother caught me driving out of the yard into the field and said if she couldn't stop me, she'd go with me.

"Fifteen minutes into the drive the horse suddenly went nuts from a fly bite, took off at a dead gallop, tipped the carriage going around a corner, and threw Mother out. The right rear wheel rolled over her leg. It was a heavy carriage."

Peggy made a sound that was half moan, half scream.

"I managed to stop him and get the carriage back to Mother. She was unconscious, and I could see bone sticking out of her jeans and lots of blood." "How far were you from help?" Peggy poured herself another brandy. I had barely touched mine, so she put the bottle back on her silver tray without offering me any. I'm not certain she was even aware she'd poured a new drink.

"A mile or more. No cell phones back then. I didn't dare move her, so I got back in the carriage and drove the gelding back to the stable, screaming all the way. They landed a helicopter in the pasture and air lifted her to Louisville. One of the farm hands drove me to the hospital to meet the chopper. I didn't know whether I'd find her alive or dead when I got here."

"I'm almost afraid to ask," Peggy said.

"She had a concussion and some bumps and bruises, but her leg was so badly mangled that at one point they were talking amputation. The only thing that prevented them was that they said I wasn't old enough to sign the consent form.

"Thank God she came around and convinced them to operate and put it back together. She was in ICU when my father stormed in shouting at me. Someone had alerted him in Virginia, and his boss had flown him in on his private jet." I gulped my brandy. I could feel the burn all the way down to my toenails. I wanted to scream all over again the way I'd screamed night after night when I dreamt my way through the whole ordeal again and again.

Still do, as a matter of fact, although I've learned to wake myself up before Hiram shows up at the hospital. Peggy leaned across and gripped my knee. "Did she? I mean . . . "

"She lived. Through half a dozen more operations and a year of physical therapy. And through divorcing my father and marrying my stepfather. He's the doctor who supervised her last two operations and her therapy. She limps and still uses a cane when she's tired." No sense in telling Peggy what a great ballroom dancer she used to be, or how I remember her at hunt balls wearing chiffon and rhinestones as she twirled in my father's arms.

"Oh, dear, so you feel responsible for the breakup of your parents' marriage on top of everything else."

"Hiram helped. I haven't held a pair of driving reins since and I don't intend to start now."

"I thought you were at a driving show when Hiram died."

"Managing it, not driving in it. I still train drivers and horses, but from the ground. I use a bullhorn and wireless microphones to talk to the reinsmen. I don't need to be riding beside the driver to teach. For years I blamed Hiram because he'd made me so angry by breaking his promise for the umpty-umpth time, but let's face it, I chose to be angry, I chose to break the rules, I damned near got us killed."

"Is that why you and Hiram were estranged? Why you called him Hiram instead of Dad?"

I shrugged. "A bunch of other stuff as well. The psychologists call it a toxic relationship."

I carefully removed Sherlock from my lap and earned a grumble. I had to use both hands on my knees to stand up, thereby earning another grumble from Watson, still on the back of my chair. Marple hadn't surfaced, but I suspected she was behind Peggy's ankles. "Don't get up," I said to Peggy. "I know the way home."

She still followed me to the back door and waited in the outside light until I shut the door of Hiram's apartment behind me.

I unhooked my bra, kicked off my shoes, fell onto the bed, pulled the quilt up to my shoulders and shut off the light, too worn out even to brush my teeth, much less to take my clothes or my makeup off.

I generally go to sleep the instant my head hits the pillow, even when I'm not exhausted and half drunk. Maybe I was *too* tired to sleep.

I'd wasted so much time hating Hiram. Hating is a choice, and one that hurts the hater much more than the hated.

Now, I had somebody new to hate the person who'd robbed me and my father of the chance to love one another again. Maybe even to totter away into old age together.

I would find out who killed my father and see justice done.

But it suddenly struck me that wasn't my only or even my greatest responsibility. Hiram had committed himself completely to his new enterprise. It was up to me to see that it didn't go down the drain.

Could I succeed in keeping his dream alive?

Chapter 14

Tuesday morning
Geoff

"Definitely murder." Geoff Wheeler laid the coroner's full report on Amos's desk, sat and stretched his legs. "But probably not first degree. If you're planning to kill somebody, there are neater ways to do it." He accepted a mug of coffee from Amos.

"Cream and two artificial sweeteners," Amos said. "Used to be sugar when we were younger."

"Used to be I wasn't fighting gut gravity in the gym and had brown hair. After I talk to you, I'm headed out to what should have been preserved as a crime scene."

"And wasn't, thanks to the state police and Sheriff Campbell."

"Any motive?"

"Not so far. Usually takes generations for real enmity to develop in Mossy Creek. We're still fighting with Bigelow over something that happened in 1836. Lackland moved into Peggy Caldwell's apartment less than a year ago."

"Money? Inheritance? Insurance?"

"His only daughter is due here any minute. The land he bought will be worth a pretty penny in a few years, but not at the moment. Insurance?" Amos spread his hands. "She seems to have a solid alibi, but she could have hired it done."

"Sex?"

Amos chuckled. "You'll have to find out for yourself. Hiram was no spring chicken, but he was attractive, courtly, and a bachelor. Much in demand among the garden club ladies."

"Any chance I could show up at their next meeting?"

"I thought you'd want to see them one at a time," Amos said.

"I'd like to announce that their extra man was murdered and see if anybody reacts. My mother ran the garden club in Athens. Those ladies make satellite communication look old-fashioned. This entire end of the state will know an hour after I see them that somebody offed their tame bachelor."

Mutt opened Amos's door and stuck his head in. "Ms Abbott's here," he whispered.

"Great," Geoff said. "Send her in." Then he looked over his shoulder at Amos. "Sorry. Your office."

Amos waved a hand at him. "Your investigation."

Mutt opened the door fully, and a second later Merry Abbott walked in.

Geoff blinked. He didn't know what he'd expected, but not this. Not that Merideth Abbott was a fashion model. But most of the professional horse women he'd met had skin like saddle leather and tended to look more like Clint Eastwood than Nicole Kidman.

This one didn't land exactly in the Kidman column, but it was close.

"Oh, I'm sorry. I'm interrupting."

Both men stood. "Not at all," Amos said. "This is Agent Geoffrey Wheeler of the Georgia Bureau of Investigation."

He offered his hand. "Sorry for your loss, Ms Abbott."

She sank into one of the wooden chairs in front of Amos's desk. "Georgia Bureau of Investigation? Peggy was right? Somebody actually murdered my father? I kept thinking she must be wrong because. . . . " Her shoulders slumped. "Hiram could be a butthead, but who'd want to kill him? Why? For what?"

"That's why I'm here, Mrs. Abbott." Geoff eased one hip onto the edge of Amos's desk, so that he looked down on her. Not quite as good as sitting behind Amos's desk, but still good. "I take it you have no ideas."

She shook her head. "If Hiram made any enemies, I wouldn't know about them. Hiram and I hadn't been exactly close the last few years. "

"Care to tell us why?"

"Divorced father, constant travel, spotty child support. We got crossways when I was a teenager and stayed that way until recently."

"What changed?"

"We got older. I got a divorce myself a couple of years back that gave me a better understanding of why marriages implode. In the meantime, he seems to have grown. We were meeting in the middle." She ran her hand along her cheek to brush away a tear. "I thought we'd have years to get to know one another again. I was sort of on my way down here to visit him when I got the sheriff's call."

"Quite a coincidence," Geoff Wheeler said. He tried to keep the disbelief out of his voice, but apparently he didn't succeed.

She glared at him. "Don't you dare go there. I've got a couple of hundred people and horses to prove that I was two hours the other side of Chattanooga all weekend."

"I wasn't implying anything."

She rolled her eyes. "Of course you were. If you're actually interested in finding out who killed him and not simply in covering it up for the governor, don't waste your time on me."

"I work for the state of Georgia, not Governor Bigelow." Geoff tried to keep his voice even, but her barb had come uncomfortably close to the truth. Neither he nor Amos was interested in covering up a murder, but the sheriff of Bigelow County had a vested interest in keeping Bigelow safe and serene for the governor and his family. The sheriff was considered semi-honest, but he liked his job. No telling how far he'd go to keep the governor from taking an interest in county politics and throwing support to opposing sheriff candidates in the election.

Next to simply sweeping a murder under the carpet if Sheriff Campbell was capable of that getting a citizen of Mossy Creek arrested and charged with capital murder would suit him just fine. Actually, Governor Bigelow would probably frame Ida Walker for murder in a heartbeat, given the chance. Everyone in the state of Georgia followed their particular feud. At the moment, Ida was ahead on points.

He changed the subject. "Your father seems to have been something of a ladies' man. Could he have been romancing a lady whose husband didn't like it?"

"Hiram was nearly seventy, but that didn't keep him from flirting. If you're asking me whether he was capable of anything beyond that, for God's sake, I'm his daughter. He's unlikely to discuss his conquests or his Viagra prescription with me. Does that mean you think he was a man did it?"

"Or a strong woman," he said, running his eyes down the strong muscles outlined by her turtleneck shirt. "Or a very small woman who had help."

"How about an entire garden club?" she snapped. "Like

Murder on the Orient Express? They got together and decided he'd become a menace to their sisterhood." She stood up without using her arms as leverage.

That took strong thighs and belly muscles. Plenty strong enough to crush a man's skull and then drop a heavy iron wheel over on him. Geoff made a mental note to find out whether all her time could be accounted for over the weekend. The drive from Chattanooga took less than three hours. She might have called her father, met him in the middle of the night, killed him, then driven back to Chattanooga. What time did she have to report for her duties as show manager? Had she spent the night in anyone's bed? Her alibi might not be so airtight after all.

"If you want to speak to me later, give me a call." She handed each man a business card. "That has my cell phone and email address. I'm on the road so much, nobody can get me at home. Now, if you'll excuse me, I have to drive to Bigelow to make arrangements for my father's funeral." She turned back as she reached the door. "If that nitwit sheriff decides not to release my father's body after all, can either of you pull some strings?"

"That shouldn't be necessary," Amos said. "Is Peggy going with you?"

Merry nodded. "I also have an appointment with Hiram's lawyer."

"To find out how much money he left you?" Geoff asked.

She sucked in a breath and snapped, "I've got four horses plus a jackass to feed and a hired hand to pay whether Hiram left any money or not. I'd really like to continue to feed myself too, but if one of us has to go hungry, it'll be me. I need to find out whether I can pay the feed bill and still buy myself the occasional cheeseburger."

"So you're only interested in the horses."

"In my world, the horses *always* come first. You know that old saying, 'dogs have owners, cats have staff?' Compare cleaning a litter box with mucking out a stall if you want to know the difference between acting as staff for a cat or groom for a horse. As a matter of fact, why don't you come out to the farm this afternoon about four when I'm doing the afternoon feeds. I'll show you some *real* manure, and not the stuff you've been shoveling at me." She slammed the door behind her.

"Whoa!" Amos said. "I think that's a point to the lady, Geoff. Reminds me of Ida."

"If she did it, she won't be easy to rattle. The only time she got upset was when I questioned her allegiance to those horses, which are not even hers."

"I don't think she killed him. You don't seriously think she killed him, do you?" Amos said softly asked.

"Ask me after I've checked out her alibi and found out how much money he left her."

Chapter 15

Tuesday Morning
Merry

"You turned off your cell phone," Peggy said as she climbed into my truck in front of her house. "I've called you a dozen times."

"Sorry. I didn't want it to ring while I was talking to Amos and his tame GBI agent."

"Everybody and his brother's been calling me asking when Hiram's funeral is scheduled. And a couple of reporters from national magazines called me when they couldn't get you. I don't know how they even found out that Hiram lived downstairs, much less discovered who I am and what my telephone number is."

"People he worked with in the business, probably. Plus the internet."

"They wanted to ask you about Hiram. I didn't realize he was such a big muckety-muck in the driving world. Oh, I knew he'd had a career, but gold medals at the Driving Worlds?"

"Three times. But not recently." I turned onto the highway leading to Bigelow. "It's a very small world. Nobody outside of driving would so much as recognize his name, although he had enough silver cups and bowls and platters to fill the average jewelry store." I glanced over at her. "Any idea what he did with them? Did he sell them for a down payment on the farm? Most of them are engraved. That must lower the value considerably. Still a lot of them were good quality sterling."

"He didn't bring them with him when he moved in. You saw what he brought. A couple of suitcases, a couple of black plastic trash bags of clothes, some harness and some books."

"I don't know where all his files are either. He kept notes on every horse he ever trained, every Coggins test he ever pulled, every shot or leg poultice. Are there any storage rental places in Mossy Creek?"

"I'm sure there are in Bigelow. Couldn't he have left all but the essentials in Aiken when he moved here?"

That did make sense. I didn't know how long he had wandered before he settled on Mossy Creek and went back to get his horses and belongings. He might have spent months looking for land before he found his forty acres.

"You said Hiram had been living in your apartment less than a year. Did he live somewhere in this area before that? Maybe camp out in that old barn while he and Jacob were putting up the new stable?"

"I think he may have, or stayed in some el cheapo motel, but I don't know for how long or how many times he'd visited the area before he bought his land. He did say he commuted from Aiken for a few months."

"That's some commute. How did he find your apartment?" I asked.

"I had my basement finished last year in hopes of bringing in a little extra income. I put an ad in the *Mossy Creek Gazette* and the following Sunday, Hiram showed up on my doorstep. He was the first and only person to look at the place. He moved in a week later. We became friends almost at once."

I looked over at her. I still wondered if they'd been more than friends, but there was nothing in her voice that said he was a lost lover. It was none of my business anyway unless it turned out to have something to do with his death.

"Turn left," she said. "Mr. Robertson's office is off the main square. I made a list of people you need to call back when we get home. I'm sure there'll be plenty of others on Hiram's answering machine."

I wouldn't be able to blow them off. I owed Hiram his obituaries. What I didn't owe anyone was answers to probing questions about the way he died. Even if I'd had answers, which I didn't.

We drove onto Bigelow's main drag and parked in front of the Victorian house that had been turned into the offices of Kauffman, Hardwick, Smithson and Robertson.

"I recommended Frederick Robertson to Hiram. He's been my lawyer since Ben and I moved down here and Ben died on me. Even in a really straightforward estate, there are things that need to be done, final tax preparation, probate . . . "

"Please," I begged. "I *so* don't want to do this."

Peggy left to do some shopping while I climbed the stairs to the offices where Frederick Robertson was a partner. I've never been to a lawyer's office in Timbuktu, but they probably import antique wood paneling, furniture, and hunting prints on the theory that their clients expect it. This office was the prototypical southern lawyer's office except for the secretary, who was a knockout redhead. She ushered me directly into Mr. Robertson's office. He was chubby, cheerful, and seated me in a leather chair that probably belonged to his grandfather.

After the usual stuff about being sorry for my loss, he templed his fingers and leaned forward. "Do you want me to continue to act for you in matters pertaining to the estate?"

"Good grief, yes!" I reached for my handbag. "Do I need to give you a check as a retainer? I just assumed . . . "

He waved pudgy fingers. "Don't worry about the retainer. I'll have Hiram's will admitted to probate, with the attesting witness statements, put the notices about payment of debts in the legal notice section of the local papers, and have twenty copies of your letters testamentary made for you. You are his sole heir without bond as well his executrix. You're also going to need at least twenty copies of his death certificate . . . "

"I beg your pardon?"

"That should do it for the immediate future. They'll be sent to the funeral home for delivery to you. You'll find yourself giving them out left and right to banks, the social security administration I'll have Eleanor make you a list. I'll file for an extension on his income taxes to give us time to file his final tax statement, although he'd already sent most of the information to his accountant."

If my head could have physically spun 360 degrees, it would have. As it was, my brain was crashing around in my skull at Mach ten. At some point I managed to shut my mouth, but I'm sure my eyes were popping like a bush baby's.

He stopped speaking and put his hand to his mouth. "Oh, dear. You've never done this before. I should have realized. I am a dumb old hound."

"Never by myself."

"This is simple as Simon." He chortled. "Getting seven warring heirs to agree to sell Hiram his land that was difficult."

"I beg your pardon?"

"Do you know anything at all about your father's estate?"

I shook my head.

He took a deep breath and leaned back in his tall leather chair. His head didn't quite reach the top of the back. *Mr. Pickwick Meets Law and Order.*

I stifled a giggle. He really would think I was brainless if I laughed. I've been cursed with the *Chuckles the Clown* syndrome all my life. Remember the old Mary Tyler Moore Show? At the somber funeral for Chuckles the Clown, Mary breaks out in hysterical laughter. That's me. Give me a disaster and I'll get the giggles. Except for the time I hurt my mother.

"Basically, Mr. Robertson," I said as I drove my fingernails into the palms of my hands, "I need to know if there is any money available right this minute so I can pay the feed bill and Jacob Yoder's salary."

"That shouldn't be a problem. Take a copy of the death certificate and a letter testamentary to the Mossy Creek Bank and transfer the funds in your father's checking and savings accounts to your name. Should be enough money for running expenses. If not, we can advance you money from the estate. We'll check with his accountant about his brokerage accounts and other savings and money market accounts, so you can have those transferred to your name as well. Have you considered what you plan to do with the property?"

The words 'sell it' froze on my lips. "Not yet."

"Should you decide to sell it, I have already received at least one discrete inquiry to sell at a profit. In this market that's amazing." He leaned forward and propped his two chins on his fists. "My advice is not to sell. Don't do anything major for a year. That's standard lawyer advice. At the moment the real estate market is in the tank, but at some point Hiram's land is going to be worth a great deal of money."

"I may not be able to afford to keep it. I'm sure the mortgage is astronomical . . . "

He frowned at me. "I keep forgetting you don't know anything. I'm getting old. When a man Hiram's age buys a valuable piece of property on which he plans to make a substantial investment, even in the crazy mortgage market we had before the sub-prime crash, lenders demand a complete physical, including some questions about mental stability." He glanced up at me to see if I understood.

"They wanted to see whether or not he had suicidal tendencies."

He nodded. "Or incipient dementia or Alzheimer's. They also require mortgage insurance. Hiram folded the cost of the new stable and arena into the mortgage. Standard operating procedure at the time, although not strictly Kosher. He'd never get away with it now. The moment Hiram died, the mortgage insurance kicked in. The property is yours free and clear. Or will be, after I shepherd the paperwork through the insurance company and file the deed."

"Free and clear?" I couldn't believe that. I'd expected to be saddled with a load of debt I wouldn't have been able to make the first payment on.

"Oh, the insurance company may make a bit of a fuss, but there's no possibility of suicide. So, unless you actually had something to do with his death . . ."

I shook my head. "I didn't."

"Of course you didn't. They may try to delay the payment, but I won't let them get away with that. You do realize that no one can profit from a crime he or she commits?"

"I have an alibi." In the space of two minutes I had gone from surprise to elation to sheer terror. Suddenly, I was the obvious suspect in my father's death. That GBI agent already thought I'd done it. How perfect was my alibi? I wished I'd accepted the proposition from that Argentinean polo player I'd met at the horse show, even if he was fifteen years younger than I am. As it was, I'd spent the night in bed alone at my motel.

Now I *had* to find out who had actually killed Hiram. And fast. I sure couldn't trust Agent Wheeler to look any further than his long snoot, and Sheriff Campbell would snap the cuffs on me just to keep the governor happy.

Chapter 16

Tuesday Afternoon
Merry

When Peggy picked me up in front of Robertson's office, I carried a stack of blue legal folders containing letters testamentary. Despite the warm April day, my teeth were chattering.

"What on earth is the matter with you?" Peggy asked. "Shall I turn on the heater?"

I managed to stammer my way through most of it while she kept the car idling.

"Good," she said and put the car in gear. "Hiram told me about the mortgage insurance. I assumed you knew. He bitterly resented having to pay it, but knew he couldn't buy the property without it. I told him that Ben took it out when we bought our house in Mossy Creek. Otherwise on my retirement income I might not have been able to keep it after Ben died so suddenly."

"Mr. Robertson seems to think Hiram also had brokerage accounts and money market accounts as well as standard bank accounts. Where did he get the money?"

"He told me he followed the advice of his rich employers over the years. On a smaller scale, of course, but when they made money, he made money."

And they definitely made money. Pots of it.

When I thought of how hard I'd fought to persuade my ex-husband Vic to help with my daughter Allie's tuition payments at the University of Kentucky, I got mad at Hiram all over again. Allie should have gone to an Ivy League School. She had the grades and had been accepted at Johns Hopkins and Brown, but we weren't quite poor enough for grant money, nor rich enough not to need it. She'd been smart enough to land an internship and then a job at her brokerage firm, but she would have had a much easier time if she'd gone to a school in the east.

I had never asked Hiram for money for her, but that was because I assumed he didn't have any. He sure didn't volunteer the information.

Why did that not surprise me? He seldom paid child support for me even before my mother married Stephen. I've never understood why so many men feel no compulsion to support their children.

"Having brokerage accounts does not necessarily mean there's money in them," Peggy said. "The way the stock market's been going lately, he may be down to his last fifty cents."

True. I'd have to hold off my anger until I knew for certain. One minute I grieved for him, the next I was ready to kill him myself. If we'd met, we could have hashed out our differences. Now, I felt as though I was stuck in an elevator with either Dr. Jekyll or Mr. Hyde, and I had no idea which.

"He wanted you to have a good life after he died," Peggy said. "Seems like bad manners to cry po-mouth when he's just made you an heiress."

"He's also made me a murder suspect!"

*

Peggy had made an appointment for us at the Mossy Creek Funeral Home. I had no problem with her taking the lead. I was happy to defer to her as much as I would have deferred to my mother in similar circumstances. I answered questions to the best of my ability, but the whole process was a blur.

"Hiram was nominally an Episcopalian," I said to the funeral director, Mr. Straley, "but I don't think he went to church." Actually, he could have haunted the local church or turned to Buddhism or Scientology for all I knew. "Can't we have a simple Episcopal graveside service? Can't he be buried in your cemetery?"

I didn't want him cremated. I know it's not supposed to matter, but I couldn't bring myself to consider it. That opened up a whole list of decisions. I had to pick out a coffin and a vault to put the coffin in, choose a gravesite, and ask the funeral director to check with the Episcopal rector to see when or if he could do the service.

"I'm afraid we don't have an Episcopal Church in Mossy Creek, but I'm sure the rector at Saint Stephen's in Bigelow would be happy to officiate at the graveside service."

Great. Somebody else to worry about.

"Now," Mr. Straley said as he shoved a sheet of paper across his desk at me, "These are the standard charges for a single plot, although I would recommend a double."

"He wasn't married."

He smiled sweetly. "Nor are you."

"Oh." Talk about stuff you don't want to think about! "No, I think at this point a single will be sufficient, than you."

He took a printed form from his desk and began to write numbers on it. "Let's see. Plot, yes. Opening and closing the grave, yes. Setting up a tent for the mourners at graveside and folding chairs, yes. Hiring the minister." He stopped. "Usually the family does that and pays him directly, but in this case, we will be delighted to schedule him for you. Shall we check on Friday morning for you?"

"Sooner, maybe?"

He sniffed. "You'll find Friday is soon enough. No doubt you will need time for family and mourners to make their ways to Mossy Creek. Standard fee?"

I nodded. I'd ask Peggy what a constituted a standard fee in Mossy Creek.

"Episcopalians do not approve of flowers on the coffin itself, but prefer the church's pall, a heavy tapestry cover. They will no doubt allow us to borrow it for the viewing, but there may be a charge for cleaning and so forth." Notation.

"Putting the obituary and death notice in the *Mossy Creek Gazette*." Notation. "We will need information about your father and a recent photograph if you have one."

I said the only pictures I knew about were the ones from driving shows that I had seen stacked against the wall in the clients' lounge. They might do for obits in the horse magazines, but not in the *Mossy Creek Gazette*.

"I have some snapshots that should do," Peggy said.

"Excellent," Mr. Staley said. "Charge for collecting deceased from the medical examiner in Bigelow, transporting him to us, embalming and preparation." Notation. "Charge for viewing room the night before the service." Notation. He looked up at me. "Will you be furnishing a burial suit or should we provide one?"

I had no idea.

"We will provide clothing," Peggy said, and reached over to

take my hand. She could see I was getting really frazzled. It might not matter how much money he had in his bank account if all those notations added up the way I was afraid they would. Somehow I'd manage to find the money. This was my daddy we were talking about.

"The book for mourners to sign at the viewing and the service." Notation. "We furnish one hundred thank-you notes and envelopes free of charge."

I could remember all the women in my family sitting around the dining room table after my grandmother's funeral drinking quantities of wine, writing notes and telling funny stories about her. I looked up. He'd asked me another question. I had no idea what.

"Do you wish the casket open or closed for the viewing?"

"Closed." Peggy said before I had a chance to answer.

"Fine." Notation. "Now, before we repair to the casket display room so that you can choose the casket of final repose for your father, Mrs. Abbott, just a few more questions. Since you are a stranger in town without a church affiliation, shall we prepare a light repast with punch and wine in the viewing room after the interment for the mourners?"

"I'll bet Hiram would prefer a steamship round of beef and a vat of Artillery punch." I heard my voice ascending into coloratura range, but I couldn't seem to control it.

Mr. Staley gaped, Peggy squeezed my hand hard, but it didn't help. I had an attack of Chuckles the Clown. I tried to head it off at the snickers stage, but it got away from me and morphed into full-blown donkey brays.

That's when Peggy caught it. Her shoulders began to shake. She snorted a couple of times and sailed off into howls of laughter.

At one point we nearly calmed down, but one look at the funeral director's horrified face and we were off again.

I couldn't breathe. Tears streamed down my cheeks. My chest hurt. I was in danger of wetting my pants.

Peggy was as bad off or worse.

The poor man had edged his chair back against the wall behind him. His fingers were searching under the lip of his desk. No doubt he had a panic button to bring on the bouncers to rid him of lunatics.

The door behind us opened and a male voice asked, "Mr. Straley, do you need assistance?"

I clapped my hand over my mouth and managed to choke myself off for a count of five before I exploded again. Peggy gulped and snorted beside me.

To give him credit, Mr. Straley smiled and waved off the man. He folded his hands on his desk and waited us out.

Eventually, of course, we subsided. If we'd kept up much longer I have no doubt the funeral director would have taken his chances and bolted past us out the door. As it was, the knuckles of his folded hands were snow white.

"Oh, my, that felt good!" Peggy said. She grabbed a handful of tissues from the box on the funeral director's desk, blew her nose and wiped her eyes. "I need a drink."

My stomach gave an ominous rumble. We hadn't eaten lunch and it was well past noon.

"Come on, Merry." She pulled me to my feet.

"But we still haven't picked out the casket and . . . "

"We'll come back tomorrow morning at nine," Peggy said as she slung her handbag over her shoulders. "It's not like he's going anywhere."

*

"That poor man," she said as she slid behind the wheel of the car. She gave a sort of yip. I clamped down on her wrist. She wasn't talking about Hiram.

"Don't start. You'll wreck the car." I giggled. "We were awful. I'm so sorry. None of that was funny."

"I doubt it's the first time he's dealt with hysteria. It will be all over town before nightfall." She pulled into traffic. "But oh, how Hiram would have loved it."

"If Hiram had his way, he'd be buried like one of those Neolithic nomads in a marathon carriage."

"Surrounded by the corpses of his slaves, his mistresses, and his horses."

"That's going a little far," I said, but the thought gave me pause. "They wouldn't actually let us bury him in a carriage, would they?"

"No doubt there are strict health regulations about that sort of thing." She pulled into a space in the lot behind Bubba Rice Lunch and Catering. "Besides, the hole would be too big. You can't afford it. However, I see no reason he can't be buried in a top hat with his whip beside him." She glanced at me. "Oh, dear, it's not my choice. I am butting in."

"Butt on. I think it's a great idea. He loved wearing his top hat," I said and began to snuffle. "He had a beautiful handmade English holly whip that he only used for formal occasions. I wonder where it is." I turned in my seat to face Peggy. "We have to find it. He has to be buried with it." I choked. "He loved that whip. Oh, God."

She wrapped her arms around me and patted my back. When I subsided into gulps and hiccups, she said, "Let's get some food into us before we both collapse."

This late we found a table and ordered a pair of chicken salad plates and iced tea. While we waited for it, Peggy reached across and laid her hand on mine. "I know how terrible this must be for you."

"It's horrible, all right, but I'm worried to death about how I'm going to pay for it all. I don't imagine many people will show up from Aiken or Southern Pines or Wellington or Ocala, but I don't want him to feel slighted." I took a gulp of my iced tea. "That is about the dumbest thing I've said recently. He's not around to care."

"The thing about funerals," Peggy said as she stirred a couple of artificial sweetener packets into her tea, "Is that they are an awful lot of fun." She caught my expression and smiled. "The only difficulty is that somebody has to die before you can have one."

I started to say something, but she held up a hand. "Think about it. The only other ceremony at which you see friends and kin you seldom see is at a wedding, and they are generally frantic and nobody gets to talk to one another. That's why God invented wakes. We get together, eat, drink, toast the deceased, remember our lives with him or her, remember how much we love the people we seldom see, do a fair amount of weeping and a lot of laughing, and hang onto one another literally for dear life."

"It's a woman thing, isn't it?" I asked. I remembered listening to the women in my grandmother's kitchen laughing as they cooked and served and cleaned up. As a child, I listened to tales of making wreaths at Christmas, and how she crocheted amazingly ugly dolls to fit over the toilet paper rolls, and the ambrosia she made every Christmas that nobody else knew how to make. At Hiram's wake I'd be surrounded by strangers. Even worse, I might be completely alone.

"Most of the ceremonies of life and death are women things, Merry. It is a skill the generations pass along to one another."

Suddenly I wanted to talk to Allie and my mother.

Chapter 17

Tuesday afternoon
Merry

"Mom, I can't come to the funeral," Allie said. "We're launching an important IPO on Friday."

She had finally returned my call, as I was driving out to Hiram's to feed the horses their afternoon hay and check on Yoder. I heard voices in the cell background. "You're still in the office. Can you talk?"

"Actually, We had such a crappy day that we took off early. I'm in a bar. I am drinking my first and only white wine and I'm with two girlfriends. I am not trolling for Mr. Goodbar."

"Glad to hear it." She was old enough to drink in bars if she wanted to, even New York bars, which television and movies always made out to be strictly for hook-ups with serial killers. I should talk. "Hey, I'm a mother. I get to worry."

"Don't. I'm much choosier than you were."

Ouch.

"Sorry. And it's not just the IPO. I'd just get in the way. I *so* did not know the man. Or how to talk to his friends or even tell stories about him. How embarrassing is that?"

Steve, my mother's husband, was the grandfather she loved and who adored her.

She knew Hiram only from an occasional photo or article in a horse magazine, and checks on her birthday and Christmas when he remembered. Maybe that was one of the reasons she'd learned to equate money with love. She hadn't learned it from me. I never had any money, although that in itself may have driven her to want wealth above all else.

"Relax. I wasn't really expecting you to come," I said and hoped I'd kept the disappointment out of my voice. "I was feeling a little overwhelmed and needed to hear your voice."

The thing that keeps me from smacking her upside her head is that she does get it eventually. "I could fly down to Atlanta on Saturday and stay until Sunday afternoon. Would that help?"

Go and pat needy mother on the shoulder. As if. "And miss

an April weekend in Manhattan with your friends? No way would I do that to you. A simple graveside service. No biggy. I'll report afterwards."

"Maybe we can do an FTF next weekend, okay?"

I smiled. I always did when she went all acronym on me. "A face-to-face might be just what the doctor ordered."

"I'll send you a time when I know my schedule. You can tell me all about it then. Mom, did somebody really kill him? I mean, nobody you actually know gets killed, much less family."

"Somebody actually did." I didn't add that at the moment I was at the head of the line as First Murderer, at least in the eyes of law enforcement.

*

Agent Stone-Face had already parked his white Crown Vic with its antenna farm and black-walled tires in front of Hiram's barn. I've never known why the cops don't simply put blazing lights on top and signs on the side. You'd have to be from Katmandu not to know you're being tailed by an unmarked police car.

Wheeler, however, wasn't sitting behind the wheel waiting for me, but back in the stable with an actual muck fork in his hands and an Atlanta Braves baseball cap on his head. He wore starched jeans and a long-sleeved t-shirt emblazoned with Georgia Bureau of Investigation. "You did say four o'clock?"

I wear a stainless steel watch that has survived a million dunkings in horse liniment. It read four minutes after four. "What about 'close enough for government work?'"

"Not the government of the state of Georgia. What am I supposed to do with this thing?" He bounced the prong end of the muck fork on the ground.

"You weren't seriously planning to pick up horse manure, were you?"

"That's why I'm here."

I took the fork. "Go sit on a hay bale. Watch and learn."

He arched an eyebrow at me. I wish I could do that. I can wiggle my ears, but that doesn't express quite the same degree of disdain.

"Where's Yoder?" he asked. He arranged the creases in his jeans and sat on a bale outside Heinzie's stall.

"No idea. He should be here." I kept my voice casual, but

my stomach clenched. If Jacob thought he was under suspicion, he might well have high-tailed it for the hills or his lady friend and left me to deal with this place alone. I prayed I was over-reacting.

I pulled the manure cart from beside the barn entrance to the front of Heinzie's stall. Since the horses spent most of the day out, only a single pile of road apples lay like a nest of brown roc's eggs in a corner of his stall. I scooped them up, picked up a small pile of wet shavings, checked the water bucket and moved across the aisle to do the next stall. "I am very good at mucking stalls. How's that for a talent to put on your tombstone?" I leaned against the wall and closed my eyes.

"You okay?"

"Blood sugar," I lied. "Move over."

He did.

"I have to figure out what to put on Hiram's tombstone."

"Name, date of birth and death, obviously."

I gulped. "He deserves more than that when some kid in the twenty-third century comes checking out old graveyards for a term paper. Something pithy so he'll say, 'Wow! What a guy.'"

"That could go either way. What a great guy or what a rotten guy. Which was he?" Wheeler asked.

I picked up the manure fork and walked into Don Qui's stall. "A guy who didn't deserve killing."

I launched the fork like a lance. It stuck into the wood below the window and quivered there. I wanted to gnaw it down to the metal like an angry beaver with a sapling.

"I've spent this whole damned day on the logistics of death and I'm not through yet. When do I get to pay attention to who killed him and why?"

He came into the stall, yanked the manure fork out of the wood and handed it to me. "You don't. I do."

"Right. Like anyone around here is interested in anything but kissing the governor's ass."

"Screw the governor's ass."

"I'd rather not." We glared at one another across my lethal weapon. I swear he broke first.

The corner of his mouth lifted. "I'd rather not as well."

He took the fork, and I followed him into the aisle. "So, who gets the money?" he asked.

"Me, as you no doubt already know." Of course he knew. No reason for Robertson not to tell him. Wills become public knowledge the moment they are probated. Why make Wheeler wait? "Now, if I just knew what money, how much, where it is, and how to get it, I'd be able to pay the funeral home mega-bucks for what they call a simple graveside service. God only knows how much a big send off in a church with an organ and a choir would cost."

"I would imagine his accountant could tell you how to locate his money."

"Robertson is setting up an appointment with him for tomorrow if he can squeeze me in." I began to stomp up and down the aisle waving the fork like a cheerleader's baton. At one point Wheeler ducked.

"Watch that thing."

"Watch yourself. Peggy and I have to go back to the funeral home at nine tomorrow to pick out a casket and a vault for Hiram, approve the grave site, find out when and if the Episcopal priest can and will perform the service and lend us his pall, check out headstones . . ."

"Pallbearers?"

"What?"

"Honorary ones, at least, to walk behind the coffin up to the gravesite from the hearse. You'll need at least one limousine to take them from the funeral home to the graveside. And one for you and Mrs. Caldwell and whatever other family attends."

I smacked myself in the head. "Pallbearers? Who on earth can I get? He didn't know anybody around here but women and Jacob Yoder."

"There's Robertson and his accountant."

"Oh, lovely bosom buddies for life. Can you have women pallbearers?"

"How about the people he knew in the horse world?"

"Nobody's going to drive over from Aiken of Southern Pines or up from Ocala and Wellington. They'll send flowers. Oh, God, flowers! I'll have to order some in case nobody else sends any. They may send memorials or telegrams or phone me, but they won't actually come."

"Thought those big guns flew private jets. They may get together and come in a group."

"That's all I need!"

"In any case, don't forget you'll need boutonnieres for them."

"What?" I yelped. "That's for weddings."

He looked so calm leaning against the wall that I wanted to clock him on that wolf snout of his. "Funerals, too. Usually white rosebuds."

"Do I get to carry a bouquet?" I heard the hysteria in my voice. Chuckles the Clown peeked over the horizon like Kilroy over the fence line. I would *not* lose my cool in front of this man.

"How big is your refrigerator?" he asked.

"Why?"

"Because by the time you get home tonight, you'll have enough chess pie and sweet potato casseroles and homemade zucchini bread to feed Mossy Creek."

"They'll all have to be thanked." I collapsed on a hay bale and dropped the fork. "In writing." I glared up at him. "You're enjoying this."

"No, I'm not. But I am an expert at what goes on after somebody dies by violence. Many times there's no body to bury. Don't let it overwhelm you. Don't you have family that could come down and help?"

"My mother would come if I begged, but I won't. She has been married to my stepfather for twenty years, I'm divorced and an only child, and *my* only child is launching an IPO in New York on Friday. I'm it. If it weren't for Peggy Caldwell, I don't know what I'd do."

"She's certainly very helpful," he said. I caught something in his voice.

"Wheeler, if it weren't for Peggy, Sheriff Shiny-Badge would have brushed Hiram's death off as an accident."

"I doubt even he could have managed that after the medical examiner's findings, but Peggy had already gotten in front of it. She did find the body, after all."

"And the person who finds the body is the killer? First you go after me, then after Peggy?"

"I'm not going after anybody. Yet. Find me another of those fork things. We'll get this done and the horses fed fast." He pushed the cart from in front of Don Qui's door. "Then I want to see the inside of the workshop."

"Don't you need a warrant?" I handed him a fork from the rack beside the door.

"It's technically a crime scene."

"But your people released it."

He dumped a small pile from Don Qui's stall into the cart and moved it down to the next stall. "Everybody watches too much *Law and Order*. I could get a court order, but it would be faster if you'd give me permission to search."

"Permission granted. But I get to watch."

"Dang," I heard and spun in time to see Jacob Yoder turning and striding away fast.

Wheeler dropped his fork and sprinted after him. "Yoder. Hold up. I want to talk to you."

"Later. I am busy."

"Now! Right there, unless you want me to violate your parole for running from an officer of the law."

Jacob stopped, but didn't turn around. "I have nothing to say to you."

"*I* sure do." I said as I came up to them. "It's four-thirty. You said you feed and pick stalls at four."

"Thirty minutes only is not much."

I could smell alcohol on him, but whether he'd been drinking beer or hard stuff, I couldn't tell. I'd have to discuss that with him, but I wasn't looking forward to it.

"*They* think it's a big deal." I waved at the five equine heads hanging over the fence as though they were on the verge of starvation. "Please finish the stalls and fill the water buckets. I'll put out the feed. Where's your list of who gets what?"

"I know what they eat." He edged around Wheeler. "I will do it." He sounded sulky, but obviously putting out feed and mucking stalls was preferable to speaking to the GBI. "You want to talk to me, you come along," he said to Wheeler.

The agent glanced at me. "Alone. Ms Abbott, please wait for me outside the workshop. I won't be long."

With those words Yoder visibly relaxed. "I know nothing."

I wanted to hear whatever constituted nothing in his book, but Wheeler lifted that damned eyebrow at me again, so I slunk off around the corner of the barn and stopped out of sight.

A moment later Wheeler stuck his head around the corner.

"Didn't your mother tell you it's not nice to eavesdrop?"

"Didn't yours tell you it's bad manners to sneak up on people?" I walked off with my head held high.

He'd said *outside* the workshop, but it *was* my workshop, after all. Or would be, once the will was probated. I left the padlock open and hanging from its hasp. The fluorescent lights under the rafters furnished Hiram plenty of light for fine work at his workbench and in the center of the barn, but the back and right side were in shadow.

I walked past the sagging vis-à-vis to the two carriages against the back wall waiting for restoration. The one on the left by the harness racks was a real beauty—an antique dogcart set up for a pair. The two horses in the pasture would fit perfectly with it.

On closer inspection, however, the upholstery leather showed bare patches, the wicker sides of the dog compartment under the seat hung ragged, and the coachwork was deeply scratched and scored as though it had been run through brambles. The singletree to which the two horses would be attached hung from one rusty chain just in front of the dashboard, and the spokes of the wheels looked as though they'd been driven through heavy brush and over tree limbs. It needed restoration, but nothing any good carriage maker couldn't handle. Whoever sent it along to Hiram was doing him a favor, giving him some income as he was getting started. Probably one of his old clients who knew how precise his work was.

Actually, in some ways he was an even better craftsman than a driver. The carriages he and his owners drove were always immaculate, and if they needed repair, he did the work himself, not generally the sort of thing one would expect of a professional driver. He'd always had a workshop wherever we lived, and I'd worked alongside him every chance I got. My mother flipped out when she found me using a circular saw when I was seven. I still have all my fingers, so Hiram was a good teacher.

The second carriage was an obvious antique doctor's buggy from the mid nineteenth century. I'd be willing to bet it had been stored in some farmer's hay barn since the last time it was used. Since doctors regularly traveled the back roads of the south by horse and buggy well into the twentieth century, it could have been stored since the nineteen twenties.

It was a wreck. God knows why anyone would want to restore it. A brand new one would be cheaper and better constructed. They aren't rare. One of the shafts that would have held the single horse leaned against the back wall. The other lay on the ground in two pieces. Both were badly warped.

The fabric of the canopy was in shreds as was the black horsehair upholstery. Varmints had appropriated most of the stuffing to line their nests. The entire equipage was filthy, and half of the spokes in the wheels were broken. All the brass was black with age. The glass in the lanterns was broken or missing. Whoever commissioned the restoration was spending a pretty penny for what had to be sentimental reasons.

I couldn't return either of them until I discovered the clients' names.

So I'd better find Hiram's records.

"Thought I told you to wait outside," Wheeler said from the doorway.

"Don't *do* that! You scared me half to death."

"Don't do what? Walk into where I told you I was going? Or don't catch you doing something you don't want me to see?"

"I am *so* not doing a thing I don't have a right to do. I was looking at the carriages Hiram was restoring. I have to find out who they belong to so I can return them."

"Shouldn't be difficult." Wheeler glanced around the barn. "Where'd he keep his paperwork?"

"Good question. You see any filing cabinets?"

"No. I'll let you know if I find anything."

"Are you dismissing me?"

"Yes. Go home. I'll come by after I finish here."

"Say what?"

He sighed. "Ms Abbott, I realize that you are staying in your father's apartment, but I do need to go over it."

"Why?"

"He may have left a note saying, 'if I should be murdered, so-and-so did it.'"

"You are one callous bastard."

He closed his eyes. "Right. Sorry."

"Simply because I don't go off into hysterics doesn't mean

I'm not grieving. He was my father, and some place inside I haven't accessed in twenty years I loved him."

"Then let me check his apartment."

"Okay, but call first or I won't open the door."

"Good enough." He walked back towards the *vis-à-vis*, then glanced at me over his shoulder. "Go away."

I did.

Jacob had finished feeding and mucking. He dumped the contents of the manure cart on top of the pile, then trundled it back into the barn. He didn't speak when he saw me waiting for him.

"What did you tell Wheeler?" I asked.

"Nothing. Cannot say what I do not know. I have an alibi."

"He going to check it?"

"That man checks he has a head on his shoulders before he climbs from bed in the morning."

"Who is she? The alibi?"

He shook his head. "None of your . . . business."

It wasn't. But that didn't mean I'd stop asking questions. I've never understood how the Jessica Fletcher types manage to be so rude and nosy and get away with it. Jacob already disliked me, so I might as well practice being rude and nosy on him. "Was Hiram worried about anything?"

"You."

"Huh?"

As he raked the aisle, I walked alongside him.

"You arriving down here to see him. Like to have worked me to death finishing the fencing and spreading the sand in the arena and staining the wood on the stalls. Trying to finish the *vis-à-vis*, too, so you could drive around town on Easter."

"He knows I don't drive."

Jacob swept the steel tines of his rake within an inch of my sneaker. He expected me to jump back. I wanted to, but managed to hold my ground. "*He* drove, did he not? He could see good as anybody up close and trotting slow. How you think him and me have been fixing the carriages? Heinzie is lazy, but he is unlikely to run into anything at a walk."

"Who owns the carriages?"

"He did." He waved a hand toward the back of the stable.

"Not the new ones. The ones in the workshop he's

restoring."

He shrugged. "Don't know. Vis-à-vis is sold to somebody out of town. Atlanta, maybe. Supposed to pick it up after Hiram used it Easter."

"What about the driving lessons he's been giving?"

Jacob snickered, pulled a tin of tobacco out of his rear pocket and started to stuff a wad of it into his cheek.

I held up a hand. "Not in the barn."

"I do not *smoke* it. Hiram never minded." He dug the rake into the clay so hard he had to yank the tines free.

"I do. I hate the stuff."

"You make too many rules." He shoved the bits of hay out the back door of the stable and onto the grass. Normally, that would bother me. I preferred to have it added to the manure pile, but I let it go.

I might need a new farm hand sooner than I thought. "The lessons?"

"The women take lessons to get close to Hiram. He made sweet talk so they came back for more." He simpered at me. Brown teeth showed between thin lips. His voice went deep. "Sweet thing, you slide on over here and let Hiram help you handle those reins." He sounded amazingly like Hiram in his southern gentleman role, and different from his usual stilted Pennsylvania voice.

I shuddered. "What about Mrs. Caldwell?" Jacob might well know if Hiram and Peggy had been more than friends.

"She is very serious about the driving. Some take to driving like they find the Holy Grail. Hiram looked to buy her a carriage and a Halflinger once he found a good deal. She is a natural driver. Good hands. He thought even of having her drive the Friesian to the vis-à-vis part of the time on Easter."

Peggy hadn't mentioned that to me, but maybe Hiram hadn't told her yet. "And the rest of the time? Not me?"

"Hiram planned to drive. You would ride with him."

Right. What was I supposed to do when he casually handed me the reins in the middle of Main Street with half the kids in Mossy Creek in the vis-à-vis and their parents watching? Sneaky old coot. I would have climbed down and left him on his own. One cripple on my conscience is way more than enough.

"Now *you'll* have to drive," I said. "I'll ride along if Peggy can't, but I will not handle the reins."

The sneaky look again. "Not in my job description."

"How about 'other duties as assigned.'"

"You pay me extra, say a hundred bucks?"

I nodded. "You have any ideas where his paperwork is?"

"Told you no. In Aiken, maybe."

"Jacob, who wanted him dead?"

He held up his hands. "Not me. I am hired labor only."

"Much more than that. You go back a long way."

"Does not mean we were close."

"Please, you worked for him. You saw things. Who did he get crossways with?"

For a moment, a foxy expression passed across his face, but was gone almost before I registered it. He did know something. Something he wasn't about to tell me.

I gave up. We went over details of the morning schedule, and I helped him put the horses out for the night. Equines, that is. Don Qui decided he wanted to stay inside, away from the Mayflies until he realized Heinzie was outside. Then he brayed until I let him out to join his buddies.

"I am going to town now," Jacob said. "I will return in the morning to feed and water." He started across the pasture but stopped ten feet away and turned back to me. "I am not a trainer," he said. "If you plan to continue running this farm as a training establishment, then either you must quickly hire someone to train or return to driving yourself." He stalked off across the pasture.

I stuck my tongue out at his retreating back. *Mind your own business.* The thing was, he was right. I couldn't afford to hire a first class trainer, certainly until I had a full barn, and I wouldn't have a full barn if I didn't hire a trainer or train myself.

I could bribe Yoder to do some of the driving, and Peggy would pitch in as well. Jacob said she was a fast learner with a real aptitude for driving, but she was still a beginner.

I enjoyed ground driving horses but no faster than a walk. Running around the arena behind a trotting horse would give me a heart attack in five minutes.

I could lunge the horses and give a student driving lessons from the ground, but that simply wasn't good enough.

I had to get back in a carriage and drive.

I leaned over the pasture fence, and all the horses wandered over to have their foreheads scratched. Don Qui wriggled in front of Heinzie and stood between his forelegs. I always carry a pocketful of sugar cubes, which really makes a mess in the washing machine if I forget to remove them. I handed sugar cubes to Don Qui and Heinzie.

"Okay, guys," I said, as the others crowded closer. I doled out cubes to the two Dutch warmbloods and the Halflinger pony. I hadn't paid attention to any of them except to feed and water them and muck their stalls. Being out in pasture instead of standing in stalls had calmed down the Dutch warmbloods, but they also hadn't been driven since Hiram's death, so they were probably hyper again. The owner had sent them to Hiram because they were unruly. Even if they behaved like angels, I had no business attempting to build my confidence behind a pair of sixteen hand high-strung warmbloods.

And Heinzie was too darned big to put to without help. Simply dragging the big Meadowbrook up behind him and lifting it over his tabletop rear end and into the tugs would take two people. No horse took kindly to being poked in the butt with a wooden shaft.

Peggy said Hiram used Golden Boy, the Halflinger, as a lesson horse for his beginning students. Those I had met were all female and middle-aged or older, so Golden Boy must be gentle and forgiving. Since he was technically small enough to be considered a pony, his Meadowbrook cart and harness were both smaller and lighter than Heinzie's. I could put him to without help.

Last, but definitely not least, he didn't have a deranged emotional attachment to a psychotic miniature donkey the way Heinzie did.

At some point, I decided, I'd put Golden Boy to his cart and attempt to drive while Jacob or Peggy stayed by the fence to monitor.

I backed up a step and stared into Golden's chocolate eyes. He seemed to understand me. I could almost hear him telling me he'd look after me.

I'd never be able to conquer my rotten phobia with anyone looking on. What if I failed? Jacob would snicker, which would be bad.

Peggy would pity me, which was worse.

I had to pick up the reins when I was alone, or not at all. Once I was confident driving Golden Boy, I could spring it on them like *Poltergeist.* "I'm baaaaccck!"

On the other hand, driving alone was as dangerous as scuba diving alone. And what about the epitaph carved on the cowboy's tombstone? "Aw, he ain't gonna do nothing."

"You won't, will you, Golden?" I said and scratched behind the Halflinger's ears.

Alone it would be. I'd walk Golden sedately into the dressage arena, an enclosed space. No trot. Once I'd broken through the taboo or the phobia make that terror I'd tell Peggy what I'd done and go from there. It wasn't as though I'd forgotten how to drive. I started handling the reins on my pony cart when I was five, and I'd been handling them with Hiram since I was three. My hands and arms still remembered, even if my brain fought to forget.

And OMG how I missed it! I hadn't admitted that even to myself. I told myself that simply working around horses was enough. That the occasional trail ride in the saddle compensated for missing long, leisurely drives or heart-stopping marathon runs.

Besides, if I drove alone and messed up, nobody else would be hurt.

That was what had taken me off the box. I couldn't bear the thought of hurting a passenger or horse. There were fewer carriage accidents than riding accidents, but the ones there were tended to be much worse.

What the heck. I had a hard hat, a cell phone, and a couple of hours of daylight left. Why wait? I might never push my courage to the sticking place again. Technically, I wouldn't even be alone. Geoff Wheeler was in the barn, although I didn't plan to let him catch me driving Golden Boy.

I stared into Golden Boy's wide brown eyes. "I can do this," I said. Golden Boy wiggled his ears in agreement. I haltered him and cross-tied him in the stable aisle. I opened the gate to the dressage arena so that I wouldn't have to get off the cart to do it once I was holding the reins. This would be a piece of cake.

None of the horses had been groomed properly in days, and once I began to curry and brush Golden Boy I realized that his natural golden color had concealed a thick layer of dirt and dander. He leaned into me as I worked, sighing in pleasure. The longer I worked, the harder I brushed, the calmer I grew.

Golden Boy stood patiently while I harnessed him and put him to the Meadowbrook, and I put on my hardhat.

I unclipped the cross ties, picked up the reins and walked around to the rear of the cart, lifted the seat and put one foot on the rear platform.

"Whoa," I said. "Stand." I lifted my other foot onto the platform and took a deep breath. I was aboard if not actually sitting down yet. *So far, so good.*

My full weight pushed the rear platform down and lifted the shafts in the tugs. Golden snorted, lifted his head and braced himself against the additional weight.

As the cart tilted backwards, I caught my breath, grabbed for the back of the seat, rammed the toe of my left shoe hard into the steel brace under the seats, and yelped in agony. Startled, Golden Boy took a little crow hop and pulled the cart out from under me.

I yanked my toe out, let go of the seat, teetered, overbalanced and fell back, tearing the reins out of my hands. I grabbed for the fender to stay upright, but missed. Both feet went out from under me. I landed on my back in the dirt and knocked the wind out of myself.

My hard hat thwacked the ground hard enough to rattle my brain. I couldn't draw a breath. My heart ceased to beat, and once I gasped it back to life, it raced.

I'd broken my toe, or maybe my foot. Or my back. Or my ribs, or my stupid fool neck. I sat up and saw the reins trailing in the dirt behind the cart.

Released from his crossties and with no one holding his reins, the pony was free to canter off with the cart behind him.

Just like Jethro.

Unlike Jethro, Golden Boy walked.

Thanking God for short-strided ponies, I dove forward, smacked my chin on the edge of the back step, grabbed the reins, and wound up face down in the dirt. I spit out the dirt and barked, "Golden Boy, whoa!"

Obligingly, he stopped and turned his head as far as he could to try to peer behind him in puzzlement. We were supposed to be going on a drive, weren't we?

I pulled myself to my feet behind the cart. My chin hurt, but I didn't feel any blood, thank God. I'd never explain blood to Peggy, but makeup would cover any bruise. I prayed Geoff hadn't heard me shout. I was embarrassed enough without a witness.

I was dying to take my right shoe off to check for broken toes, but was afraid to look. I unhooked the hard-hat without letting go of the reins and tossed it behind me onto the wash rack. It bounced.

"Was it good for you too?" I asked Golden Boy. "Personally, I had a *whee* of a time."

He snorted, anxious to move off.

"Sorry, guy, not gonna happen." Not this afternoon and probably not in the future.

I'd been damn lucky. Thanks to Hiram's training and a good-natured pony, nothing bad had happened. Nothing except that I had totally freaked and dropped the reins on an unsecured pony put to a cart. If I'd done that during a show, I'd have been kicked off the grounds.

This time there was no show committee to blame.

I'd tried and failed miserably. I didn't plan to try again.

Chapter 18

Tuesday evening
Merry

I managed to sneak my truck past Geoff's and down the driveway without his seeing me. I'd brushed as much dust as possible off my clothes, but my face was filthy.

As I turned left on the country road that intersected with the main road to Mossy Creek, I nearly sideswiped an empty silver Beemer parked along the narrow shoulder fifty yards from Hiram's driveway. The car blended dangerously into the evening shadows. Who'd be wandering around out here at five-thirty on an April afternoon?

I wasn't aware of any open hunting season in Georgia this late in the spring. Besides, who takes a Beemer on a hunting trip? By the time I thought to write down the license plate number I was around the curve where I couldn't see the car in my rearview mirror. I made a mental note to ask Peggy if she knew anyone who drove that kind of car, then decided I was being paranoid. The car wasn't on Hiram's property or even on his side of the road.

Hiram's property started on the right side of the road and climbed up the hill. Somebody must own the land on the other side of the road that continued down the hill. Whoever owned it was simply checking it out, although I didn't see a soul. I also didn't see a 'for sale' sign anywhere along the road on that side, and at first glance couldn't see any viable use for the parcel. It looked to be made up of old growth woods, scrub pines and thick vines and underbrush that grew straight down the mountain. There was probably a streambed at the bottom, but it was much too far away to see or hear.

No good for farming. Any *house* would have to be built on stilts sunk deep enough into concrete so that the house wouldn't slide down the hill during the first big rainstorm. Construction would cost a fortune. Logging would be next to impossible, since any logs would have to be hauled straight up the hill to the road. Hunting would be brutal. I'd seen several deer trails disappearing down into the woods on that side, but any hunter who shot a deer down there would have to haul the carcass up the hill though poison oak and sumac. And snakes. I do not do snakes.

If the original farmers who owned Hiram's land had owned that land as well, I suspected their heirs would be stuck with it forever unless they turned it into a nature conservancy. Good thing they hadn't tried to force Hiram to buy that parcel when he bought his farm.

*

Peggy had asked me to stop for a drink when I made it home. As I drove up I saw a number of packages on her front porch. I parked my truck, went in the kitchen door, and told her about them.

"Oh, Lord. Food. I put the car in the garage when I came home from Marilee's and didn't look out when I turned the front porch light on. I didn't even see them. We'd better bring them in."

We found several covered aluminum dishes and throwaway plastic containers on Peggy's front porch, as well as a couple of cakes and loafs of zucchini bread. Just as Geoff Wheeler said.

I guess the people that dropped them off didn't want to take the chance of leaving them in the driveway outside my door, so they left them on Peggy's front porch. They might well have assumed she was feeding me anyway. In any case they knew *her* and didn't know *me*. It took the two of us a couple of trips to bring them in off the porch and set them out on her kitchen counters and table.

Peggy brought a yellow legal pad and a pen from her desk in the library and handed it to me. "I'll read you the name of the person who sent the dish and what they sent. That way you'll have a list to use when we write thank-you notes after the funeral."

The names meant nothing to me, of course, but I dutifully listed them as she read them to me.

"You can have the Lady Baltimore cake," she said. "I've never liked white cake. I'll fight you for the Sock-it-to-me cake. I don't believe in any dessert that's not chocolate. The apple pie we can split."

Someone sent a pan of green beans with canned fried onions

on top, already starting to sog up. My grandmother fixed them every Thanksgiving and Christmas along with her sweet potato casserole covered with marshmallows. Peggy could have them with my compliments.

I ate one of the pecan brownies and drank a Diet Coke while I wrote the names she read me from the cards attached to the dishes.

One container held slices of spiral cut ham and sliced turkey. Perfect for sandwiches. "I'd be happy with a sandwich for dinner," I said.

Peggy nodded. "Me, too, but we should probably eat the tuna casserole while it's fresh and still warm." She shoved Sherlock off the chair at the head of the table before he could get to the throwaway aluminum pan that held cream tuna with breadcrumbs on top. I'm sure to a cat it smelled like ambrosia. "Bad cat. Go away."

He meowed at her, swearing that nobody cared that he was starving too.

Peggy picked up the aluminum pan of tuna casserole and looked under the bottom. "Drat. No card. Maybe it fell off on the porch." I'll put the rest of this stuff away while you look." I checked our path from the front door, the porch, the front steps, and walked down the driveway to the street. No card or masking tape that might have come off the bottom of the pan.

As I closed the front door behind me, I heard Peggy yell, "No!" followed by a crash and a thud. Something yellow streaked across the floor and disappeared into the library followed by three other streaks. Peggy ran after the four cats brandishing a metal serving spoon. "Sherlock Caldwell, I will throttle you!" She stopped when she saw me. "He's greedier than Jabba the Hutt."

"What?"

"Come see."

The aluminum bottom of the upended tuna casserole pan glinted from the floor. Tuna, cheese and noodles lay in globs around it.

"I turned my back for one second to put the green beans in the refrigerator," she said, "and the next thing I know Sherlock's up on the table with a faceful of tuna casserole. He freaked when he saw me and knocked the whole thing on the floor. What a God awful mess!"

The next second we heard an ear splitting yowl from the library. Dashiell lumbered back toward the kitchen as fast as his arthritic legs could carry him. Behind him the yowls continued.

Cats have a special howl when they're in pain that is impossible to mistake. "That's Sherlock," Peggy said.

Dashiell jumped onto the chair, then the table, and put his paws on Peggy's shoulders, obviously trying to tell her something was wrong.

He didn't need to convince either of us.

She tore off her apron and tossed it to me. "Clean that mess up," she said and ran to the library with Dashiell in her arms.

I got down on the kitchen floor, picked up the casserole pan and shoveled tuna, noodles and breadcrumbs back into it with both hands. We couldn't eat it now, and from those yowls, neither should any other mammal. I shoved the pan into the cold oven and slammed the oven door on it, pulled the entire roll of paper towels off the rack and scrubbed the floor to get the last bits of casserole, then tossed the used towels into the covered metal trash can with the cat proof lid.

Peggy rushed back in. "Sherlock's under my chair vomiting and shaking. Call Hank Blackshear. He's our vet. His number's on the wall by the telephone. Tell him we'll meet him at the clinic in ten minutes." She disappeared while I made the call. It was after hours. Of course, I got his answering service.

"If you'll tell me the nature of your problem," the telephone lady said, "I'll call Dr. Blackshear and have him call you back."

"No time for that. Tell him to meet Peggy Caldwell and Sherlock at his clinic. It's an emergency. I think he's been poisoned."

I was afraid we wouldn't be able to catch Sherlock, but he huddled miserably under Peggy's chair until I got down on my hands and knees and pulled him out. He didn't even try to claw me.

I handed him to Peggy, who wrapped him in towels and cradled him like a baby.

"I'll drive, you navigate," I said and reached for my purse. "I'll be there in a second." I went back into the kitchen, unceremoniously dumped the brownies out of their throwaway plastic container and onto one of Peggy's plates, scooped some of the tuna casserole into the empty container, popped the lid on and raced for my truck.

Jacob had told me that Hiram used Dr. Blackshear for his vet work, but I'd never met the man and had no idea where his clinic was located. If Mutt caught me speeding around the square, he'd have a fit and give me a ticket. I prayed he wasn't around, because I didn't intend to stop for anything less than a roadblock manned by Mutt and a fifty-caliber assault rifle.

Sherlock had stopped squirming and yowling. That was bad. I'd rather he tried to claw his way out of Peggy's arms. Peggy sobbed and cooed, but neither of us said what we were thinking. I couldn't talk and drive, and I don't think she had breath left over for speech other than to mumble the occasional direction.

We rolled into the clinic as the vet arrived in his truck.

Peggy leapt out before I'd stopped, and raced inside as he switched on the lights. I picked up the bowl of casserole and ran after them.

She handed the cat in his nest of towels to the doctor. "Merry Abbott, Hank Blackshear," Peggy said.

"Hey," he said.

"Merry. Maybe I can help."

The next half hour Hank intubated, intravenoused, shot, drew blood, and shoved nasty black charcoal stuff down Sherlock's throat while I held him and Peggy alternately cried and crooned.

"What did he get into?" Hank asked me.

"Tuna casserole. Someone left it on Peggy's front porch for us because of my dad's death. Either we lost the card or it never had one, so we don't have a clue who sent it."

"Tuna casserole is normally pretty harmless to cats, even when they stuff themselves," he said.

"He didn't take but one bite," Peggy sobbed. "I chased him away before he could gorge himself. He got sick almost within a couple of minutes. Could it have gone bad sitting on the front porch?"

"Not in this weather," Hank said. "Unless it's been sitting there for a couple of days, and even Botulism wouldn't act this quickly."

"It wasn't out there more than a couple of hours," I said.

"It's not simple food poisoning or salmonella. this one

might just have some unusual ingredients," Hank said.

"Something actually poisonous?" I asked.

"Surely not on purpose," Peggy said. "Somebody made a mistake and put in something they didn't plan to."

"Peggy," Hank said, "Whatever it was made Sherlock real sick real fast."

"He only had one bite," Peggy wailed. "But he takes big bites."

"It's not corrosive," Hank said. "His throat's not burned. His gums were white when you brought him in, now they're a tad pinker than when we started."

He hadn't dared give Sherlock a sedative, although his heart had been racing when he first listened to it. Peggy smoothed the broad, flat space between Sherlock's big yellow ears. "Poor little boy, I yelled at him and chased him away." She broke down again.

"Good thing you did," Hank said. "Any of the other cats eat it?"

"Sherlock knocked it off the table and scared them off," I said. "I cleaned it up before we left, but I brought some with us so you could test it."

"I'll give it a try. It acted so fast, I'd guess some sort of emetic. Ipecac, maybe, or *nux vomica*. Make a human being vomit and get very sick, but can kill a cat."

"There were mushrooms in the casserole," I said. "Could somebody have put a toadstool in by mistake?"

"Unlikely. This doesn't seem like mushroom poisoning. It doesn't act this fast either. We've got plenty of death angel Amanitas around here, but it' too early for them. They usually come up late in the summer and early fall."

He ran his hand over Sherlock's golden flank and picked up the skin on his shoulder. It snapped back into place when he took his hand away. "His gums are nearly normal and he's rehydrated. Unless there's something latent going on, I'd say he's over the worst of it."

"Thank God," Peggy said, bent over and butted heads with Sherlock. He managed to lift his head to respond weakly.

"We'll need to keep him a couple of days to monitor his liver function," Hank said. "I want to culture that casserole, see if we can find out what he ingested."

"Surely it was a mistake," Peggy said. "What else could it be?"

"Heck of a mistake, if you ask me. More likely some busy cook just grabbed the wrong jar. Hope your mystery cook didn't make two casseroles. One to feed her own family and one to give you," Hank said. "If anybody shows up tonight or tomorrow at the emergency room with the same symptoms, we may be able to trace the cook who made the casserole. Otherwise, we may never know."

"But you can figure out what was in it that caused Sherlock's symptoms, can't you?" Peggy asked.

Hank shook his head. "Not necessarily. If I can't pin it down, I can send off a sample to the state lab, but it won't rate high on their priority list."

"What about a private lab?" I asked. "Don't you use private labs to test for parasite infestations and to process your Coggins tests on horses?"

"Faster, but costs money."

"I don't give a damn about the money," Peggy snapped. "If *you* can't figure out what's in that blasted casserole that made Sherlock sick, you can send a sample to the State of Georgia, a half dozen private labs and the CDC for all I care."

"You got it," Hank said with a grin and a glance at me. "If I can't figure out what made fat Sherlock sick by noon tomorrow, I'll call in the big guns."

Twenty minutes later, Sherlock lay bedded down in one of the clinic's hospital cages. He'd stopped shaking and no longer labored to breathe. When Peggy knelt beside him and rubbed her hand along his body, he purred groggily.

I left her beside Sherlock while I brought the tuna container to Hank. He put it in his refrigerator with a note taped to it saying, "*Specimen, do not touch. This means you.*" He drew a rough skull and crossbones on the lid with a magic marker. "You have no idea who could have sent it?" he asked.

"I looked all over the porch, the driveway and the street in case the label came off and was lying outside. I doubt there was a card in the first place. What would it have said? 'Here's to getting your just desserts?' Only it wasn't a dessert."

"You don't think it was an accident," Hank said. It wasn't a question.

I shook my head. "You don't either, do you?"

"The only accident was Sherlock's big mouth. If he hadn't eaten that casserole, you and Peggy would have."

"Unless it tasted weird, and Sherlock thought it tasted great." I'd been running on adrenaline since Sherlock's first howl, now without warning my legs turned to warm butter. I grabbed for the straight chair beside the examining table, sank into it and dropped my head into my hands.

"You okay?" Hank asked and laid a big, gentle hand on my shoulder.

I took a deep breath and sat up straight. "No, I am not okay. I am scared spitless and madder than homemade sin. Unless there's a cook in Mossy Creek who believes a big glug of poison adds special flavor to her recipes, there's a good chance somebody tried to kill Peggy and me tonight."

Neither of us had heard Peggy come back. She stood in the doorway with her hand braced against the jamb and her face the pearl gray Sherlock's gums had been when we brought him in. "Why?" she whispered.

Hank wrapped his arms around her. I stood and shoved her into the chair I'd just vacated. She grabbed my hand. "It's the same person who killed Hiram," she said. "He's after you now, Merry."

"Us," I said grimly.

She shivered and hunched her shoulders.

"Don't go off half-cocked until I find out what's in the thing," Hank said. "Could be the worst that happened would be you spent the night in the bathroom throwing up. Or in the emergency room having your stomachs pumped out."

"We have to call Amos," Peggy said.

"I can't do much until tomorrow morning," Hank said, and eased his hip onto the edge of the examining table. The kindly vet was gone and in his place was a concerned man.

"If it had been left there for any length of time, one of the neighborhood dogs could have gotten into it," Peggy said. She turned to me. "We don't pay that much attention to leash laws. A small dog or roaming cat that ate much of it might have died."

"Then there's the squirrels, the raccoons, the possums . . . Whoever left it didn't give a damn who got hurt." Hank reached for the phone on the wall. "I'm calling Amos's cell phone."

First Hank talked to Amos, then he handed the phone to Peggy, who explained as much as she knew. When she hung up, she said, "Merry, he'll meet us at home in fifteen minutes to pick up the rest of the stuff and the container it came in." She turned to Hank and hugged him. "I know I can trust you to look after Sherlock."

"We'll check his liver function in the morning. Casey will call you with an update. With luck you can pick him up after lunch." He walked us to our truck, turning off the clinic lights as he went. "Nice to meet you, Merry, although not like this."

"Nice to meet you too," I said over my shoulder. "I hope I don't need you until we do regular shots at the barn in a couple of months." I'd already decided to continue using him for Hiram's horses, assuming I hadn't sent them all home by that time. Hank had proved how conscientious he was with small animals, and Hiram had trusted him with the horses. I would too.

"I hope I don't see you either until then, although I could use the money." He grinned. He was a very handsome man. Amazing how many male veterinarians are good looking. I wonder if anyone has ever done a study on that. They do studies on much dumber things.

The night was chill, but clear. "Thanks for coming in," Peggy said.

"No problem."

As I was getting in the truck, I had an idea. "Hank, do you think your wife might be interested in a driving lesson?"

Peggy had mentioned that his wife, Casey, had been an athlete until she was left a paraplegic.

He glanced at Peggy, then back at me. I guess to see whether Peggy had told me. "She's in a wheelchair most of the time."

"I know," I said. "Lots of people in wheelchairs drive carriages. Several companies design and build carriages and carts specifically for paralyzed drivers. Think she'd like to try it? You'd have to help us get her in."

"I'll ask her, but yeah, I think she might like that a lot."

On our way home, Peggy leaned her head back against the seat. "That was sweet of you."

"He deserved it."

"Sherlock could have died."

"What about *us*? We could be lying on matching gurneys on our way to the hospital."

"Or the morgue," Peggy said in a very small voice.

"What have I gotten you into?"

"You have it backwards. I don't know what I stirred up, but somebody assumed Hiram's death would be called an accident. They are not happy the police called it murder."

"Now that he's gone, they want to get rid of *me*. I wish to heaven I knew why."

*

We hadn't expected to answer that question so fast. The small window pane beside the lock in Peggy's back door lay in shards on the kitchen floor. The door was slightly open, the chain was unhooked and the lock open.

"The cats!" Peggy said. "Dashiell! Marple! Watson!" She waved her hand. "Get the cat treats out of the cabinet beside the sink. If they're still inside they'll come for treats." She bent to look at the broken glass.

"Any blood on the glass?" I asked and handed her the treats.

"None visible. If I touch anything Amos will kill me. Here, kitty, kitty, kitty." She gave me a handful of treats and started toward the dining room. I headed for the library.

I stopped dead on the threshold. The room was a bigger mess than my apartment, first, because Peggy had more books, magazines, and papers than Hiram, and second, because whoever broke in had smashed both Peggy's and Hiram's laptop computers. I'd locked mine out of sight under the seat of my truck after Sunday night, so it was safe for the moment.

"Oh, my sweet Lord," Peggy whispered. "Why not simply take the computers? Why smash them?"

"Check the other rooms. The TVs in here and in the kitchen haven't been touched. How about your jewelry?"

Peggy came back in after five minutes. "More paper strewn around, but nothing taken that I can see." She collapsed into her big chair. "This is simply insane. What are these lunatics after?"

Dashiell materialized from behind her chair and landed on her shoulder. We both jumped, then Peggy handed him a treat. A moment later two small heads peeped out from under the sofa. "Watson, Marple," she crooned. They jumped into her lap. She gave them treats as well. "Thank God."

Ten minutes later Amos arrived. He sat Peggy and me down at the kitchen table with all three cats on our laps while he went over the house. "Your computers insured?" he asked when he finally joined us.

"Mine's on a rider to my home owner's insurance," Peggy said and looked at me.

"No idea, but I doubt it," I said.

"Are we agreed that somebody was probably searching for something?" he asked. "The books on the lower shelves were dumped, but not on the upper ones." He looked at me. "Somebody about your height," he said. "Couldn't reach the top shelves without the library ladder and didn't take the time to get it."

"We have alibis, Amos, unless you think we had a high old time doing this together before we took Sherlock to Hank's."

"Now, Peggy, don't get your back up. That was an observation, not an accusation."

"What about fingerprints?" Peggy asked.

"Not much chance, although I've dusted the back door. I'll take both of yours to rule them out, but I doubt it'll do any good. Most thieves wear gloves."

"Why not steal the laptops?" Peggy said. "Why break them?"

"Pure-D nastiness. You'd be surprised. You're lucky they didn't hurt the other cats."

Just what Peggy needed to hear. She was already on the verge of hysterics.

"What about the tuna casserole?" I asked. "That was meant for us, not Sherlock."

"Won't know 'til we find out what's in it, will we?" Amos asked. I'm sure he was generally a calming influence, but I wasn't in the mood to be calmed. He turned to Peggy. "Anything that might have that kind of effect growing this early in the poison garden?"

"I beg your pardon?" I turned to stare at her.

"Amos Royden, you know darned well I tore it out a couple of years ago after my granddaughter figured out how to climb the gate." She ran her hands through her hair. She looked exhausted and her eyes were swollen. "All I have now are wild flowers."

"Some of which are pretty poisonous themselves," Amos said.

"Lots of plants are poisonous," Peggy said. "But I promise you I didn't do this."

"Nobody's saying you did." He put a reassuring hand on her shoulder. "But you have a better knowledge of vegetable poisons than most people around here, so put your mind to it and see what you come up with. In the meantime, I'm taking the rest of the tuna with me. If Hank doesn't come up with what's in it by noon, I'll FedEx it to the GBI lab in Atlanta."

The cats disappeared when he opened his fingerprint kit. Probably didn't like the smell. While we washed the ink goop off at the kitchen sink, he checked the kitchen door. "Got any plywood you can put over this broken pane?" he asked. "Mighty thoughtful intruder. Broke only one pane, reached in, unhooked the chain and the lock. I take it the deadbolt wasn't locked?"

Peggy raised her wet hands, palms out. "I know, I know, but I never can find the key, so I only ever use the latch."

"Well, find the key, keep it on your key chain, and from now on, use the dad-blasted deadbolt. Give me a roll of aluminum foil and a stapler. Think you can find that in all this mess?"

She made a rude gesture, but dug out a small stapler from the junk drawer in her kitchen. Amos made a pad of foil and stapled it over the empty pane in Peggy's window. "Not what I'd call secure, but it'll keep the cold air out and the cats in."

We thanked him and watched him drive away without lights and siren.

"Thank heaven," Peggy said. "One squawk from his siren or flashing blue light and we'd have the entire neighborhood down here to find out what happened."

"I should move out tomorrow," I said as I dumped the shards into the trashcan under the sink.

She rounded on me. "Oh, no you don't! You're not going anywhere, young lady. This was already personal. Now I'm well and truly angry. Nobody hurts my cats and gets away with it." She glared at me, then her eyes widened. "These people kill human beings, and here I am worrying about cats."

"That's why *I* should . . . "

"We have no idea which of us is the actual target. When they couldn't locate what they wanted in Hiram's apartment, they sent that tuna casserole to make us so sick we'd go to the hospital so the house would be empty and they could search."

"We don't know that," I said as I swept the broken glass from the laptop screens into the dustpan.

"So two sets of people hate us? I don't *think* so." She sank into a kitchen chair. "Leave it. Leave it all until tomorrow. I am flat worn out." I wanted to soak in a hot tub and sleep. Despite everything, I was also hungry. Peggy knew who had sent the ham and turkey, so I took a couple of sandwiches down to the apartment with me and devoured them in front of something mindless on TV.

I had a bazillion more phone calls to return, emails to answer, and lists to make, but they could wait until tomorrow. Mostly I needed time to mourn. So far I'd been too busy. I suspect that's the point of the logistical nightmare entailed in funerals.

My mother warned me when Gram died that the death of a parent means the death of possibility. All the words we thought we had time to say will go unsaid. All the family stories that should have been passed down will be lost forever like the recipe for Gram's ambrosia.

Grief felt strange when Hiram and I hadn't seen one another for so many years and had only begun to reconnect in the last few months, but his death left an unexpectedly big hole in my life. I had been a daddy's girl until I was seventeen.

He had been a wanderer since Mom divorced him, and I had become rootless after my divorce. He had finally rooted himself in Mossy Creek and asked me to be part of his world again.

No one else shared our memories. Who did we have except one another?

I cried big, gulping, sobbing, gut-wrenching, agonized, empty wails of loss and longing for the way we thought our lives would turn out.

Eventually I gulped and hiccupped into silence and curled into a fetal position on the couch.

I could accept his death by accident or disease, even if I resented it. But someone who was theoretically a human being had cut my father down. Had he been frightened? Known he was dying? Cried out for pity or help? Had he been tortured?

Nobody had the right to kill to solve a problem. The moment that human agency crushed the life out of Hiram, it had ceased to be human, had become something truly 'other'. It should be easily recognizable, wear a 'C' for 'Criminal' on its forehead. But the 'C' was in the soul and didn't show on the outside. Could I unmask the person who had committed the one crime that could not be expiated?

And had my impending visit been a catalyst? Without realizing it, had I somehow caused my father's death?

Chapter 19

Late Tuesday afternoon
Geoff

Ideally, Geoff should have had a team of three or four forensic techs to work the barn and the surrounding area, but then ideally he should have done this search while the body was still *in situ.*

He set his kit beside him, pulled on his gloves, turned on his flashlight, and began to walk the grid. He knew about the blood where Lackland's head had lain, but no one had discovered the weapon that caused the crack in his skull. Actually, no one had looked.

After a step-by-step search of the dirt floor, Geoff turned off the overhead lights and clicked on his Lumalight. Luminol spray was not only toxic, but expensive, so he wanted to narrow down the possible murder weapons before he used it. He slipped a painter's mask over his mouth and nose. If he'd been spraying extensively in an enclosed space, he'd have used a respirator, although most CSIs were pretty casual. In this large open space, however, he figured the small mask was sufficient.

None of the hand or power tools carefully laid out on the workbench and hung on pegs above it showed blood. Lackland was meticulous about his tools. They were all clean, polished, and in their proper places. A newly polished murder weapon wouldn't show up under ordinary light. Using the Lumalight, he checked for specks of blood where handles joined heads.

Nothing. So that he could tell a jury that he had checked personally, he sprayed the wheel from the vis-à-vis.

Blood from the thin cut across Lackland's throat stained the rim and seeped down two of the wooden spokes. The circle of blood in the dirt under where his head had lain was larger.

So what had the killer used to incapacitate Lackland? Had he brought his murder weapon and taken it away? Had he come planning to kill Lackland?

The medical examiner's report said the weapon was wooden and longish. Flecks of black paint were embedded in the scalp.

Possibly something like a baseball bat.

Hiram either had been caught unawares or had trusted his assailant enough to turn his back on him. Or her. A woman could crush a man's skull with a baseball bat. Laying out the man's unconscious body and dropping the wheel on him took time, but not a lot of strength.

Geoff got down on hands and knees and went over the wheel spoke by spoke searching for fingerprints. Nothing. Either the assailant had worn gloves or wiped the wheel clean. He was about to give up when he noticed several places on the spokes where the dust lay thinner. Flat on his stomach, he gently brushed the top layer of dust aside.

He took a second to realize what he was looking at. The print of the toe of a trainer or athletic shoe. Medium size. Hard to say whether it belonged to a man or a woman. He wasn't certain he could pick up the impression, but he pulled his tape out of his case and lifted what was there. With luck he could bring up the shoe print and identify tread and size. He brushed fingerprint powder over it and took several photos.

He sat back on his heels. Looked as though he had knocked Hiram out, arranged his unconscious body, dropped the wheel so that the rim fell across his throat, and then *stood on the spokes* close to the rim to increase the pressure until the hyoid bone was crushed.

The throat wound had bled, but that alone had not killed him. He had essentially been strangled, although he might well have died from his crushed skull.

Callous bastard, whoever he was.

So who had Hiram trusted? Peggy Caldwell. If Merry Abbott had showed up early in the storm or the middle of the night, he would have welcomed her. Jacob Yoder. Hiram had perceived no physical threat from whoever struck him.

By the time Geoff had crisscrossed the room foot by foot and reached the two carriages along the back wall, his knees ached, his back ached, and his head throbbed from the toxic fumes. He should have used a respirator.

He checked the carriages only so that he could say he'd done it. He was about to give up when he looked at the carriage shaft from the doctor's buggy. It was six feet long at least, but when he touched it, he discovered it weighed much less than he'd suspected. He sprayed along its length and used the light. Nothing.

Where was the second shaft? He found it under the carriage in two pieces, but the break in the wood looked old.

He knelt and pulled the two pieces out, then sprayed them and clicked on the light.

Five inches of the thick end piece lit up like a bottle of lavender fireflies.

"My, my." He left the piece untouched, brought his camera from his bag, packed the Lumalight and Luminol spray and picked up his brushes and fingerprint power.

The other shaft was extremely dusty, but streaks along this one showed it had been wiped clean within the last three or four days. "Can't win 'em all," he said. A nice set of fingerprints would have been helpful.

He slipped the wooden piece of shaft into paper evidence bags one from the top, one from the bottom so that they met in the middle. He didn't have a single bag long enough. He taped them together, signed and dated his makeshift package, then sealed it. Amos could send it down to Atlanta to the lab for confirmation of the blood and DNA typing to prove it came from Hiram.

He called Merry's number, but received no answer. He figured she'd be upstairs with Peggy, so he swung by anyway. By the time he reached the Caldwell house and knocked on Merry's door it was dark, he was hungry, achy and grimy from crawling all over Hiram's workshop. He was also very late.

He was about to knock a second time when he heard the chain rattle. A moment later Merry opened the door and walked away from him into the small living room.

"You look like hell," he said when she turned to face him.

"So do you."

"I'm just dirty. You've been crying."

She curled up in a corner of the sofa. "You bet. And raging against the dying of the light."

"Got any teabags?" He opened cabinets in the small kitchen.

"I have no idea. I'm supposed to make you tea? Sorry, I'm fresh out of crumpets."

"Here we are." He ran water in the sink, soaked the teabags and wrung them out, then handed them to her in a paper towel.

"Lie back and put these on your eyes."

"So I can't watch you plant evidence?"

"So tomorrow morning you don't look like a fighter after ten rounds with Mike Tyson." He shrugged. "Even with your eyes wide open I could still plant evidence. You'd never catch me."

She snorted, leaned back and laid the teabags on her eyes. "What were you intending to plant?"

"If I knew that I'd do it."

She sat up and dropped the teabag into the palm of her hand. "You haven't talked to Amos recently, have you?"

He came instantly alert. "Not since before I drove out to your farm. Why? What's happened?"

She pointed to the leather chair across from the couch she sat on and told him.

Halfway through he came to his feet and began to pace. "I ought to toss you and Ms. Caldwell both into jail."

"What have *we* done?"

"At least you'd be safe."

She waved him away. "I've been searched, Peggy's been searched. I'd guess Hiram's barn was searched. We're probably safer here than we'd be in that bread box of a jail where we'd be sitting ducks, thank you very much."

"So leave town."

She fell back against the sofa and began to laugh. "Even if Amos or the sheriff of Bigelow County would let me, which I doubt, I'm not going anywhere until after Hiram's funeral, and maybe not then. Hiram was never there for me when I needed him. I intend to be here for him now."

"That makes no sense."

She shrugged. "Makes sense to me. I'm here until Hiram's killer is caught, or until I run out of money, whichever comes first."

"Talk with your eyes closed."

She slid the teabags back into place, and leaned back.

"When you were burgled Sunday evening, could you tell if anything was stolen?" he asked.

She shook her head without disturbing the teabags. "Who knows? We found old driving magazines, some bills, some junk mail . . ."

"Personal letters?"

"I would have remembered, or maybe I wouldn't. I was pretty wasted by that time. Peggy came down and straightened up Monday morning while I was down at Amos's with you."

"So she could have removed anything that incriminated her?"

She sat up, peeled off the teabags and frowned at him. "Why would she write him when she could bang on his door?"

"Well . . . 'I hate you and never want to see you again. Get out of my apartment.' Easier to do on paper than face to face. Safer, too."

"Get real. Hiram wasn't violent. They didn't fight."

"Who told you that? Ms Caldwell? Where was he planning for you to sleep? Was he planning to bunk in with her?"

"Peggy has offered *me* her guest room, but this sofa makes into a queen-sized bed. I suspect he would have given me his bed and slept on the couch. We've both slept on a bunch worse. He never mentioned he would move out while I was visiting, certainly not upstairs."

Geoff sat in the club chair across from her. "My father and I have gone through some rough times, but we still talk to one another at least a couple of times a week."

She laid the teabags on her eyes again. "If that is your subtle way of asking me whether we were estranged because he abused me when I was a child, you can forget it. I adored him when I was little. Hiram was not God's gift to marital fidelity, but he liked his women rich, beautiful, adult, and preferably married."

"You don't just drift apart from a parent. What caused the estrangement?"

"Why is that any of your business?" Merry asked. He was getting into tough territory.

Good. He waited. Few people could endure silence.

She couldn't. She folded her arms tight across her chest, oblivious to the damp teabags that fell onto her polo shirt. "I didn't realize how low my mother and I were on Hiram's totem pole until I was a teenager. After her accident and the divorce, I went with her to St. Louis to live with my stepfather. Hiram was in Virginia or North Carolina or Florida most of the time. He had no facilities to look after a teenager. I couldn't visit, and he seldom came as far west as St. Louis.

"The couple of times he did come to town and take me out to dinner, he tried to act like the authoritarian father." She rolled her eyes. "He didn't know a damned thing about me. He certainly had no right to tell me what to do with my life."

"What accident?" he asked. Something in her tone had alerted him. Maybe Hiram had hurt her mother. On purpose.

"She fell off a carriage I was driving and nearly lost her leg."

"So he was not responsible?"

"Depends on your point of view. He wasn't around, if that's what you're asking. I walked away from driving and even gave up horses completely for a while until I realized I couldn't bear life without them and went back to working with them. I'd probably still be married and a damned sight richer if I hadn't. Seductive beasts."

"Why do you call him Hiram?"

"Started as a put-down, then became a habit. Saying he wasn't really my father."

"Did he resent it?"

"If he did he never mentioned it."

"Okay. Put the teabags back. I'll be quiet while I search."

"Leave my stuff alone, please. It wasn't here when Hiram lived here, so it's not part of your crime scene or whatever you call it. What's not hung up is still in my suitcase at the foot of the bed."

"No problem." She'd never notice a quick check. He knew how to search.

An hour later he had found nothing of interest, no personal correspondence, no files, nothing to give him an inkling of why anyone would want to kill Lackland. Whoever had burgled the place either found what he was looking for and took it, or didn't find what he was looking for because it wasn't here.

He turned off the light in the bedroom and saw that Merry had fallen asleep on the couch with the teabags over her eyes.

He hoped she wasn't guilty of anything, and that Peggy Caldwell wasn't guilty of anything either. Merry needed a friend she could trust. She seemed completely alone.

He went back into the bedroom, pulled the quilt off the bed and draped it over Merry. She'd have a sore neck in the morning, but he couldn't see disturbing her. He let himself out quietly and made sure the door locked behind him.

As he walked up the driveway to his car, the back door of the house opened and Peggy walked out on the stoop.

"Good evening," she said. "Could I interest you in a glass of iced tea and a sandwich? There's something you need to see."

Geoff's stomach gave a mighty growl. His watch said ten o'clock. His stomach said he hadn't had anything to eat since noon.

"I don't plan either to poison or seduce you," Peggy said. "I might even run to a piece of homemade apple pie. Or pumpkin if you'd prefer. I have several."

"With cheese?"

"Melted cheddar with ice cream."

"Consider me seduced." He stopped on the stoop. He pointed to the open space now covered by a square of aluminum foil. "Is this where they broke in? Merry told me what happened.

"That's what you need to see." Four cats met him in her kitchen. Peggy introduced them.

"I wish I could take credit for the pie," Peggy said. "It's from one of the members of the garden club."

"I don't want . . . "

Peggy laughed. "I have much more than Merry and I can eat, Agent Wheeler. It is Agent Wheeler, isn't it?"

He nodded.

"I saw you at Amos's, but we weren't introduced. Is Merry all right?"

"She's asleep on the couch."

"Poor child hasn't had a minute's peace what with the funeral arrangements and the lawyer and the horses and I don't know what all. I've been helping as much as I can, but I can't do anything for the horses, and I can't make decisions for her." She brought him a ham and cheese sandwich and a glass of iced tea on a tray. "The pie's in the warming oven. I'm ready for another piece myself. Merry took sandwiches down with her, but I don't know whether she ate them. She's exhausted and grieving. So far she's carried it off with that flip attitude, but deep down she's hurting. At some point the dam is going to burst."

"It burst tonight. She's been crying."

"Good." She busied herself apportioning the pie.

"Were you sleeping with him?" he asked.

"Good Lord, no!" The pie server clattered against the plate. "We were friends."

"In amazing health for a man his age, if you count his medications. Only aspirin and Viagra." He felt a thud against his thigh and looked into the moon face of the large gray tabby.

"Shove him down," Peggy said. "He'll climb onto the table if you let him."

Geoff reached down and scratched behind the cat's ears, then gently removed his paws from the thighs of his pants and lifted him onto the floor. He looked up to find he'd been served enough pie for three men plus the cat. "About the Viagra?" he asked. "Great pie."

"He didn't use the Viagra on me, but I can't vouch for the rest of the ladies in Mossy Creek."

"Would you know the possibles?" He finished his pie as Peggy finished her much smaller slice.

"In Mossy Creek? Probably. In Bigelow or the other towns within easy driving distance, probably not."

"Was he often gone overnight?"

She rinsed the plates and put them in the dishwasher. "I didn't keep tabs on him. If I looked out in the morning and didn't see his truck, I assumed he'd already left for the barn."

"But you went looking for him on Saturday."

"That was different. He was supposed to come up for breakfast Saturday morning, after which we were going antiquing. He was always on the lookout for old buggies or carriage lamps or horse brasses and such like. I knew he'd been on his mountain Friday night, and I couldn't get him on his cell phone. What else could I do but go hunting for him? At our age, we learn to check on our friends when they aren't where they're supposed to be. How about some coffee? At this hour, it's decaf."

He nodded. He wanted to keep her talking, and this seemed an easy way to do it. "What time did you find him and what did you think had happened?"

She gave him a mug of coffee and set a cream pitcher, sugar bowl and packets of artificial sweetener on the table in front of him.

She didn't answer, but went to the refrigerator and opened a can of fishy cat food, which the cats smelled immediately. They eddied around her feet and meowed, while she spooned small amounts into three bowls on a mat in the corner, rinsed the tin and the spoon, put the spoon in the dishwasher and dropped the can into the trash compactor. He'd decided she didn't plan to answer him when she said, "I got to the barn around eleven Saturday morning. I was afraid he'd had a heart attack or an accident. He was already cold. His face felt like marble."

So rigor mortis had begun to set in by that point. In that chill he could have been dead as long as four hours or as short a time as two. Whatever the television shows said, time of death was not yet an exact science. "You told the state trooper he'd been murdered."

"That's after I realized he couldn't have fallen the way he was laid out."

"Did you see any drag marks or footprints in the dirt?"

"By the time I started looking, we'd been tramping around. I suppose he could have been dragged. He was certainly *arranged*."

Geoff had seen the crime scene photos that Peggy had given to Amos. They weren't bad for an amateur. She hadn't noticed the broken shaft under the buggy at the back, but neither had anybody else until he'd found it. Of course, he and Peggy were really the only ones looking at the place like a crime scene.

"What do you think happened?" he asked. That was one of the questions he liked to ask of suspects. Amazing how often they revealed they knew more than they should know.

"Am I being interrogated? Should I ask for a lawyer?"

"You're being interviewed. We interview witnesses. We interrogate suspects."

"Subtle difference."

"We Mirandize suspects before we interrogate them." He finished his coffee. She raised her eyebrows to ask whether he wanted more. He shook his head. "So, what do you think happened?"

"Hiram was as tough as old boots. He and Jacob Yoder built that whole place from scratch, practically single, well, dual handed. I can't conceive of a stranger driving up that scary road in hopes of finding somebody to rob, much less kill, so he must have known his killer. He was hit over the head and knocked unconscious, so he must have turned his back on whoever hit him. Not somebody he was concerned about. A friend, or at least an acquaintance, business or otherwise."

"Then what?"

She shrugged. "The person or persons—there might have been more than one—laid him out, shoved the wheel off the vis-à-vis so that it fell on him, cleaned up any mess, and drove away."

"Not walked?"

"They could have left their car or truck down on the road and walked up, but why would they? Someone might see it and remember it."

"How about over the fields and down through the other property that Hiram didn't own?"

"Good grief, anybody who didn't know that area thoroughly would be so lost by the time they got down the other side of the mountain, you'd still be looking for a missing person. Who would be dead of snake bite or a broken neck."

He nodded. "Thanks for the food. You'll check on Merry, I mean, Ms. Abbott, in the morning?"

"Just a minute before you leave." She took a deep breath. "I plied you with food on false pretenses. Come look at the library." At the threshold, she waved a hand and said, "Breaking the computers was pure meanness."

He looked at the mess, and asked, "Either you or Hiram have a backup on a flash drive?"

"We both did, but they were attached to the back of our computers."

"So they're gone?"

Peggy nodded. "I suppose we should have kept them locked up separately, but I figured, and I'm sure Hiram did too, that we were backing up to save ourselves from crashes and viruses, not vandalism."

He'd see about that. "Leave the computers, please. We may be able to reconstruct the hard drives. I'll have someone pick them up tomorrow."

She followed him out onto the front stoop and pulled the door almost closed behind her. "Actually, I was planning to call you in the morning anyway. The Mossy Creek Garden club is meeting at Ida Walker's at eleven-thirty tomorrow morning. If you want to meet the usual suspects in Hiram's love life, most of them will be there."

"Can I just show up?"

"Of course. They'll be thrilled."

Thrilled? He drove away shaking his head.

On the way to his hotel he stopped by the police station and took his paper bag inside to be signed and sent to Forensics.

Later, lying catty-cornered across his king-sized bed in the Hamilton Inn, his mind refused to turn off. He wouldn't sleep well until he knew who had killed Hiram Lackland and how he was going to convict the killer. Once he'd made the arrest, he'd go home and sleep for fourteen hours.

He was letting these people get to him. He liked Peggy and Merry. Big mistake. He liked what he'd seen of Mossy Creek. Bigger mistake. Too easy to overlook or miss something important working alone, without allowing personalities to intrude. He needed to do what he always did—concentrate on the victim. He had great faith in forensics, but they operated best when pointed in the right direction.

He'd overseen the arrest and conviction of a number of killers he'd liked. Psychopaths were frequently charming until you got in their way. Some nice folks snapped and found themselves horrified by what they'd done.

But if any of these nice people from Mossy Creek had killed Hiram Lackland, he'd arrest and convict them without a qualm.

Chapter 20

Wednesday morning
Geoff

The next morning when Geoff called Amos to ask for directions to the mayor's house, Amos said, "Be careful, old buddy. They may look like little old ladies in tennis shoes, but they'll eat you alive."

Ida Walker met him at the door to what he could only call her mansion. No wonder Amos was smitten. She might be older than Amos, but she was hotter than most women Amos's age or younger.

She ushered him into a garden room that stretched across the back of the house and looked out on gardens already blazing with tulips and azaleas.

The LOLITS's ranged from Peggy in jeans and a plaid shirt to an aged elf named Mimsy Allen in what his mother called a lady dress with lace collar and cuffs. They looked innocent enough.

They'd no doubt been discussing the murder before he got there. Peggy handed him a cup of fruit punch and introduced him. "He wants to ask us some questions about Hiram," she said.

He prayed she'd stop there. Now that he faced them all, he was hesitant to bring up Hiram's love life. It was like talking dirty to his Sunday school teacher. He might have to rethink his strategy of interviewing them as a group.

"Have something to eat," Peggy said. A round table covered with a lace cloth groaned under silver trays and chafing dishes of hors d'oeuvres.

"Thanks, maybe later."

The crystal punch bowl and cups probably dated from the eighteen hundreds. Normally, he loathed fruit punch. It reminded him of his mother's boring garden parties. Intending to set his cup surreptitiously on the nearest end table, he tasted his punch to find it surprisingly good and not too sweet.

His mouth felt dry; his palms felt wet. Principal's office

syndrome. He drank the punch, and the smiling elf handed him a full cup. They had been milling around, but froze when he walked in. He couldn't decide whether they looked like a bunch of chickens that had spotted a fox, or a group of foxes lying in wait for an unsuspecting rooster.

Now one of them in chinos and deck shoes stepped forward and offered her hand. He swapped his punch cup to his left and shook hands with her.

"I'm Louise Sawyer. My husband Charlie and Hiram shared woodworking secrets."

"Did he ever go up to Hiram's workshop?"

She followed him over to the wall of windows. "Several times. Charlie crafts lovely furniture," Louise said. "Keeps him out of my hair now that he's retired. They glommed onto one another five minutes after we met Hiram at somebody's dinner party. Charlie has a top-of-the-line planer. Hiram planned to use him after the restoration part of the business got going. And pay him, which thrilled Charlie no end." She stared out at the garden and sighed. "I don't know how Ida does it. My azaleas bloom leggy and my tulips are downright squatty."

"Did you take any driving lessons?" he asked her. In other words, was she alone with Hiram on that mountain?

Everyone around them laughed. Louise frowned at them. "I don't have time for horses. I herd sheep."

"She means she has horses *already*, only she calls them Bouviers, and they allow her to live in their house," Ida said.

"We go to sheepherding contests and train during the week." She glared at the group. "We win, too. They are perfectly well-behaved dogs."

"Oh, sure," Ida said. "*Now.*"

He felt a strong hand on his sleeve and turned to meet a tall woman with hair that would have made Lucille Ball's look beige. "I'm Eleanor Abercrombie. I'm taking lessons. Hiram was a wonderful teacher. Once, I nearly ran us into a ditch and the pony kept slipping and Hiram had to get out and back the pony by his bridle. He was so sweet about it." She blushed. "My dear husband would have berated me for years."

He wondered whether Dear Husband was still around or no longer in Berating Mode.

The punch really was remarkably good. His cup never

seemed to be empty.

"Any of the rest of you ladies take lessons?" he asked.

"You know about me already," Peggy said.

"Not my thing," Ida said. "Hiram was a great extra man at a party, though. If more men learned to dance, there'd be more happy marriages in this world."

"He could dance?"

General oohs. "Could he ever!" Eleanor said. "You remember that tango in *Scent of a Woman*? Hiram made Al Pacino look like a walrus on tranquilizers." She fanned herself with her hand. "Whoo-ee."

"Such a great bridge player," said little Mimsy. "I learned on my honeymoon never to play bridge with my husband. If I made a teeny mistake I never heard the end of it. Why I remember once I bid two no-trump and . . . "

"Yes, dear," said Louise and patted her hand.

"The point is," Mimsy huffed, daring the other lady to interrupt, "one night when I was playing with Hiram I ruffed a club when I had a heart left and had to renege and we went down two tricks on a grand slam. He told me it could happen to anyone. He was so sweet."

Peggy leaned over to him and whispered, "Happens to *her* all the time, bless her heart."

He smiled beatifically around at them all. None of these sweet creatures could possibly have killed Hiram. Still, he'd have to interview them one at a time later in their own homes. He'd been wrong to try to interview them in a group. They'd never admit to doing the nasty with Hiram in front of their friends. He couldn't conceive of it either, although his mother always told him that almost everyone has much more sex than anyone believes. He snickered.

"Did you have breakfast?" Peggy whispered. He turned to answer her and blinked. His vision did a little bounce before he focused.

Oh, God. "What's in the punch?" he whispered back.

"We always have Mimosas before lunch," Mimsy said. "Of course, we don't use mixes. Fresh-squeezed orange juice. We have our own recipe." She giggled. Then she patted him on the back. On the butt, actually. He jumped.

"Maybe you should have a little something to eat," Louise

said. "It's time for lunch anyway."

He looked around the room at the ladies smiling benignly at him.

He suddenly saw them as bunch of slavering wolves ready to bite his head off and devour his carcass along with their mimosas and ham biscuits. He had to get away before he fell on his face and broke his nose. Or one of the windows, whichever was closer.

"Uh, actually, I have an appointment for lunch with Amos." He straightened his shoulders. "If you'd excuse me." He'd busted lots of drunk drivers early in his career and recognized his careful walk. This was going to be a problem. All these women must realize he was only one step from knee-walking.

Ida and Peggy followed him to the front door as the ladies converged on the luncheon table and the punchbowl. He heard them twittering, no doubt talking about him.

"I'll drive you to Amos's," Peggy said as she took his arm. "You shouldn't get behind the wheel."

He started to protest, then mutely surrendered his car keys.

"We'll take my car," she said. "Amos can send Mutt and Sandi out for yours."

As they drove away, he leaned his head back. It spun. "You were all at that punch before I got there and they're back there still going strong." He sat up quickly, too quickly. He felt his gorge rise. "Are *you* sober?"

"I am today's designated driver," she said. "We rotate."

"So they knew I was drunk?"

"Lord, honey," she said and patted his knee. His knee, this time, and not his thigh or his rump. "God Himself knows you're drunk. I should have warned you. That punch is lethal. We're all used to it and we eat big greasy breakfasts before we come."

He leaned his head back against the seat and closed his eyes. "Damn right you should have warned me. Amos should have warned me. *Somebody* should have warned me! They think I'm a stupid sot."

Another knee pat. "No they don't. They did want a little time to assess you before they opened up to you, though."

"Time to get their stories straight, you mean." He opened his eyes and tried to focus on the road. "You all ambushed me."

"We didn't really plan to."

Riiigght. "Better drop me at the hotel."

"What about Amos?" Peggy asked. "Isn't he expecting you for lunch?"

"That was the first excuse I could come up with. Can you get me the names, addresses and phone numbers of the garden club so that I can call on them singly?" *If I dare face them.*

"Sure. We're all in the phonebook." She pulled up in front of the Hamilton Inn. "I'll drop your car keys off at the police station so they can deliver your car."

"No! I'll catch a cab to Ida's."

"If you're worried the police department will find out about this, they will regardless of whatever precautions you take, and they'll sympathize. You're not the first and you won't be the last." She leaned across him and opened his door. "Take some aspirin before you collapse. Helps the hangover."

Five minutes later he staggered into his room and fell face down across his bed. Then he draped one arm over the side to touch the floor and stop the room from spinning. He seldom drank anything stronger than the occasional lite beer or glass of wine, and never before lunch. How could he have been so stupid? He hadn't expected a ladies garden club to be drinking alcohol in quantity at eleven in the morning.

But whatever they used in those Mimosas did *not* taste of champagne. Vodka. Had to be. Lots of Vodka. Vats of Vodka. It was about the best damned punch he'd every had. Too bad it punched back.

He'd have the Godzilla of all hangovers when and if he woke up. At this point, death seemed a better option.

Chapter 21

Wednesday
Merry

I left the funeral home with most of the arrangements for Hiram's funeral finished.

Now all I had to worry about was finding the honorary pallbearers and paying for all this. Maybe I should have cremated Hiram after all.

No. Somehow I'd pay the costs, even if I had to borrow money from Mr. Robertson. At the moment, American Express was on the hook for more than my yearly bill had been last year.

An hour later I left Hiram's accountant's office a happier camper. I would indeed be able to pay off American Express, and keep the farm's expenses up to date as well.

Actually, after I eventually transferred all the accounts to my name, I wouldn't be rich, but I would be comfortable. Hiram had done better than I would have imagined. He'd invested wisely and made money through the years. He had hefty checking and savings accounts not only in Bigelow, but in Aiken.

Mr. Haywood, the accountant, gave me copies of Hiram's previous tax return and agreed to do his final tax return as well as to contact his investment accounts and social security for me.

He did not, however, have any of Hiram's records for the current year, nor know where they were. Frustrated again.

I couldn't transfer Hiram's checking and savings accounts without copies of his death certificate. Mr. Robertson said they'd be sent directly from the state to the funeral home and wouldn't arrive for a week or so. As soon as I got the funeral out of the way, I needed to start trying to find a lock box or storage shed in Mossy Creek or Bigelow in Hiram's name. Then I'd have to start in Southern Pines and Aiken.

I hoped the death certificates would arrive before my bill for the funeral did or my credit would be shot to hell. I picked up a turkey sub and a couple of six packs of diet soda and drove straight back to the apartment. On the way I called Jacob

Yoder's cell phone. When he answered, he sounded morose and grumpy, but sober.

Probably the reason he was morose and grumpy.

"Yeah, I handled it all this morning, and I will handle it this evening and tomorrow morning." He sighed deeply. Much put upon. Of course, it was his job, but that didn't make him any happier about doing it. "When's the funeral?"

I told him and asked him to be an honorary pallbearer.

"Got no suit. You will spring for one?"

I could see him buying an expensive Italian suit on my dollar. "Sorry, not in the budget. Wear whatever you wear to take your lady friend out on the weekends."

Silence. "Very well. I suppose."

"I'm up to my ears until the funeral's over, Jacob. If I can count on you, I promise I'll add another hundred to the Easter driving." What was another piddly hundred bucks compared to what I'd already spent?

Another silence. "Very well."

"Sober. Drunk doesn't count."

I hung up before he could protest. What I needed now was lunch, a nap, my laptop and a telephone.

Answering machines being what they are, the last call recorded was the first to play back. I listened to them all and wrote down the ones I needed to return on a memo pad, crossed out duplications from Peggy's list, then started from the bottom to work my way up.

The horse magazines were easy. They already had obituaries for present and past celebrities on file, so I only had to bring them up to date about the new farm. I didn't mention murder. They offered to post notices including the time and place of the funeral on their web sites.

Katie Bell at the *Mossy Creek Gazette* was tougher. I had to promise her an in depth interview after the funeral. I also sicced her onto Geoff Wheeler and Amos Royden. Amos was undoubtedly used to fending her off. I didn't even know what *I* was supposed to know, much less what Amos wanted let out to the media.

Next I called acquaintances in the driving community. I started in Wellington, Florida, outside of Palm Beach, where a great many rich horse people and their employees spent their winters showing their horses or playing polo.

Since I was calling in the middle of the afternoon, I got a large proportion of answering machines. I worked out a short message to thank them for caring and gave them the basics about Hiram's death and the funeral arrangements. I mentioned that we were having only a private graveside service. I didn't quite emphasize private, but I hoped they got the message.

I also didn't actually say Hiram had an accident or a heart attack, but if they got that impression, I didn't tell them different.

Finally after two hours, four diet sodas loaded with caffeine, most of a gigantic bag of Cheetos, a left ear that was probably coming down with gangrene, and a telephone bill I didn't even want to think about, I checked off the last acquaintance call.

That left the few people whose names I recognized either as former employers, or that Hiram had called real friends. And former mistresses, of course, but females weren't necessarily his mistresses simply because they were female. Hiram loved women whether he slept with them or not. Old or young, fat or thin, beautiful or horse-faced, even rich or poor, he enjoyed them all so long as they made no demands on him like fatherhood or marital fidelity.

I was casually acquainted with most through shows I'd managed, but only three had known me before Hiram and my mother divorced, when I was still driving, which meant they knew *why* I no longer drove.

Chances were that Dick Fitzgibbons, Hiram's last and longest employer, would know more about his recent affairs than any of the others, so I started with him. A retired corporate CEO, Dick would be home in his elaborate stable or out in his dressage arena exercising one of his horses.

He gravitated towards matched teams of blood bay Danish warmbloods. Hiram had picked out his last pair in Denmark, brought them to Dick's and trained them.

Hiram seldom made mistakes about horses, even when they were young. That's not as easy as it sounds. Fillies and colts grow in stairsteps, first the front end outgrows the rear, then the rear end outgrows the front. Even the most beautiful youngster goes through stages when he'd make Don Qui look like Secretariat. Hiram could look beyond that gawkiness to see how the horse would mature. I was never as good as he was.

He could also gauge whether the horse would take to driving. Some horses feel the first tug, freak out, jump the nearest fence, destroy the breaking cart or truck tire tied behind them and never recover emotionally. No matter how carefully they are nurtured, they'll never be trustworthy to a carriage. Hiram could tell by his own brand of horse ESP.

I saw Dick last a couple of years back at a carriage show north of Lexington, Kentucky, where I lived. That day Dick told me that Hiram had retired from driving competitively because of his eyes. First time I'd heard that.

"Can't say that I blamed him for retiring. No way to thread a team through cones or drive them at a dead gallop around marathon obstacles without perfect depth perception," Dick had said. "Hiram can still drive and train horses, but he can't take the chances he used to take, and that means time penalties and knocking over cones."

And no blue ribbons. For Dick, winning was the only thing, as somebody famous once said.

This afternoon when Dick answered, he said, "I'm in my arena driving my new Halflinger to a piddling little Meadowbrook. Oh, how far have the mighty fallen."

"How're your warmbloods?"

"Much better. Hiram came over here a while back to tune on them for a couple of days. Tune on *me*, that is. Nothing wrong with the horses. I'm not looking to repeat my performance around the cones in Lexington."

I burst out laughing.

A moment later he joined me, but his laughter sounded rueful. "I almost gave up driving after that little fiasco. It was the first show I ever drove without Hiram there to coach me. I do hate making a fool of myself in public."

"Oh, come on, Dick. You didn't make a fool of yourself."

"We both know you're lying through your teeth, an unbecoming trait in a lady," he said. "I knew in the warm-up ring I was out of my depth. By the time we trotted through the in-gate and started through the cones, they'd decided if they had to drive with an idiot on the reins, they'd get it over as fast as possible, and in whatever order they picked." He sighed. "My record for the number of cones knocked down and the times off course is not likely to be bested in this century. Not the way I'd like to be remembered."

By rights, the judge should have excused Dick halfway through for being off course, but she must have been as stunned by the mayhem as the rest of us and figured he couldn't stop anyway.

"Took the crew twenty minutes to reset and remeasure the course," Dick said.

I remembered. The looks they gave Dick would have melted tar in a blizzard.

I'll say this for him. He had not blamed his horses, and he'd climbed down off the box laughing. "I got to call Hiram right now," he'd said as his groom led his team away. "He'll bust a gut when he hears how well I did without him. Maybe if that new place of his goes under, he'll come back to me."

That was how I'd first learned Hiram had bought land in North Georgia for his own place. I'd assumed he'd be at the show. Frankly, I still don't know if I hoped to meet him or to avoid him.

Now Dick said with a catch in his voice, "Hell, Merry, I can't believe he's gone."

Neither could I. No one had mentioned Hiram had been away from Mossy Creek recently. He must have left Jacob in charge, which meant that Hiram trusted him, even if I didn't. "Did he seem worried about anything when he came to Aiken?"

"Seemed in high spirits. Said he'd found something that somebody was going to pay him big bucks for. When I pressed him, he smiled and clammed up."

"What sort of thing? A horse?"

"Don't know. He said he'd bought it for a song. I figured it was a carriage. He working on anything interesting?"

"An old doctor's buggy that's on its last legs and a late nineteenth century dog cart that needs a lot of work. And a vis-à-vis, but I think it's already sold. To you?"

"Nope. Not my style."

"Dick, did he leave anything with you?"

"What kind of thing?"

"I can't find any of his old logbooks or files. Surely he didn't throw that stuff away when he moved, did he?"

"He wouldn't do that. Let me check the storage room over

the barn. I seldom go up there, so he might have left a half dozen file cabinets without my knowing. You in a hurry?"

"I need to find out who owns the horses we've got, for one thing."

"Heinzie and Don Qui are mine."

"Oh. That's new. When did you switch to Friesians? And a donkey? Come on, Dick. You driving a VSE? Can you come get them?"

"Unless you've pulled a miracle and weaned Don Qui away from Heinzie, I'd rather leave them with you. Can't show a horse in the ring with a donkey attached to him like a limpet."

"Surely it isn't that bad."

"Oh, no? Try driving a dressage test with that little demon at the in gate or locked in a stall screaming his head off."

"Why were they ever allowed to get that close in the first place? Heinzie's what? Three?"

"Coming five. Heinzie's mother died when he was less than a week old. We hand raised him and brought in Don Qui as a baby to keep him company. As a stud colt Heinzie couldn't go out with the mares, so they grew up together. Heinzie gets separation anxiety unless he can either see or hear Don Qui while he drives. Don Qui goes straight to rage if you try to keep them apart."

"I don't know if I can be much help."

"Give it a shot. Hiram said Heinzie's come a long way. He planned to use him to drive a big carriage at some event or other."

Easter. "Hiram was supposed to take people on carriage rides on Easter afternoon." That meant I'd have to get the wheel put back on the vis-à-vis and check out and tighten everything else. Then I'd have to keep Jacob sober to drive around Mossy Creek with everyone's children. "Did he say what he was planning to do with the donkey while he drove Heinzie in town?"

"Leave him in the trailer where Heinzie could hear him, probably."

One more thing to worry about. To show just how distracted I was, I hadn't heard Dick's last sentence and had to ask him to repeat it.

"I said," Dick said, "Like most Friesians Heinzie's very

quiet and good natured, but I'd have Don Qui close by when the farrier comes to trim and shoe. Hiram was giving lessons to a couple of his more advanced pupils with him." We talked some more, then I rang off.

The *farrier*. The horses' feet looked in pretty good shape, but I didn't know when they'd last been trimmed and shod, and I had no idea who'd been doing the work. Hiram could trim hooves, but not shoe. Maybe Jacob did the work. If not, would Jacob know who had?

The more I got into this running Hiram's operation, the more I realized I needed Jacob.

Maybe I'd actually get around to finding out who killed my father sometime in the next millennium.

Chapter 22

Wednesday evening
Merry

Peggy dropped by the apartment about five with a bottle of good sherry and a plate of room-temperature Brie and crackers "Thought we might have a drink on your patio since the weather's so nice," she said. "We're supposed to have rain the next two days."

Perfect weather for an outdoor funeral.

"Have you lined up the pallbearers yet?" she asked after she'd handed me a glass of sherry and settled herself in the chaise longue.

"I can't think of a soul except Jacob Yoder. Do we really have to have pallbearers for a graveside service?"

"Don't see why. They usually follow the coffin from the church to the hearse. The funeral home will have it all set up at the graveside before we get there."

I closed my eyes. "I'll call Mr. Straley first thing tomorrow morning and nix the pallbearers."

"What are you wearing?" Peggy asked.

I sat up and stared at her with my mouth open.

"Uh-oh," she said.

I had brought no skirts, just jeans and one good pair of gray slacks. Somehow muddy paddock boots didn't seem quite the thing to wear at a funeral. Since I'd come from a horse show, I didn't even have a pair of pantyhose, and I certainly didn't have a pair of black pumps with me.

"Tomorrow morning, we'll go to Bigelow," Peggy said. "We should be able to find you a decent black dress and some inexpensive black shoes."

Some women, no, a *lot* of women enjoy shopping. I am not one of them. I have charge accounts at four on-line tack shops. What I can't buy from Dover or Stateline, I buy from Meador or Dressage Extensions. I shop online from Land's End or L. L. Bean. I did have a couple of decent black dresses, but they were hanging in my closet in Kentucky. Even if I could trust the super of my townhouse complex to find the right dress, I didn't even have time for FedEx Overnight. I didn't have a single friend in Lexington I could call on. Nobody except my condo manager had a spare key.

"I can't keep imposing on you like this," I said.

"So you'll know where to shop and how to find the stores by yourself?" she said. "You're not imposing. Call this my payback to Hiram for not finding him before some maniac killed him."

"If you'd walked in on it, your daughter and I might be planning a funeral for two parents instead of one."

"Marilee would be very angry at me if I got myself killed," Peggy said. So far as I could tell, she was dead serious, no pun intended.

*

April is not the best time to find a plain black daytime dress, but we managed at the third specialty shop. It cost more than I would have liked, but it would do later for exhibitors' parties. I also found a pair of inexpensive black pumps that didn't have five-inch heels. How on earth can women walk in those things? I tried on a couple of pairs and nearly fell flat on my nose. The little Chinese ladies with their bound feet couldn't have been much more uncomfortable.

I bought three pairs of black pantyhose at the same store. I'd be bound to snag a run in one when I put them on. The second pair would get me to the funeral, then I'd snag them. I'd keep the third pair in my handbag to change into before the reception. If I ran true to form, I'd have to toss all three pairs into the trash the minute I walked in the apartment door. Pantyhose and I do not get along.

I sincerely hoped the black dress wouldn't see any more funerals in the near future. We stopped by the funeral home to make certain that Hiram's body had arrived from the morgue, to give Mr. Straley the items we had selected for his burial. His eyebrows went up almost to his receding hairline when I handed him Hiram's carriage whip and top hat.

"I was under the impression that you wished a closed coffin, Mrs. Abbott," he said. He took the hat, but merely stared at the whip.

"That's right, but I don't want him to spend eternity

underdressed."

"He will be wearing the suit you selected."

"Hiram needs his top hat and his whip. Be glad I didn't bring his brown driving gloves and his top boots."

"Oh, I am," he breathed. "Would you like to inspect the viewing room, Mrs. Abbott? Your father is already in place, but of course we will make the, ah, adjustments you have requested. I hope you approve of the casket. It's not too late to upgrade, you know."

I didn't even want to think of what this mid-range coffin and the lead-lined vault would cost. Seeing it and knowing that Hiram was in it was the last thing I wanted, but I felt as though I had to.

I was surprised there were several flower arrangements around the room. Avoiding looking at the big brown oblong box that sat in the corner, I checked the cards from the arrangements.

"Should I send flowers?" I asked Peggy.

She shook her head. "Here's one from Ida."

Beautiful roses. A wonderful dark red that was nearly blue. Not at all funerally. I appreciated that.

"The garden club sent spring flowers. Well, they would, wouldn't they?" Peggy said.

"Peggy, you sent flowers?" I asked. I showed her the card. "You've done so much already. He did love yellow roses."

Peggy sniffled. "I know. He really was a sweet man, you know."

Sure he was, to his clients and his women.

*

As we walked back toward the foyer, Mr. Straley said, "The funeral ladies will be here at ten tomorrow morning to set up for the reception after the interment."

"Funeral ladies?" I asked.

"Oh, yes. The same group of ladies has done all our in-house receptions for many years. Since you will not be having a sit down luncheon buffet, they will provide assorted hors d'oeuvres, deviled eggs, finger sandwiches, desserts, coffee, tea, and fruit punch. Since you did not stipulate, we decided not to offer wine, but we can, of course, include white or red or both. There's still time to make arrangements."

Behind him, Peggy shook her head and mouthed, "No wine."

"So long as the fruit punch isn't that nasty stuff with lime sherbet," I said.

"Certainly not," Mr. huffed. "The punch will be light and not too sweet."

"And not pink," Peggy said.

He glanced at her. "Very well. Not pink. Nor green, it would seem. Would pale yellow be acceptable?"

I could just see the funeral ladies ladling out cups of urine-colored punch. "I'm happy with pink," I said. "So long as it's pale pink." Cups of blood didn't seem appropriate either.

"We will open the room for viewing at six this evening if that is convenient," he said. "We generally close at ten, but arrangements can be made to stay open longer if you prefer."

"God no!" I caught my breath. With luck nobody would show up this evening. Then I'd have only four hours alone to commune with my father's casket in the corner. Could I possibly sneak a book in? Otherwise, what would I do? Any chat would be one-sided and not to be overheard by Mr. Straley or his minions.

"She means four hours will be ample," Peggy said.

"Of course. Now, I'll have one of my assistants drive you up to show you the plot you selected on the site map for your father's eternal resting place. It lies at the top of a gentle rise. The view, especially at this time of the year when the azaleas are in bloom, is quite lovely."

"I'm sure he'll enjoy it." I mentally kicked Chuckles in the crotch and hoped he'd double over in pain.

Mr. Straley knew darned well he was being got, but he was really, really good at this. He never cracked a smile. "If you prefer, we can return to my office and I can give you the virtual video tour."

Chuckles was recovering fast. I didn't dare look at Peggy.

"Thank you," she said, "That won't be necessary." She grabbed my arm and began to pull me toward the front door.

"You have to know where the service is being held." I could hear an edge of desperation creeping into his voice.

"We'll follow the hearse," she said as we bolted.

We dove into her car and spun rubber getting out of the

parking lot. I was afraid to turn around for fear Mr. Straley was trotting behind us demanding that we take the virtual tour.

Suddenly I didn't feel like laughing. "I can't do this," I said.

"Of course you can. I'll be there."

"Can I bring a deck of cards so we can play gin rummy if nobody shows up?"

"They'll show up all right. Mossy Creek goes in big for visiting before, during and after funerals, and there'll be a bunch of Bigelow folks as well, some of whom may never have met Hiram."

"Why would they come?"

"There's a cadre that attends all the funerals. Mostly widow ladies with nothing better to do. And, I'm afraid, the combination of his international reputation and being murdered has put Hiram on the local map."

"Tell me we won't have television cameras?"

"Probably not, but you promised the *Mossy Creek Gazette* an interview."

"Do I have to wear that dress tonight? If so, I better stop for some more pantyhose."

"Slacks will be fine."

"What gets me is that there's more to-do about Hiram now that he's dead then there was when he was alive. I am running around like a chicken with my head cut off scandalizing Mr. Straley with Hiram's hat and whip."

"It's your job."

"No, my job is to decide what I'm going to do with the farm and the equipment and the horses and Jacob Yoder and get back some semblance of my life before all this happened. I want to remember Hiram alive, not continue to deal with Hiram's death."

My cell phone rang. I jumped. I almost always do. I don't wear one of those Men from Mars things behind my ear, but I can't ever leave a telephone unanswered, even when I'm certain from the number that it's a magazine subscription salesman. In this case I recognized Dick Fitzgibbons's number.

"Got your goodies," he said. "Two big filing cabinets, one filled with paperwork and log books. On cursory examination, they seem out of date. You know old stuff."

"So I'm still missing Hiram's current stuff. The only thing I can think of is a storage locker down here and maybe a lock box, but what on earth would he have that should go in a lockbox?"

"How about deeds? Ownership papers on the horses and the carriages? Insurance documents. A copy of his will."

"Yeah, yeah, yeah. I'll have to wait to go hunting for a lock box or storage locker locally until I have death certificates to present."

"You didn't let me finish about the filing cabinets. The other is stuffed with silver bowls and platters black with tarnish. Want me to get a couple of my boys to polish them up for you so you can auction them off on eBay? Some of the early things are Sterling. Might fetch a pretty penny."

"EBay is a wicked good idea," I said.

Peggy glanced over at me and lifted her eyebrows.

"Tell you later," I whispered. "Dick, can you hang on to them for a while? The viewing's tonight, the funeral and the reception at the funeral home, afterwards, is tomorrow."

"Episcopal funeral ladies or plain old ecumenical ones?"

"You know about funeral ladies?"

"Indeed, yes. I know a great deal about funeral ladies."

I could have kicked myself. His wife of forty some-odd years had died five years ago. What he'd gone through before her death and afterwards made my deal with Hiram seem like a walker in this case a carriage ride in the park.

"Want me to drive up to hold your hand?" he asked.

"Not necessary. I'd love to see you when I come over to get Hiram's stuff, but that may be a couple of weeks. I have to get Yoder to finish cleaning up the vis-à-vis and then make certain he's available to drive it and Heinzie around Mossy Creek on Easter Sunday afternoon."

"Have you decided what to do with Don Qui while you're in town?"

"Not yet."

"If you get desperate," he said, "call me. I wouldn't mind driving ole Heinzie around your village. He's a good guy."

Peggy drove me out to Hiram's, although I told her she should drop me at the apartment so that I could pick up my truck and save her gas. "I'd rather come with you," she said. "I really don't like your being alone with Jacob Yoder out there, and it's not simply because he's a jail bird. There's something of the toad about him."

"With some rat and weasel genes tossed in for good measure. Geoff must have checked his alibi by now. If it's full of holes, he is the perfect choice for First Murderer."

Chapter 23

Wednesday
Geoff

"Miss Sallie Sue Jones swears that she and Jacob Yoder spent Friday night, all day Saturday, and most of Sunday together in her apartment in Bigelow." Geoff sat in the straight chair on front of Amos's desk and arranged the perfect creases in his slacks, then shrugged and propped his calves across heels on the rim of the metal wastebasket.

"You believe her?" Amos asked.

"From what she says, she and Yoder were both drunk as skunks. The woman lives in a sty a pig would turn up his nose at, but I don't believe Jacob could have driven out to Hiram's, killed him and driven back without Miss Sallie Sue being aware that he was gone a bit longer than necessary for a liquor store run."

"Even in the middle of the night? Was she covering for him?"

Geoff shook his head. "Doesn't look like it. Couple of other weekend juking lushes swear his truck never left from in front of her apartment building, and her car's in the shop. Perennially, from all accounts. Not much in the way of public transportation out to Lackland's area." He sighed. "A real pity." He pulled his gold Parker pen out of his breast pocket and began idly working it over and under the fingers of his left hand, gambler fashion. "Guy's a real prince. I'm going out to talk to him again this afternoon to find out precisely why Lackland hired him right out of jail."

Amos stood and casually kicked the wastebasket from under Geoff's feet. "Come on, ole buddy. Time to make the rounds to protect and serve."

"Protect from what and serve whom?"

"In both cases the good citizens of Mossy Creek. You'd be surprised what shenanigans they can get up to if I'm not around to remind them I'm around. I like to police by walking and riding around. You can come along, then I might be persuaded to buy you a cheap lunch."

As they strolled away from the station, Amos said, "Okay, tell me about Jacob Yoder." He nodded to the lady with the Lucille Ball hair. Geoff didn't remember her name, but he winced when he thought of all those mimosas.

"Rap sheet's not as long as your entire arm, but I'd bet it would stretch above your elbow," Geoff said. He managed a smile, although he wanted to avoid eye contact with the woman. Was that a smile or a sardonic grin she gave him? He collected his thoughts and said, "Jacob started with minor vandalism up around Intercourse where he's from."

"Amish. I guessed as much."

"Got caught at sixteen painting naked ladies on barns under the hex signs. An Amish version of tagging. His kin would probably have taken care of that one with a buggy whip, except that he made the mistake of picking on some non-Amish barns, got caught, and the police were brought in."

"Actually, that's kind of funny," Amos said.

"Juvenile authorities must have thought so too. He was put on diversion and given to his parents. He had to paint over all his naked ladies."

"Great loss to the world of art." Amos waved at Ingrid Beechum at her bakery. Bob the Chihuahua barked at him.

"Damn dog thinks he's a real dog," Amos said. "Even after he got picked up by the hawk. He just *never* got the memo about being more rodent than guard dog."

Geoff cut his eyes at Amos. He knew Amos wanted him to ask about Bob and the hawk, so he didn't. Since college Amos had found ways to drop bombs into the conversation while he fought the urge to act interested or ask questions. He'd driven Amos nuts that way since college. He wasn't about to let his guard down now. "So. Next Yoder steals a car and wrecks it. His family paid, so he was given probation."

"Tough on a teen-aged boy to be a motor head when your family's mode of transportation is a horse drawn carriage," Amos said. He nodded toward the bakery. "Incidentally, that woman makes the best cream cake in six counties."

"Uh-huh. The next car he stole belonged to a young man who was boarding with the Yoders to learn everything about carriages. Guess what his name was?"

"Wouldn't be Lackland, now would it?" Amos asked. He walked across the street, sat on a bench and stretched his legs out.

Geoff sat beside him. "Indeed it was Lackland. Only this time he wrecked the car and killed the teenaged town girl he'd persuaded to go partying with him. Her father was a lawyer. Yoder got two years for vehicular homicide."

"What happened when he came out? I've heard those folks shun family members who get above their raisin'."

"I don't know who ditched whom, but he disappeared," Geoff said.

Nearly everybody that walked by nodded and smiled at Amos. He nodded and smiled back, but didn't invite anyone into their conversation and nobody came over. That, Geoff assumed, was because he, the outsider, was sitting beside Amos.

"Was Lackland still living with the Yoders when Yoder went to jail?" Amos asked.

"Don't know. I'm having one of my people in Atlanta see if he can get me work history on Lackland. I suspect, however, judging by Merry Abbott's age, Hiram was gone and married before Yoder got out of prison. He served the whole two years, by the way. Let us say he did not adjust well to prison life."

"He must have turned into a real bad ass."

"Not quite enough to get his sentence extended, but enough to keep him from parole. After that he seems to have kept his nose clean for a few years."

"Wife? Children?"

"Not on record. Even if he'd wanted to come home, I doubt his community was into killing the fatted calf for the returning prodigal."

"So at this point he's what, thirty?"

"About," Geoff said. "That's when he committed a couple of robberies with violence. Held up some liquor stores. Got caught."

"Pennsylvania?" Amos asked.

"Nope. Georgia. Did a dime out of twenty. After that a bunch of Joe jobs. I talked to a couple of his ex-employers. The ones that remember him say that he was a hard worker when he was sober. Painter, roofer, construction, drywall, the kind of guy who can fix anything including cars and trucks."

"And when he was drunk?" Amos asked. He stood and walked away without checking to see that Geoff was following.

Geoff caught up with him. "Bar room brawls, drunk and disorderlies, and domestics. The last time he sent his current girlfriend and her new girlfriend to the hospital for serious surgeries. That turned into grievous bodily harm and three years."

"Did he hunt up Lackland or did Lackland seek him out?"

"Yoder says that he saw a write-up about Lackland moving down to Mossy Creek in a local paper a year and a half ago. Started corresponding. Lackland needed somebody to help him build the place. Whether he brought pressure to bear or not, Lackland went before the parole board and offered him a job. When he got out, he came down here to finish his sentence, where, to hear him tell it, he and Lackland worked like navvies. Says Lackland promised him a working partnership. Seems really pissed that Lackland got himself murdered."

"So, what if Lackland reneged on the offer once Merry Abbott agreed to visit him?"

"Wouldn't be the first time Yoder reacted with violence. Lackland says *no* to the partnership, Yoder picks up that broken shaft and hits him, then either believes he's dead or decides that he's got a better chance of keeping out of jail again if he finishes the job and sets it up to look like an accident."

"What about his alibi?" Amos asked.

"I've got a call into the M.E. in Bigelow to see how much fudge factor there is in Lackland's time of death. As cold as it was Friday night, and with the storm, it's possible Lackland died earlier than originally thought. We don't know what time he had his last meal since he brought sandwiches with him, so we can't judge by that. The last time anyone admits to seeing him is mid-afternoon Friday. If he was killed earlier than Saturday morning, Yoder might have killed him before he drove down the mountain to meet Sallie Sue."

"How?" Amos asked.

"Beg your pardon?"

"Yoder parks his old truck over in the trees by his trailer. So how does he get down the mountain without driving through the pasture and down Hiram's gravel road?"

"Good question. How about we drive out there and find

out."

The men walked around to the parking area behind the police station, picked up Amos's squad car and headed out the road to Lackland's farm. "What's all that about Lackland owing him?" Amos asked as he swung out onto the street.

"Wouldn't say, but I'm thinking maybe Yoder didn't actually steal that car in which the girl was killed. Maybe Lackland was driving."

"Why would Yoder take the blame?"

"Money? Promise of wealth to come? I do not know, but the man is slimy as an eel and capable of killing Lackland in a fit of anger."

"Trigger?" Amos asked.

"Again, I don't know. Yoder would blackmail St. Peter. I'm sure he knows more than he's telling, but he's not going say a word unless he figures he can't make a buck out of it."

"Then I hope he knows what he's doing," Amos said.

Chapter 24

Thursday afternoon
Geoff

Peggy Caldwell's truck was parked in front of the barn beside Hiram's white dually and trailer. When they walked around to the stable, the two men saw Merry Abbott and Peggy Caldwell harnessing the big black horse to a two-wheeled wooden cart. Yoder leaned against the open stable door watching, but making no attempt to help. The miniature donkey leaned shoulder to knee against the big black horse like a four-legged gray wart.

"There," Merry said as she buckled the padded girth around the horse's big middle. He seemed to have gone to sleep. His head drooped, and his eyes were half closed. The donkey's ears twitched but not much else.

Geoff had never seen a horse and carriage close up, and had only a vague idea of how a harness worked. The instant Yoder saw the two men he pushed away from the door of the barn and drifted inside.

Geoff let him go. At least he hadn't absconded yet.

"Come back, Jacob," Merry called after him. "You're going to help drive. We've got to get Heinzie and Peggy ready for Easter Sunday."

"You taking the jackass along?" Yoder asked.

Merry patted the cross on the donkey's back. "More appropriate for Palm Sunday. I can't believe he's actually that big a problem."

Yoder snickered. "Hiram tried to wean him off ever since they got here. Heinzie got better. The jackass did not."

Geoff wondered what they were talking about. Both horse and donkey seemed to be dozing.

"Still got one axle to pack on the vis-à-vis," Jacob said. "Need to move her outside where we can scrub her down too. Needs a paint job."

"That will have to wait a bit, but we can pack the axle, wash the carriage and practice drive it tomorrow afternoon after the funeral," Merry said. "With Don Qui locked in his stall. In the meantime, give us a hand putting Heinzie to the Meadowbrook."

Geoff figured he and Amos were being ignored on purpose. The Meadowbrook, a medium-sized two wheeled cart with a black leather-covered bench split into two seats, sat behind the horse with its shafts resting on a wooden sawhorse.

He watched the complicated procedure of putting the horse into the harness and the carriage to the horse. Then Peggy climbed in from the rear and took up the reins.

A long buggy whip stood upright in a shiny brass holder at the right hand side of the front of the carriage, but Peggy didn't touch it. "Heinzie, walk on." Peggy's voice sounded shaky, but Heinzie obligingly ambled off. The cart bounced slightly every time it rolled over a stone or a minor bump.

Don Qui nearly fell over when his leaning post walked away from him, but came instantly awake and marched beside Heinzie's left front leg.

"I've seen Dalmatians trot under carriages," Merry said, "But this is ridiculous."

Geoff thought the wooden cart looked light and fragile, as though it might take flight at anything faster than a walk.

Peggy walked Heinzie into the dressage arena. Don Qui kept pace.

Merry walked to the center of the arena where she could call to Peggy as she drove.

Heinzie was as large as the teams of Clydesdales and Percherons he'd watched in parades. Long feathers of hair trailed down over his hooves, which were as wide as soup tureens. His black mane flowed below his shoulder and eddied in the late afternoon breeze. He seemed content simply to walk around the arena, and Don Qui seemed content to walk beside him.

If the horse ever decided to take off at a gallop, however, he'd be unstoppable and the donkey would be left far behind.

"Move him up into a trot," Merry said.

Peggy glanced over at her. Geoff saw her jaw set. "Tur-rot on," she said.

Heinzie walked.

"Trot on, blast it."

Heinzie walked.

Peggy frowned, Yoder, leered, Merry laughed.

"Pick up your whip and tap him on his flank when you say trot," Merry said. "Tap, don't whack."

"Oh, dear," Peggy whispered, but she did as she was told. "Trot *on.* "

Heinzie opened his eyes wide at the touch of the whip against his shoulder, snorted once, and trotted. He ate up the space around the arena with his long stride.

"*Yeah*, baby. Go," Peggy said.

Don Qui managed to keep up with the big horse, although his short legs worked like sewing machine needles.

"Easy," Merry said.

Heinzie apparently heard her because he dropped into a slower trot. He lowered his head, arched his neck, and swung his broad hindquarters from side to side as though he were dancing a samba.

"Shoot, that looks like fun," Amos said.

A couple of more figure eights and Peggy pulled Heinzie down to a walk as she came abreast of the two men. "Jacob, I can handle this. Amos, climb aboard."

"O-kay."

Yoder climbed out and held the seat up so Amos could get in and sit.

"Trot on," Peggy said. This time Heinzie trotted at the sound of Peggy's voice. Merry came to stand beside Geoff with her hands in the pockets of her jeans and a broad grin on her face. "You're next."

"I'm not dressed for it," Geoff said.

"Sure you are. If you drive in a show you'll have to wear a top hat or a bowler." She stared him up and down. "You look like a top hat guy. Today, however, you get to be safe." She handed him a black helmet with a chinstrap. "It's a hard hat to protect your thick skull."

He glanced down at Merry as she watched the horse and carriage trot lazy figure eights around the arena and caught his breath. He didn't think he'd ever seen such naked longing. No more like lust. She ached to be out there holding those reins instead of Peggy.

So why wasn't she?

When he changed places with Amos, he found the sight of Heinzie's oversized butt sashaying from side to side as his mega-hooves clopped felt almost hypnotic. Maybe after all this was over, nah. Atlanta was too far away to drive up here for lessons, and he didn't think he'd enjoy them unless Merry was teaching them.

"Heinzie, strong trot," Peggy said. The big black horse moved to a much faster gear instantly.

Geoff grabbed the wooden fender over the wheel.

Crack!

Without warning, the Meadowbrook gave a sickening lurch to the left, collapsed underneath him and threw his body against the wheel. His left shoulder connected with the metal rim. He felt as though somebody had whacked him with a crowbar.

The rim of his hard hat connected with the edge of the wooden fender with a jolt that rattled his teeth and crossed his eyes.

Peggy screamed, fell against him, and crushed him against the wheel with all her weight.

Ahead of him Heinzie reared, bucked and struggled to stay on his feet while the carriage, now canted over on its left side, dragged through the sand at a forty-five degree angle.

"Whoa!" Merry raced past the cart, grabbed Heinzie's reins and shouted, "Heinzie, stand!"

More running feet, and a moment later, Peggy's weight shifted off him as Amos dragged her back toward the right side of the cart. "Geoff, crawl out," Amos shouted.

"I'm stuck."

"Can you twist around far enough to give me your right hand?" Merry's voice. He rotated his right shoulder back and felt Merry's strong hands grasping his wrist across the back of the seat. "Slide forward so I can lower the seat back."

She sounded remarkably calm. Who was looking after the horse? He spared a glance and saw Heinzie trying desperately to keep the carriage upright.

"He won't move," Merry said. "Not for a minute, anyway. We need to make this quick. Amos, you have Peggy?"

"Got her," Amos said. "Come on, Peggy, upsy-daisy."

Geoff braced both feet against the dashboard to push himself toward the back of the carriage as Merry hauled on his right arm with both hands. For a moment he stuck, then he slid forward and landed face down on top of Merry. For a moment they were nose-to-nose before she shoved him off and rolled away from him. Even in his present state, he had time to register the soft cushion of her body.

"Come on." She rolled to her feet. "We've got to hold the carriage upright long enough for me to get Heinzie loose. Can you hold up the wheel?"

He rubbed his shoulder and nodded. The wheel was no longer round, but had collapsed into an ovoid with a bent rim. He could see several broken spokes.

"Peggy, are you all right?" Merry said as she ran past Geoff toward Heinzie's head.

"I'm fine, but Amos probably has a double hernia from hauling me out."

Amos grabbed the rim of the wheel next to Geoff, grinned at him and hefted half the load. Geoff was amazed that after his initial terrified buck, the horse had fought to stay on his feet without fussing or trying to run away.

"Heinzie, good boy, walk forward," Merry said. Geoff could see her on the left and Peggy on the right by the horse's head. "Good boy. That's it."

A moment later the horse was free of the shafts. The weight on Geoff's hands and arms lessened. Then Merry and Peggy lowered the shafts to the ground.

"Heinzie, whoa. Stand." Merry said. She called to the men, "Let the wheel down easy. Try not to let the carriage tip all the way over."

Throughout, her voice had remained calm and steady. Amazing. Everybody else himself included, he suspected, had been screaming and shouting. As he and Amos both released the wheel, Merry touched Geoff's shoulder. "How's your head?"

"I thought you were crazy to make me wear this stupid hat," he said as he unclipped it and pulled it off. "Thanks."

"What the hell happened?" Amos asked.

Geoff dropped to his knees. "Some spokes broke."

A moment later Merry knelt in the sand beside him. "Not like that, they didn't. Spokes break, all right, but not in the middle, and not three at once." She propped herself on her right elbow to look at the back of the wheel. He heard her breath catch. "Geoff, look at this." She scooted back to give him room. "Peggy, reach me the spares box. I don't want this cart falling on our heads."

Peggy handed Merry the heavy wooden box from behind the driver's seat. Merry forced it under the back of the carriage to take weight off the broken wheel.

Geoff propped himself on his right arm, then lay down on his back and slid behind the wheel. His left arm and shoulder felt bruised and sore, but with his right he felt along and broken spokes. "Hell," he whispered and slid away. "Amos, you better take a look at this too."

"What?" Peggy asked and bent down. "All I see is three fractured spokes."

Amos checked behind the wheel, stood up and brushed off his no-longer immaculate uniform. "Uh-huh," he said.

"Look, I have to get Heinzie out of his harness, check to see he hasn't hurt himself, and put him out in the pasture with the others," Merry said. "I'll meet you in the stable in ten minutes."

"You go with them," Peggy said. "I'll look after Heinzie." She pointed to the donkey, who stood once more shoulder to knee with Heinzie. "Don Qui too."

"But . . ."

"Go."

"Leave the harness on the fence," Merry said. "I can wash it and put it away later."

Peggy nodded, rolled up Heinzie's reins from where they trailed behind him, tucked the traces under his britchin, and led him away toward the pasture. Don Qui trotted along behind.

Merry stalked off toward the stable with her head held high and her chin stuck out a mile.

Geoff and Amos followed.

"That's one steady horse," Amos said. "He could have totally freaked and hurt himself, not to mention Peggy and old Geoff here."

Merry whirled to glare at him. "*Whoa* means do not move a foot until I tell you different. I knew he'd stand. My *daddy* trained him." She brushed her fingertips along her cheeks and turned away. "Hiram may not have been the world's best father, but he was one hell of a horse trainer."

The three walked into the stable and down to the hay bales

that constituted the only place to sit down. Merry sank onto the nearest bale and wrapped her arms around herself.

Geoff could tell she was crashing fast.

"Somebody sabotaged your cart," Geoff said. He leaned against the stall and rubbed his sore shoulder. His fingers still tingled. "Unless you're in the habit of sawing kerfs straight across the backside of three spokes."

"Why didn't it break the minute Peggy and Yoder started driving?" Amos asked and took up a position two bales down from Merry's.

"Whoever did this is either sneaky, lucky, or knows his way around carriages and hand tools," Geoff said. "Cuts weren't deep. They might have held up fine, even with two people in the carriage, at a nice sedate walk, although I doubt it. Not for long."

"Might have lasted longer if Peggy had been driving from the left, too," Merry said. "Although anyone with driving knowledge would know the driver traditionally sits on the right." She turned to Amos. "Yoder is skinny and you're not a heavy man. Even weakened and at a slow trot, the spokes apparently held."

"From the jagged edges where they broke, however, I'd say they were already starting to split," Geoff said. "My weight was enough to finish the job the minute the horse started to trot with me in the left seat."

"But why?" Merry cried. "You could have broken your neck."

He came across, hunkered down in front of Merry and took both her hands. "Who other than Peggy knows you don't drive any longer?"

She looked confused. "I suppose Hiram could have told someone. He probably told Yoder, but I don't know who else. It wasn't exactly secret in driving circles. Peggy didn't know until I told her."

"But you did announce that you'd be resuming Hiram's teaching schedule, didn't you?"

"Sure. So?"

"So, wouldn't someone who didn't know about your driving problem assume you'd be riding left seat during the lessons?"

He watched her eyes widen.

"Me? You think someone was out to hurt *me*?" She began to shake her head. "No way. Of all the wacko, inefficient, stupid ways . . ." She glared at him. "I'll have you know I do not weigh nearly as much as you do."

"I doubt whoever sliced those spokes did beta testing on how much weight it would take to break them."

At that moment Peggy walked into the front of the barn. "Heinzie's out in the pasture discussing his adventures with Don Qui. What have I missed?"

"Geoff thinks somebody was out to hurt *me,*" Merry said.

Peggy nodded at Geoff. "Makes sense."

"Makes no sense at all!" Merry said. She strode up and down the aisle. "The only person I know around here other than you all is Jacob, and he *wants* me in one piece so I can keep paying him. Besides, he knows I don't drive."

Geoff got to his feet and put out an arm to stop Merry. "Whoever sabotaged that carriage didn't do it for their health."

"Or yours," Peggy added.

Chapter 25

Thursday evening
Merry

By the time we arrived at the mortuary for the viewing—although the coffin would remain closed—heavy clouds were rolling in across the mountains to the west, and drum rolls of thunder followed lightning.

Mountain storms are different from flatland storms. Flatlanders come at you from far away. Plenty of warning to head for the storm cellar or an inside closet with cats, dogs and children and hope there's no tornado around.

Mountain storms roar down at you from behind hilltops and catch you flatfooted. Of course, they normally don't bring tornadoes with them, but they can sure touch off forest fires, not something I'm used to. No danger of that this early in the year.

NOAA weather is marvelous and saves a great many lives. Still, I sometimes miss sitting on my front porch enjoying a good old thunderstorm that begins with that buttered toast smell when the first raindrop hits dry dirt and drops the temperature twenty degrees in twenty minutes.

Now, we huddle around our portable television sets looking for hook echoes on the radar. Much safer, but not nearly as much fun.

"Rain in ten minutes," Peggy said as we pulled into the parking lot at the funeral home. "The weather forecast says it's going to be a wet Friday."

"Perfect weather for a graveside service. I don't suppose I can wear my muck boots with my black dress."

She slammed her car door and trotted toward the funeral home entrance. "Dig your pumps into the mud like everybody else," she said over her shoulder.

The first drops hit the metal roof over the funeral home entrance as we opened the door to the hall. "Mr. Straley has left for the evening," said his assistant. He peered at Peggy and me and kept his distance. Straley must have warned him we could erupt into hysteria. "A number of ladies have dropped dishes by."

"Funeral ladies?" I asked.

"Oh, no. The funeral ladies won't arrive until mid-morning tomorrow to set up. These are Mossy Creek ladies. They said they wanted to be sure we had snacks, and since you weren't home . . . Well, they brought them here."

"Don't worry," Peggy whispered. "We'll make sure they all signed the book, although I can't see anybody trying to poison an entire group in public."

Not much chance of wasting away from grief. At least not for a while.

Looking at the array of tiny quiches and individual cheesecakes the ladies had brought, as well as chips, dip, and one elegantly arranged veggie tray, I hoped we'd have a few people show up.

The funeral home had furnished a coffeemaker with cream, sugar, and artificial sweetener on a credenza opposite the casket. The Styrofoam cups and plastic spoons spoiled the effect, but you can't have everything. I wondered how much I was paying for it.

We'd barely stashed our purses out of sight behind the red velvet drapes when our first visitor arrived.

"Oh, Lord," Peggy whispered. "What's *he* doing here?"

Had to be a politician or a banker. Something that allowed him to get that light brown hair with its hint of gray at the temples razor cut by the same caliber of barber that did John Edwards. A real GQ kind of guy. He wore a pale blue shirt that matched his eyes, a red power tie, a dark gray suit that had been made for him by someone who knew his fabrics, and spit-shined Italian loafers with tassels. I always check out the shoes.

My heart did not ache with despair when I saw his wide platinum wedding band. He was entirely too pretty for my taste. I don't do pretty. I prefer the Tommie Lee Jones craggy-faced guys who never use moisturizers or pluck their eyebrows.

He came toward us with his hand outstretched. I saw Peggy hesitate a moment before she took it. Interesting that he was so obviously trying to be socially correct when he didn't know that a woman always offers her hand first, if she chooses to do so. I doubt Peggy would have.

He clasped her hand with his right and covered it with his

left. "Mrs. Caldwell, how nice to see you, even under these dreadful circumstances."

Peggy withdrew her hand and tossed him a micro-expression of distaste before she smiled. He didn't pick up on it, but I sure did. "Good evening, Ken," she said, slightly emphasizing the use of his first name.

He couldn't really be named Ken, could he? He was such a perfect Ken that I longed to grab his crotch to see if he actually had genitalia.

"Merry, this is Governor Bigelow's henchman, Ken Whitehead. Ken, Merideth Lackland Abbott."

He chortled. "Right hand man, Mrs. Caldwell. Henchman sounds nasty." He did the two handed thing with me, but let go before I had a chance to pull my hand away. His hands were a bunch softer than mine. I didn't look down at his nails, but I'd bet he had a manicure every week when he had that hair trimmed. "Such a terrible thing, Mrs. Abbott. I assure you Bigelow is one of the safest counties in the state the whole region."

Tell that to Hiram.

"No doubt some tramp wandering through, and now long gone. Terrible thing. Terrible."

"Yeah, Hiram did like a good tramp. Or is that dirty tramp? I always get that confused."

Duh, the old 'wandering tramp' scenario. This guy was one big cliché.

Then I looked into those too-pale blue eyes and caught Peggy watching him as though he were a six-foot water moccasin coiled to strike. I could certainly see him holding his own among the power brokers, but I wondered how he handled himself among the good ole boys. Probably switched to jeans, a Wal-Mart polo shirt, muddy work boots, a John Deere baseball cap, and a completely different syntax. I couldn't see him going so far as to rub dirt into those immaculate cuticles.

I made a sound that he might take for assent. "How nice of you to come. Did you know my father well?"

He reached for my hand again, but this time I was too fast for him. I stuck both hands in the pockets of my blazer.

"You wouldn't know, of course. I represent the consortium that owns the acreage that abuts Mr. Lackland's property. We are neighbors."

This time he was too quick for me. He slid his hand under my elbow and cut me away from Peggy as expertly as a wrangler with a prize heifer. At that moment several other people I didn't know walked in and Peggy went to meet them.

She glared at Ken over her shoulder and gave me a tiny shake of her head that I took to mean "do not buy property in the Everglades from this man."

"This is a trying time for you, Mrs. Abbott. May I call you Merry?" He didn't wait for me to say yes or *hell* no. "I know you must be overwhelmed. The governor and I stand ready to do everything we can to alleviate your difficulties in such a sad time."

And if I didn't already have difficulties, he'd be happy to provide them for me. "Uh, thank you," I said.

"We all know that the real estate market is at the bottom of a deep pit at the moment." He shook his head and gave a little cluck. "You may not be able to unload Mr. Lackland's property for a very long while working with a Realtor, even a good one. Meanwhile, the debt piles up, then come taxes, utilities, upkeep of the horses and equipment, mortgage payments on the new stable . . . " He shook his head sadly. "On top of that, you have a home in Kentucky."

How in heck did he know that?

"Plus a daughter just starting her career and apt to need your support both financial and otherwise in this down market. You're a woman on your own, completely responsible for your own welfare. You live a peripatetic lifestyle, traveling from horse show to horse show, horse farm to horse farm. Without even alimony . . . "

He'd gone way beyond Google. The governor's man had developed a dossier on me. Why? And why was he letting me know how much he knew? I started to snap his head off, then I saw Peggy across the room watching us, calmed down and decided to hear him out. I nodded and gave him my sad puppy stare. I actually brushed his cashmere sleeve with my fingertips.

"How long are you planning to stay in Mossy Creek after the funeral?" he asked.

"I haven't made up my mind," I sniffed. "I do have so much paperwork to go through."

He snapped to as though I'd hit him in the rump with a cattle prod. "Paperwork? I'm in Bigelow looking after some of the Governor's interests for a while. I'd be most happy to help you organize . . ."

"Oh, no. It's just final taxes and such. My father had a wonderful accountant and an excellent lawyer."

"Yes, of course." He'd gone somewhere else for the moment, but he came back to himself and brought his attention back to me. "Let's have lunch at my club in Bigelow one day next week. Say, Tuesday? I'll have my girl call up and confirm. I think I can solve all your problems." He glittered at me. "Maybe the governor can even put a word in the proper ears in New York for your daughter."

Was that a promise or a threat? My skin crawled. I do not anger easily, but if he tried to use Allie's career as leverage against me, I'd kill him *and* the governor. Besides, I absolutely hate people who call their secretaries and assistants 'my girl.' I spent too many years when Allie was growing up being somebody's girl. I managed to smile, however, and nod with a hint of tears. "I'd be so grateful," I said and hated myself.

He patted my hand one final time. For a moment I thought he was going to give me an air kiss and braced myself not to recoil, but he caught himself at the last minute and patted my shoulder instead.

"Now, I'm afraid I have to leave so I can get home to read the kids their bedtime story." Before he slammed the dungeon door shut on them for the night, no doubt.

He tossed Peggy a little wave and swept out of the room while everyone watched him go. He moved as though he was expecting applause.

I walked over to Peggy and leaned over to whisper, "Who was that masked man?"

"Not the Lone Ranger, that's for damn sure. What did he want?"

"I don't guess it's anything to my advantage."

"He's the kind of man who helps old ladies across the street, shoves them under a bus, then sues the bus company."

"Lawyer, then?"

"The term shyster does not begin to encompass him."

"He knew a darned sight too much about me." I said.

Interesting that he apparently did *not* know that the mortgage insurance would leave the farm free and clear. Good old Mr. Robertson. Had Whitehead's been the offer Mr. Robertson had mentioned? Would he tell me if I asked?

Peggy took me around and introduced me to the people who had come to pay their respects. They were mostly Mossy Creek Garden Club ladies, several of whom I had met at Mama's restaurant. They all wanted to know how soon I could start teaching them to drive.

I was surprised when Geoff Wheeler walked in. "Are you still on the clock or is this purely social?" I asked.

"An officer of the law is always on the clock," he said. "Protect and serve twenty-four-seven."

"Must play hell with your sex life." Why on earth did I say things like that?

"What sex life? We take oaths of poverty, celibacy and obedience to authority like monks."

"Of *course* you do."

He didn't wear a wedding ring, but plenty of married men didn't. Most of the policemen I'd met did, although I imagine the last thing a detective would want a criminal to know is that he has hostages to fortune stashed somewhere.

"Your wife must be very understanding."

"The poverty part caused the divorce. She's a hotshot corporate lawyer in Atlanta and makes more in a month than I do in a year. She didn't like supporting her lifestyle on my paycheck."

"So who pays whom child support?" I asked.

He actually smiled down at me. I thought of the crocodile from Alice in Wonderland who welcomes little fishies in with gently smiling jaws.

Most men can't look down on me *physically* even if they do other ways. He could. "Ask me straight out, why don't you?" he said. "This 'when did you stop beating your wife' method of interrogation went out with rubber hoses."

"Okay. Children?"

"None. No alimony, although I would like her to pay me some."

"My mother says early divorces are best because you don't have either possessions or children to fight over."

"Did you follow Mom's advice?"

"You know I didn't. Whether you or Ken Whitehead developed the dossier on me, I'll bet you shared."

"I beg your pardon?" Although his expression didn't change, he went instantly from banter to *really* serious.

"The governor's pit bull just left. He knew gew-gobs more about me and my family than he should have. He issued a gentle threat along the lines of 'keep a low profile and do what we tell you, Missy. We know where you live.'"

"What precisely did he say?"

"The words don't sound threatening."

He waved a hand. "Tell me."

So I did. I expected him to blow me off. Instead he steered me through the people standing around drinking coffee into the hall and around a corner where we were alone.

"Do as he says."

"You would say that. You play for his team," I said.

He grabbed my upper arms. I thought he was going to shake me like a beagle with a dead rabbit, but he held me at arm's length and growled at me.

"I'm talking about the low profile part, dammit. Keep your head down and do not play Nancy Drew or someone may remove it from your shoulders. That would annoy me."

"We wouldn't want that, would we?" My heart was racing and my stomach was doing flip flops.

"No, we would not want that. It would add to my workload, possibly screw up my career, complicate my life, and generally piss me off."

I thought the man was going to kiss me right in front of God and all the corpses. I wanted him to. I hadn't reacted to a man that way since I fell for Vic, and look how *that* turned out.

"There you are," said Peggy's cheerful voice. "Everyone's been looking for you."

Geoff dropped my arms, stepped back, ran his hand over his nearly non-existent hair and walked away.

"Oops," she whispered. "Sorry."

"Don't be." Or not *very* sorry, at any rate. "Who's looking for me?"

"I have four ladies in there wanting to schedule driving lessons this weekend."

"Oh, God. Do they know I can only coach them, not drive *for* them?"

"I told them, but not why. They assume it's your special teaching technique."

"You've driven the Haflinger, right?"

"Golden Boy, yes. He is a truly lovely pony. Also, he doesn't come joined at the hip to a donkey. Hiram used him for all the beginner lessons, even though he was planning on using Heinzie on Easter to pull the vis-à-vis."

"What was he planning to do with Don Qui?"

"Lock him in a stall and leave him where he couldn't hear him yell, although Don Qui has been known to open his own stall and go hunting for his buddy. Heinzie's not the problem. When Don Qui's not with him, he may whinny a couple of times, then he settles down and does as he's told. Don Qui, on the other hand . . . Well, you saw and heard. Heinzie is not the brightest star in the equine firmament. Don Qui is. They're like the old Shore Patrol—two men, the big one and the smart one. Guess which Don Qui considers himself?"

"What happens if we take him with us to Mossy Creek? Will he wander off or kick the children?"

"I doubt it. He'll stay as close to Heinzie as he can get. Hiram was working Heinzie away from the stable. I know he drove him down the driveway and along the road a couple of times while Don Qui yelled his head off from his stall. Like most donkeys, however, Don Qui laid in wait for Hiram and stomped on his foot. Broke his little toe."

"Donkeys are big on revenge," I said. "Mules are even worse. They'll wait years to savage somebody who hurt them. Okay, we'll try Hiram's technique. We'll start driving Heinzie down the road with Don Qui locked in his stall, and endure the noise."

"And watch our backs," she said.

Chapter 26

Friday morning
Merry

Friday's weather dawned appropriately soggy, and according to early television weather, intended to get wetter before it blew over. At least Hiram's cemetery plot was high enough so that it wouldn't flood out the few mourners, but getting to the tent would entail a slog from the winding road up the muddy hill. Great.

I wear a dress and heels so seldom that I felt as though I were playing dress up in my mother's clothes. I had absolutely refused to wear a hat, and I don't own an umbrella. With luck I wouldn't break my ankle and wind up in the emergency room. The weather was cold enough so that I wore my black blazer over my black dress.

The umbrella Peggy held over her head was big enough for both of us. I turned the heater on full blast as we backed out of her driveway and headed for the cemetery. The rain had turned the weather chill as well as soggy, but my shivers weren't due to the outside temperature as much as my own internal shakiness.

Friends have warned me that burying a parent is breaking one of life's ultimate connections. What possessed me to spend so much time and energy keeping him out of my life?

Now it was too late. The only saving grace was that we had reconnected before he died.

I'd never gotten a chance to hug him, to feel the strength and warmth of his arms around me, to hear his heart beating one last time, to see that shit-kicking grin that had enthralled everybody who met him, to smell his verbena aftershave that smelled like fresh lemons even in the midst of winter. We'd never had the chance to find our way back to one another.

Death sucks. Murder sucks worse.

The funeral home people had laid a three-foot wide strip of indoor-outdoor carpet from the road up the hill to the tent where the service would take place. I'd pay for that too.

The cemetery wasn't large, so Peggy and I been able to spot the green tent from the funeral home parking lot. Good thing, because the hearse had already delivered Hiram's casket to the graveside, and the cemetery staff had set it up on the hydraulic lift that would lower it into the earth.

We parked, but I made no move to open the door. I wrapped my arms around the steering wheel of my truck, put my head down and leaked. Peggy was smart enough to sit there quietly and let me have at it.

Finally I hiccupped into silence. "Stupid rain. If the sun was shining I could wear sunglasses so nobody could see my eyes," I said.

"Wear them anyway." Peggy handed me a big white men's handkerchief. "This was Ben's. Tissues won't cut it. This won't fall apart on you."

"We don't have hysterics at funerals in my family. Very bad form."

"Who said you planned to have hysterics? It's okay to weep at your father's funeral." She pulled out the twin of my handkerchief and held it to her eyes. "I certainly plan to do more than weep. More like sob. Come on. People are arriving. Time to go. It's almost over."

"After the funeral, I'll have time to figure out who did this to him."

"We will, you mean." She opened her door, stuck her umbrella out and opened it. "You'll just have to get wet until you come around to my side of the truck."

Twenty chairs had been set up under the tent and the flowers had already been moved from the viewing room to the graveside. The Episcopal pall had been removed and probably sent to the cleaners. The priest was Peggy's size with a cheerful round face that matched his round belly. I'm sure he introduced himself to me and said all the right things, but I don't even remember his name. Everybody's voice seemed to be coming at me through a synthesizer or from under water.

Peggy steered me to the center seat and sat beside me. People I didn't know came up the hill, shook my hand and took their places. The garden club ladies showed up. A couple brought husbands or significant others. Geoff Wheeler and Amos Royden came together and stood at the back.

I almost didn't recognize Jacob Yoder. He was squeaky clean, freshly shaven, and wore a black jacket with clean jeans, a white shirt and a black tie. I could believe he'd been raised Amish. Impossible to tell whether his eyes were red-rimmed from booze or tears, but he looked genuinely upset. He shook my hand in his callused one. Even his nails were clean. He'd made a real effort to show my father respect. I appreciated that.

The nice thing about the Episcopal graveside service is that there's no eulogy. I think that's because death equalizes us. After the final Amen everyone else walked down the hill to the cars. Peggy glanced at me and started to follow, but I stopped her. I waited until the coffin was lowered, then picked up a handful of dirt and dropped it onto the casket. Old English custom. The thud of finality. Peggy did the same.

Walking down that hill to my truck I felt as alone as though I were the only being on Mars. I knew tons of people from Colorado to Maine, had a mother, a step-father, a daughter, even an ex-husband, yet the only person beside me was a woman I'd met less than a week earlier. Whose fault was that? I'd always assumed it was theirs, but now I wondered if I'd been the one doing the pushing away.

Had I refused to take the chance of caring for anybody for fear they could hurt me as Hiram had hurt me? If so, then I'd shortchanged both them and me.

When we reached the funeral home, I told Peggy to go ahead. I sat behind the wheel and called my mother. Naturally, I got her email. "I love you." I said.

I left the same message for Allie.

I only had two people who mattered enough to me to call. I vowed that in a year on the anniversary of Hiram's funeral I would have more calls to make, more people I cared about and who cared about me.

The funeral ladies had done themselves and Hiram proud. The spread was more like a luncheon than snacks, with people filling their plates. I was beginning to recognize people and even know their names, but I'd not met the funeral ladies before. They fluttered around pouring punch (neither hot pink nor pale yellow and not alcoholic) and coffee, offering ham biscuits and finger sandwiches, hot meatballs, deviled eggs, half a dozen different types of cakes, and tarts and I don't know what all. I didn't pay that much attention. I'm lucky I remember as much as I do.

Everyone seemed to be having a good time. I suddenly felt starved, but I couldn't chow down with everyone watching. Since Peggy and I had to stay to the bitter end anyway, I planned to take leftovers home with us.

A tall, lanky young man with a mop of hair the color of the carrots on the veggie tray walked in and stood in the doorway staring as though he'd wandered into the wrong funeral.

He spotted me and headed straight for me. I didn't recognize him either from the viewing or the service. Who could miss that hair?

"You Miz Abbott?" he asked. He did not offer his hand. I wondered for a moment if he was a process server, and somebody was suing me.

He said, "I need to come pick up Momma's carriage out to your place."

A thin woman nearly as tall as the man materialized at his elbow. Her hair must have been the same color as his when she was younger, but had faded to a pale shrimp pink. It was drawn into a tight bun at the nape of her neck. One of the funeral ladies I hadn't met. "Tom," she whispered. "This is not the time."

He removed her hand from his arm, none too gently. "That's your carriage, Momma. I'm gettin' it back."

"Which carriage would that be?" I directed my question to the lady. The man was obviously her son.

"You know danged well which carriage," he said. His veneer of politeness apparently covered a red-headed temper. "That buggy belongs to my momma. Since Lackland's dead, I want it back. Promised he'd have it done by now so's we could sell it."

"I'm apologize for my bad-mannered son, Mrs. Abbott," the woman said and stuck out her hand. "I'm Imogene Darnell and this is Tom." She turned so that I couldn't see what she whispered to him, but it must have been effective because he took a step back and subsided.

When she turned back to me, she said with a tight smile, "A funeral's no place to talk business. I raised Tom better than that."

"You're the one let him take it," Tom said. "He's had it a

month." He turned to me. "Well, is it finished? *Supposed* to be finished."

The only buggy at Hiram's barn was a long way from finished. "I'm sorry, Mr. Darnell, but I can't let you have it until my father's will is probated. Then you make a claim against the estate and . . . "

"Jesus H. Christ, no way I'm waiting for some damn will. I'm coming out to get it this weekend."

"You'll waste a trip," said a voice at my shoulder. Geoff Wheeler moved in beside me. "That entire barn is a crime scene. Nothing can be removed until I say it can, and I say it *can't* for the foreseeable future."

"Who the hell are you?"

"Geoffrey Wheeler, Georgia Bureau of Investigation."

"And I am Amos Royden," said Amos from my other side.

"Sheriff Campbell can tell y'all what you can do with y'all's crime scene."

"No, he won't," Geoff said mildly. "Why are you so anxious to remove that carriage from Mr. Lackland's *locked* barn?"

"It's mine. I can't be waitin' forever for it to be fixed up."

"No, Thomas Darnell, it is *mine*," Mrs. Darnell said. "I choose to leave it with Mrs. Abbott. I'm sure she can find someone to restore it properly now that Mr. Lackland is gone. Why don't you go wait in the car while we straighten up?"

He made an unpleasant sound and shook off her hand. "I got to get back to work." He glared at his mother. "Come on. I don't have time to wait on you." He turned on his heel and stalked out.

Mrs. Darnell shook her head. "I am so sorry. He's under a great deal of strain at the moment with a new job and a new baby, and you know what the economy's like with layoffs and such. Don't you worry about that carriage, Mrs. Abbott. I'll call you sometime next week, so we can discuss it." She looked around. "Now, where did I put my purse? I swear I'd lose my head if it wasn't glued on. Old age is dreadful. I can't even drive these days because of my cataracts. Tom gets annoyed having to tote me anywhere I need to go. Oh, there it is in the corner." She threw me a smile over her shoulder, swooped down on her handbag and bolted out the door.

"What was all that about?" I asked.

"He wants his carriage big time," Geoff said. "Assuming it *is* his."

"Huh?"

"He furnish proof of ownership? For all you know, it might belong to somebody in North Carolina."

"Or to Hiram," Amos added as he stepped closer. "He could have bought outright it to refurbish and sell, and Darnell sees his chance to get it back and keep the purchase price."

"You familiar with him?" Geoff asked.

Amos shook his head. "Not yet, but I intend to check him out. I don't like the way he treats his mother. A man who'll fuss at his mother in public is capable of anything. Even murder."

*

In the end I packed up enough food to keep Peggy and me out of Ingles for a couple of days, as well as a big package to take to Jacob Yoder. An anemic sun peeped through the remaining clouds as we stopped by Peggy's to change clothes. I drove on to Hiram's—I suppose I should say *my*—place.

Peggy stayed home to take a nap. Shoot, I wanted a nap too, but couldn't spare the time. She said the cats weren't speaking to her because she'd been gone so much.

"And when Dashiell is angry, all the cat treats in the universe won't get me back into his good graces," she said. "Sherlock ought to carry a sign that says, 'will forgive for food,' but Marple and Watson tend to follow Dashiell's lead. I need to cosset them for a while, especially Sherlock. He still doesn't understand what happened to him at Dr. Blackshear's. I'll be out to the farm late this afternoon if you want to hitch up Heinzie and see if I can drive him to the vis-à-vis."

"You'll do fine. Jacob will share the driving and keep you out of trouble."

"What about Don Qui?"

"We'll put Heinzie to the Meadowbrook and drive him down to the road and back starting tomorrow morning," I said. "We'll try leaving Don Qui in the pasture with the others. He can watch until Heinzie's out of sight. He can't jump a fence that high or open that gate."

"He'll bray."

"Let him. Bring ear plugs."

At the farm Jacob had changed to his grubby overalls. I

found him lifting the vis-à-vis wheel, the one that killed Hiram, onto its hub. I would love to have burned it, but the wheel hadn't committed any crime. Besides, it was the only wheel big enough to fit.

"There's a care package of food from the funeral on the front seat of my truck for you," I said. "You've already re-packed the axle? Fast work."

"Thirty minutes."

"Can I give you a hand lifting the wheel?"

"Let me be." He sounded grumpy. If he had been the one who forced that wheel onto Hiram's throat, he might well hate mounting it. Once it was on the hub, he fastened the bolts, came to his feet, pulled a dirty rag out of his pocket and wiped the oil off his hands. "Let down the jack and pull out the chocks."

I did as I was told, tossed the chocks on the floor of the carriage and held up the shafts while he moved the sawhorse holding them up out to the parking lot, then came back to help me pull the carriage outside. It wasn't nearly as heavy as it looked, and so beautifully balanced on its four wheels that I could have rolled it outside alone. We set the shafts back on the sawhorse and stood back to assess what we needed to do to get it ready for Easter.

"Needs a scrub and paint what's left," Jacob said. "Hiram and me already did the sanding."

"I thought I saw a paint sprayer under his workbench."

He nodded. "Plenty of black lacquer. Two coats, she will be as good as new."

"Upholstery's dirty and ripped in a couple of places," I said. "I wonder if Peggy has a steam cleaner."

"Staple some new vinyl over the old seats," Jacob said. "Add trim next week when we have time."

"Sounds good."

"I have replaced the broken spokes in the Meadowbrook wheel as well," he said. "They must be varnished, but otherwise, no one can tell they were broken."

Would wonders never cease? The man must actually want to keep his job. "When did you have time to do all that?"

"Last night. Didn't go into town. Used Hiram's lathe." He pointed to the front corner beside the workbench. "Not that hard. I learned turning on a gas-powered lathe when I was a boy. Took out the broken ones and glued in the new ones. Should be dry by now. Good as new."

That was the longest speech I'd ever heard Jacob make. Maybe cleaning up for Hiram's funeral had uncovered some long-buried work ethic in him.

"Hose connection is over there," Jacob pointed. "I will bring the barn hose so we can wash the vis-à-vis." He strode toward the stable, then stopped and looked at me from over his shoulder. "You selling the place or staying?"

"When I know, you'll know. For the foreseeable future, I'm staying. I hope you are too." I did. He might be a curmudgeon, and he might be crooked, but so far he'd been a competent worker. If he wanted to get blotto on the weekends, I couldn't say anything unless his drinking interfered with his work on the weekdays. "Jacob?" I called. "How'd you get into the workshop? I thought I locked it."

He smirked. "Days are long in prison. One must do something to occupy one's time, and there are always those who would teach."

"In other words, you learned to pick locks in prison."

He shrugged. "If you say so." He shut the door behind him and I sat down on the step of the vis-à-vis. The first day I came out to the farm, Jacob had made a big fuss about the workshop's being padlocked, when obviously he could have unlocked the padlock and gone in any time he liked.

Had he? If so, what had he found? What had he removed? Why had he let me in on his little secret today? Did he finally trust me? Or did he simply not think I'd pick up on his talent? Hiram said he was a good worker. I hadn't asked him to fix either the vis-à-vis or the Meadowbrook. Maybe he was responsible for the kerfed spokes in the first place, and fixed them to allay suspicion. What had changed his attitude? Did he actually want to stay here?

If he had killed Hiram, then I wanted him working for me and not off in the wind somewhere where we'd never find him. In the meantime, I wouldn't let down my guard. Or even let him know I had him on the suspect list.

After I called her, Peggy brought her steam cleaner when she showed up in the middle of the afternoon. The newly washed vis-à-vis had dried in the sun, and already looked pretty good. A couple of coats of lacquer, and she'd be really handsome again.

"I brought my electric stapler, a tack hammer and upholstery tacks," Peggy said, "and dug out some old red vinyl I planned to use to make cushions for my patio chairs but never got around to. You're welcome to it if it's enough."

We spread it out over the facing seats. We had more than enough. "Let me pay you for it at least," I said.

"It's been so long since I bought it, I don't even know what it cost. Fold it back up and put it in the barn where it won't get rained on and let's steam clean those seats."

By the time we had finished, the sun was setting. Too late to put Heinzie to.

The horses knew dinner was late. Equines have an unerring sense of time and total devotion to routine. Don Qui had so far refrained from braying, probably because he could see us working on the carriage and was interested in what we were doing. The moment we rolled it back inside, however, and padlocked the barn doors, he tuned up and ran back to where Jacob was crossing the pasture.

"This time you bring Heinzie in," I said to Jacob. "Leave him and Don Qui for last. Can you put a halter on Don Qui?"

"Why?"

"Can you?"

"Maybe."

"Please do. And attach a lead line. Then halter Heinzie and wait by the gate."

"Heinzie won't like it."

"He won't care," I said.

"The jackass will care." He gave me a sardonic smile, but I hardened my heart and my resolve.

Ten minutes later only Heinzie and Don Qui remained in the pasture, while the others were already chowing down in their stalls. Jacob passed me Don Qui's lead line and took Heinzie's.

"Lead Heinzie to his stall. We'll follow," I said.

I am *very* strong. I assumed I'd be able to handle the donkey easily. I held his lead line close to his chin and waited until Heinzie disappeared. At that point Don Qui dragged me into the stable after him as though I were a water skier and he was a powerboat. I left two distinct boot tracks where I'd leaned back with all my weight against him while he dragged me forward like an elephant pulling a teak tree out of a Malayan rainforest.

Once inside, where he could see his buddy eating, he relaxed and walked into his own stall. I unclipped the lead line so that he could eat and stepped back.

He whirled, stood straight up, all three feet of him, and came down with one of his hooves on my left instep, the foot I'd already jammed on Golden Boy's cart. I yelped and fell back into the aisle.

He glowered at me, then turned back to his bucket and began eating.

"Make his point, did he?" Jacob said. "Break your foot?"

"Help me up, dammit!"

He pulled me to my feet, foot, actually, since I was afraid to rest any weight on my left, the one Don Qui landed on. I sank onto a bale of hay and pulled off my left paddock boot and sock.

"What happened?" Peggy said from the doorway.

Jacob told her.

"Oh, dear, that wicked beast did the same thing to Hiram," she said. "Let me see."

"Ow!" I said as she flexed my toes and massaged my foot.

"I think he broke your little toe," Peggy said.

I didn't tell her that the toe probably came from my encounter with the Meadowbrook.

"Those little hooves are sharp. Nothing to be done about a broken small toe. Your foot's not broken, but you're going to have swelling and a bad bruise on your instep. We'll soak your foot in Epsom salts, then treat it with Arnica and liniment. You'll be better tomorrow morning, but you may limp for a couple of days. Better put your boot on while you still can."

Cussing a blue streak, I hobbled to my truck while Jacob stood in the stable door and snickered. Just when I had decided to like the man.

I could drive my truck right-footed, but I let Peggy lead while I followed at a sedate pace. I vowed I would get back at that donkey if it was the last thing I did. I no longer cared that he and Heinzie were raised together. Heinzie *would* drive without him. Enough was enough.

*

Since Jacob had informed me he'd be spending Friday evening until Sunday afternoon evening juking with his Bigelow girlfriend, I was left to handle the chores alone. Peggy had her own chores to do on Saturday and lunch with her daughter and granddaughter, but agreed to come out mid-afternoon to try her hand at driving Heinzie to the vis-à-vis in the dressage arena. Once she felt comfortable doing that with Don Qui trotting along, we could start driving the big horse down the driveway in the Meadowbrook on Monday when Jacob was around to help.

The morning felt clear and chill from the cold front that had brought the rain with it. Peggy had asked that I check to be sure I had cell phone coverage from the top of the hill. Today in clear weather I did.

I was looking forward to puttering around doing chores and enjoying the solitude. To make Peggy happy, I slipped the thirty-eight pistol I carry in the center console of my truck into my belt holster under my sweat shirt where I could reach it in a hurry, but I didn't expect trouble. Despite what Ken Whitehead said, Hiram was not killed by a wandering tramp, and nobody could drive up that driveway without the gravel crunch giving him away.

I never feel lonely when I'm around horses. This morning I let Don Qui trot into the stable after Heinzie, so he made no attempt to stomp my other foot. As long as I allowed him to do exactly what he wanted, we could maintain an *entente cordiale*. If I interfered, we wouldn't have *any* entente, cordiale or otherwise.

Okay. I'd bide my time. No donkey was going to outsmart me. While they ate, I swept the clients' lounge, feed and tack rooms, and ran the hose over the wash rack floor.

When I went back to open the front doors, Don Qui met me in the aisle. His stall door stood wide open. I knew I'd closed and latched it.

"You little troll, how'd you do that?"

He smirked at me. Just for that, I took Golden Boy and the two warmbloods back to the pasture first. Heinzie didn't care, but Don Qui trotted to the pasture gate and back again each trip. By the time I took Heinzie from his stall, Don Qui was glaring at me. I made sure my feet were out of his way.

He trotted after Heinzie and waited at the gate while I took the Friesian's halter off.

Calmly, Don Qui walked into the pasture after his big buddy, then, just as I turned to close the gate, he whipped around and kicked out at me with both hind feet.

Instead of my thigh, he connected with one of the metal pipes on the gate with a humongous clang. Satisfied that he'd made his point, he trotted off after Heinzie. "You little demon," I called after him. Before I met Don Qui I'd always loved miniature donkeys. They're so cute and cuddly, and Don Qui had let me scratch behind his ears and love all over him.

Now that he had decided I was bound and determined to break up his happy family (which I was), no more Mr. Nice Guy.

Most of my friends keep their IPods in their ears or play radios while they work. Often I do too, but sometimes I enjoy the peace and relative quiet. The country is never truly quiet, especially in the spring when birds are looking for mates, but birdsong, soughing trees and hoof falls beat city noise any day.

This was a catching up day. First I picked the wet shavings and road apples from the stalls and dumped them onto the manure pile. In another month, we could spread them over the pastures.

Hiram's truck hadn't been started for nearly a week, and diesels don't like sitting idle. The key ring Peggy gave me included his truck key and a key to the trailer lock. Good thing, since a hitch lock is nearly impossible to get off without the key and is an effective bar to theft.

When I opened his driver's side door and smelled the faint scent of Hiram's expensive British verbena aftershave still trapped inside, I nearly lost it and had to wait until the scent dissipated before I slid in and inserted the ignition key.

The truck started without a grumble, so I drove it down to the road and back before parking it again. I found some receipts for oats in the center console, as well as a vet bill from Dr. Blackshear for spring vaccinations. Both were marked paid.

I wouldn't have to locate a farrier since Jacob told me he did the trims and sets for extra pay.

I didn't really need to clean out the trailer before we loaded Heinzie and the vis-à-vis for the Easter afternoon drive around

Mossy Creek. Hiram never left road apples in his trailer. The acid and damp rot the floorboards. Usually, some groom was around to do the cleanup for him, but in any case, the trailer probably hadn't been used since he brought the horses from Aiken.

Time to go through the workshop carefully. I had no idea why he would have hidden his records, but if he had, the barn had more hidey-holes than the new stable. Jacob might have done some searching, but I could see no reason for him to want old medication logs.

I left the big front doors wide open to air the place out and give me as much natural light as possible to supplement the fluorescents.

After I searched the place more thoroughly than I had before, I planned to start on the covers for the vis-à-vis seats. Carriage seats wear out or tear or get mildew and dry rot and have to be replaced often, so I've gotten pretty good at upholstery. I wouldn't actually tear these seats down to the frames, but new covers should do nicely and really spiff up the carriage.

Jacob and I had parked the carriage directly over the place where Hiram had died. Unconsciously, I think we wanted to avoid stepping on that spot. The barn seemed to pulse with Hiram's energy. I don't believe in ghosts, but I swear I could almost hear him. I know I could feel his presence.

I ran. Stupid, right? I leaned on the hood of my truck and hyperventilated until I had sense enough to bend over and catch my breath. I didn't have any handy paper bags to breathe into, and I had no intention of passing out on the gravel. My foot was in bad enough shape without adding gravel scrapes on my knees and elbows.

So much for the peace of the country. I needed some noise.

Hiram had an old radio and CD player on his workbench, and I always carry a bunch of CDs with me because I travel so much, so I went back inside, put on some blue grass and turned the volume up. Even if Hiram's spirit still inhabited the barn and I didn't for a moment believe that I had nothing to fear.

I used his hand lantern to check out the doctor's buggy that Tom Darnell was so desperate to get his hands on, but didn't see anything interesting or unusual about it except that for some reason part of one of the shafts was missing. Shafts get broken frequently. No big deal to either buy or make a new one.

It might be easier to replace the wheels than replace the spokes, but Darnell wanted the carriage restored, not recreated, although I had no idea why that was important.

And if it was so darned important, how come they'd let it get into this shape in the first place? Even restored, it wouldn't be worth more than four or five thousand dollars. However, if things were as tight for Tom Darnell as his mother thought, even a couple of thousand might make a great difference to his family.

If it were up to me, I'd give him the thing back right now, but Geoff didn't want it removed.

By the time I'd brushed the festoons of cobwebs off, I was filthy. The canopy needed replacing, and all the metal parts needed cleaning and oiling. The brass was a combination black and green, but should polish up nicely. No doubt the axles needed to be packed as well. Still, it was a job worth doing. Restoration, rather than rebuilding, would put it right. Jacob and I could probably handle the job. In the meantime, I'd have to find out who truly owned the blasted thing.

Next I moved to the dog cart. There are a number of versions of dog carts. The only thing they have in common is that the seats are high enough up so that cages for the dogs fit underneath. And, of course, dogs have to breathe. This little beauty's cage was caned. Not a good idea to leave bored dogs for a long time with anything they can get their teeth around, as the owner of this cart had discovered. They had shredded the cane and left holes big enough for terriers—or *terrors*, as they are known by those of us who deal with them often—to escape through easily.

Carriage dogs come in several types. Dalmatians were bred to run underneath the carriage, not behind. They have incredible stamina and can keep pace with the horses for hours. Then there are the dogs that ride on the seats or in the laps or the drivers. Finally, there are the beagles and bassets used for rabbiting, and terriers used to dig out vermin and fox. Legend has it that British Parson Jack Russell created Jack Russells from a single male he found beside the road. Their tails are traditionally docked at four or five inches, just the span or a hand.

In this country it's a disaster if hunters kill a fox. We don't have enough to spare, for one thing, and we love our foxes. But in England, the huntsman who is the professional member of the hunting staff sometimes carries a Jack Russell in the pocket of his jacket. When the fox goes to ground, he hauls the terrier out by his hand-span tail and throws him at the hole to dig the fox out.

Those are the dogs that are generally carried under the seat of the carriage. I hoped the owner of this carriage didn't want the cages recaned. Maybe since he grew up Amish, Jacob knew how to cane, but I certainly didn't.

What owner? I had to find Hiram's paperwork.

I was on my hands and knees looking at the undercarriage of the dog cart when I heard a male voice call, "Hello, is anyone here?"

I reared up so fast I banged my head and saw stars. So much for being safe from unannounced visitors. I loosened my thirty-eight in its holster before I went to see who had walked in on me.

"I was out checking our property and thought I'd drop by, neighbor." Ken Whitehead held out his hand. I didn't offer mine. For one thing, it was filthy. He stepped closer. Too close. "Surely you're not alone out here? After what happened to your father. It's not safe. Anyone could walk in on you." As he had.

He'd chosen to park his BMW at the far edge of the parking area, right at the brow of the hill. The blue grass had covered the sound of his arrival, but wouldn't have if he'd parked between my truck and Hiram's.

The BMW was the one I had seen down on the road or its twin.

"Why should I be worried? I thought you said the tramp who killed my father was long gone by now," I said. "Where does your property start?" I raised my arm to the sore spot on my head, which casually lifted the tail of my shirt. When he saw my thirty-eight, he blinked and took a step backwards.

He waved a hand to indicate that his land was somewhere back of Hiram's property. So why was he on my side of the hill at all? Peggy said his drive up to that land started on the other side of the hill. Fairly close as the crow flew, but a good ten miles by road.

"I know we discussed lunch," he said, "but I thought I'd strike while the iron is hot. We'd like to buy your land."

"Who's we?"

"The consortium of businessmen I represent."

"Including Governor Bigelow?"

"I'm not really at liberty to name the principals, but I have carte blanche to make the deal."

"Why didn't you buy it before Hiram did?"

"Could we sit down?"

I looked around. "The only place to sit is in the vis-à-vis. You might get your trousers dirty."

He gave me a grin that chilled my blood. "Why, fair lady, I'd definitely mess up my trousers if it means I can sit with you."

"Across from me, actually." I climbed up into the carriage. He followed. It is not a good idea to sit in a carriage without a horse supporting its shafts, but this carriage had four wheels, so sitting in it was safe.

I repeated my question.

"Unfortunately, we didn't find out this parcel was for sale until Mr. Lackland had already purchased it." The smile this time was rueful.

"What'd he say when you tried to buy it from him?"

"Who says we did?" He shifted and grimaced. He'd found the loose spring under his butt. I had picked my side carefully.

"He told you to go to hell, right?"

"Not quite in those terms, but yes. We offered him a very good deal, plenty of money to buy even more property closer to Mossy Creek where the land is flatter."

"Now he's built a stable, restored the barn, graded and graveled the driveway, fenced the pastures and added a driving arena."

"We would of course take into consideration the improvements to the property." He looked into the distance and said with studied casualness, "By the way, you haven't come across any reports from surveyors and suchlike, have you? No sense in paying twice for the same report, is there?"

"Haven't found a thing, but then I haven't had time to look."

"I would appreciate a call when you do. Just paperwork, but extremely technical. Nothing a non-professional would understand. In the meantime, please consider our offer."

He hadn't actually used that old southern phrase, "Now, don't bother your pretty little head . . . " But he might as well have. "What offer?" I asked. Now I was mad. "You haven't made one yet. Okay, here's the deal. You make your offer in writing to Mr. Robertson, my attorney. When I get around to it, I'll give you an answer." I climbed down from the carriage.

"Can't we just agree in principle right now? Shake hands on it? Then we can leave the lawyering to the lawyers." He reached out to touch my shoulder, but I twisted away from him. No way was this guy touching me, and definitely not that close to my neck.

"Either Louis B. Mayer or Jack Warner said that an oral agreement isn't worth the paper it's written on," I said. "Besides, my hands are dirty."

He clambered awkwardly after me and patted his bottom as though he needed to restart the circulation.

"I'm afraid I've got work to do. Nice of you to drop by," I said as I walked to the door. He was forced to follow me outside. I stopped beside his car. "Great car. I liked it when I saw it parked down on the road the other day."

He jerked. "Couldn't have been me. I was in Atlanta."

"Uh-huh." But he hadn't asked me which day I'd seen it.

He opened his door, slid under the wheel and glared up at me, the first time his smile had slipped. "You'll regret not coming to an agreement. You might not find having mansions and a golf course next door quite so pleasant. Wealthy neighbors can get extremely nasty about the flies and smells horses generate. An attractive nuisance, I think they call it. Zoning regulations, you know."

"Not when we're grandfathered in," I said. "We came first."

"I've heard driving horses can be real dangerous," he said. "Lot of accidents. Things break. Hope you have good health and liability insurance. I'd hate to see a long stay in the hospital or a lawsuit for negligence toss that tight little rear of yours into bankruptcy." The man actually wiggled his eyebrows.

I gritted my teeth and made no attempt to return his smile. "How kind. By the way, if you make your offer on this property to Mr. Robertson, it might be nice if you provided an actual figure in dollars and cents." I shut his door for him and went back inside.

And shook. He stood too close, but many sales types invaded personal space to make a point. He didn't openly threaten, but the implication was there. I could see him sabotaging my carriage. More likely he'd hire somebody else to do it, so he didn't get the knees of those tailor-made trousers dirty.

Had he been expecting the place to be empty so he could have the run of it to search or do something else nasty? Had he been the one that had searched Hiram's apartment and Peggy's library? Used Poison? Busted computers? He must have seen my truck parked in front of the barn, and he'd come in anyway. Now, *that* was scary. Good thing I'd had my gun.

If I were dead, this place and everything else I owned would go to Allie. She was a city girl and would certainly sell at the first good offer, so she could invest the money and make her first or maybe her second million.

Had I been in actual physical danger from Whitehead? He had definitely backed up when he saw my pistol. And if I'd been unarmed? Men like Whitehead never expect a woman to fight them and win, and a right cross to the jaw will take out most women before they have a chance either to run or fight.

If he'd really come to make me an offer, he'd have been better prepared. He didn't even have a figure in mind. He was also more interested in those reports than he let on. What were they? More important, *where* were they? And how did they threaten the Ken doll and his consortium?

*

True to her word, Peggy came out at two. We fitted Heinzie into his harness and put him to the vis-à-vis. She was hesitant about driving him alone, but in reality, a four-wheel carriage is easier to drive than a two wheel, and soon she, Heinzie, and his long-eared wart were trotting happily around the dressage arena.

"Piece of cake," she said when at last she climbed down. "Now all we have to do is get Heinzie to Mossy Creek on Easter afternoon all by himself."

"You game to drive Heinzie down to the road tomorrow morning without Jacob?" I asked.

"I'd really rather not unless you come along to rescue me if I get into trouble."

"Sorry, not gonna happen, but I can follow you in my truck. Jacob should be over his hangover by noon on Monday. We'll try then. I can watch Don Qui in the barn. I'd really like to see how he lets himself out of his stall."

She laughed. "Hiram never did find out. He finally gave up and let him wander in the aisle after he finished eating."

We stripped Heinzie of his tack, fed and let the horses out. Then we moved the vis-à-vis back into the workroom and started work on the seats. Either Hiram or Jacob had sprayed oil on the bolts that held them to the carriage, so they were relatively easy to remove.

We worked companionably. Peggy told me about her career as a professor of English, her husband, Ben, and how they moved to Mossy Creek. She told me tales of the Garden Club ladies and how Ida had wound up taking anger management courses. She told me about the history of Mossy Creek and its long-standing feud with Bigelow.

She described how Bob, the Chihuahua, had been shot out of the claws of a hawk by Sandy, the Mossy Creek police dispatcher, and the matches, unmatches, and rematches Creekites made. She told me about her boyfriend, Carlyle, who had retired and moved to Seattle to create a new city garden.

She told me about Hiram, and how he had showed up on her doorstep one rainy Sunday afternoon after seeing her *studio apartment for rent* ad in the *Mossy Creek Gazette* classified ads, and how they'd grown into the habit of going to estate sales, yard sales and antique stores looking for old carriages and their fittings.

I had lived in my townhouse in Lexington, Kentucky, nearly as long as she'd lived in Mossy Creek, but I knew practically nothing about my neighbors.

I was gone a good deal of the time, but I couldn't have told her a single story about them or their families and friends. When had I become *"the cat who walks by himself, and all places are alike to him?"*

*

Geoff

"Merry Abbott called me," Geoff told Amos. "Had a visit from Ken Whitehead while she was alone out at the farm. She thinks he came out to search the place, but when he found her alone instead, she thinks he made threats."

"How can you *think* something's a threat?" Mutt said. The three men were finishing lunch at Mama's.

"If she thinks she was threatened, she was threatened," Amos said. "Women have good radar about that kind of thing." He handed out the checks. The men left tip money on the table and strolled to the cash register.

"Then how come they let their husbands beat up on them?" Mutt said.

"That's a whole other issue," Amos said. "Mostly they know it's coming. They either don't trust their instincts or are afraid to leave. You interested in a trip to Bigelow?" he asked Geoff.

"Not yet. I want to find out what kind of reports Whitehead was talking about first. Hiram may have found out he and his little consortium considered themselves owners of acreage actually in the parcel Hiram paid for. Somebody in Atlanta should have the original survey, the deeds, titles, all that stuff. If we're lucky, Hiram's lawyer will have copies. I'll have someone in my office check in Atlanta."

"Won't get much info until Monday," Amos said as they walked back to the police station. "Nobody mans those offices on the weekend."

"Hey, ve haf our methods," Geoff said in an exaggerated German accent. "May not be able to get anyone in the office, but those records are probably on computer. What's on the state's computers, the state's agents can access, even on Saturday."

"Robertson won't be in his office either."

"If I can reach him at home, I'll drive over and talk to him. This is murder. He's an officer of the court. I think he likes Merry anyway, so he'll probably see me."

*

Robertson lived in a big, foursquare house, probably built around the turn of the last century, in an affluent section of Bigelow referred to as the garden district. Big old trees met over the streets, and the houses all sported well-tended lawns and gardens. Old money spent wisely. Robertson himself opened his front door and ushered Geoff in.

"Janeen's out shopping. We can go into my office. Want a

beer?"

Geoff followed him toward the back of the house. He wore elderly chinos belted slightly below his bulging tummy and a faded maroon polo shirt that his wife probably wanted to throw away. The hair on his chest was white. Geoff hadn't met him previously, and liked him on sight. His eyes were kindly, but shrewd. He'd be a formidable opponent in the courtroom and probably the board room as well.

Geoff accepted a Stella Artois from a small fridge in the room that obviously doubled as office and male retreat. The walls were lined with bookcases that held matched sets of law books, except for a fifty-inch flat screen TV mounted across from the desk. The oriental on the floor was fine but threadbare, and the big desk was a tad battered. This was a room that a man kept for himself and refused to allow even the most house-proud wife to change.

Geoff told him what he wanted. He expected to have to dance around his questions, but Robertson answered straight away.

"We did have a few bobbles in the title search on Hiram's land," Robertson said. "But we got it squared away."

"Why was the land sold in two parcels?"

Robertson leaned back in the black leather chair that looked as though it had been made for a much bigger man. He rested his head against the back, steepled his fingers, and settled in.

Geoff recognized a raconteur when he saw one. He might be in for a long story, but he doubted it would be a pointless one.

"After the Josephsons died within six months of one another . . ."

"Suspicious?" Geoff asked.

Robertson frowned at him. "Natural old age. They were in the same nursing home, had been for five years or so."

He swung his chair gently from side to side as he talked. "That land was originally titled in two parcels and taxed that way for fifty years. Nobody bothered to change it. The kids all went their separate ways. None of them went to farming. They didn't care about the place. Didn't even care when the house burned down a year or so after the parents died."

"Arson?"

"Lightning. It was empty. Nothing suspicious, Agent

Wheeler. Merely stupid."

"In what way?"

Robertson offered one hand, then the other. "Daddy's will left everything to Momma." Left hand up. "Momma's will left everything to the kids equally." Right hand up. "Her will said they all had to agree before any of the land could be sold, and if any one of them died, their *children* had to agree. Stupid! I guess she thought the land would bring them together. Instead, it made them hate each other worse."

"They couldn't agree?"

"Nosirree." Robertson leaned farther back and crossed his ankles on the corner of the desk. He was wearing aged Topsiders with no socks. Like many tubby men, he had extremely small, neat feet. "Got offer after offer. This piece, that piece, half and half. Good offers, although not as good as lately when land prices skyrocketed out there. Then the eldest sister died childless. Apparently, she'd been the hold-up. The others had kids that needed college tuition and such like. They got together and agreed to sell the smaller piece, the forty acres Hiram bought. They didn't tell a living soul except Julie Honeycutt from Mossy Creek Mountain Realty, the best Realtor in Mossy Creek. She'd been working long distance with Hiram Lackland for over a year. She called him, he drove over from Aiken, wrote up a contract for cash, and before nightfall the deal was signed, sealed, and the next day when the money was transferred, it was delivered and the deed filed."

"I thought he had mortgage insurance," Geoff said. "Merry Abbott says the land is free and clear now, but not that it's been that way all along."

"That's where the title work came in. He quietly borrowed part of the original cash from his boss in Aiken to add to what he had to make a down payment. Then, he went through all the to-do with health check, mortgage insurance, folding in extra money for the improvements he planned to make, got the mortgage and returned the original cash to the man he borrowed it from. Left him with a manageable mortgage payment and nice equity. Very, very slick. Wish I had friends that rich and that trusting."

"What kind of money are we talking?"

"For the land? A hundred and forty thousand. Thirty-five

hundred an acre for forty acres with no improvements and no domicile. Real bargain. It's a matter of record. So's the mortgage."

"Who was the rich friend?"

"Man by the name of Richard Fitzgibbons in Aiken, South Carolina. Hiram worked for him for years."

"How did the other parcel get sold?"

Robertson laughed. He sounded as though he were gloating. Not a fan of Governor Bigelow, obviously. "When the governor's bunch saw the notice of transfer in the *Mossy Creek Gazette*, they had a cat fit. Tried to keep Hiram from getting a mortgage, to screw up the zoning, which is agricultural and always has been. Offered Hiram a bunch of money and said they'd make his life hell if he didn't sell."

"Really. Would that be a man named Whitehead?"

"Ah, you've met him. When I was growing up and you got acne, you either got blackheads or whiteheads. Both were filled with pus."

"Did they keep up the pressure?"

"They calmed down once they convinced the family to sell them the other parcel. Much bigger. Over a hundred acres and prettier too, for a resort and a golf course. Not so good for horses. They paid more per acre than Hiram did, which made Whitehead even madder." He chortled. "I enjoyed that. Always thought it was kind of strange Whitehead backed off on harassing Hiram about his property. He doesn't usually fail. He'll do just about anything to impress the Governor and make sure he's indispensible. His master has a short temper and has been known to whack him on his tail when he doesn't deliver. He knows the Governor has plans for the future. Thinks he can go to Washington, God help us."

"Would Whitehead go so far as to kill Hiram?"

"Why?" Robertson's feet came off his desk and he sat up straight. "Place goes to his daughter, and it's free and clear now."

"Because she might be more willing to sell? Funny that he'd be killed just before she came to visit."

Robertson nodded. "Thought about that myself. Doesn't seem like the kind of lady to back off from a fight, and I get the feeling she might actually stay around and run the place."

"But Whitehead may not have known that. He might have thought the death would lead to a quick sale."

"He didn't know about the mortgage insurance." Robertson snickered. "Mad as a wet hen when he found out, not from me, let me tell you."

"Would you happen to know who inherits if she dies?"

Robertson took a deep breath. "I don't know for certain, but she has a daughter who is a newly-hatched broker in New York City."

"And probably would sell."

"Might well. Want another beer?"

"No thanks." Geoff waved his empty bottle. Robertson nodded toward a leather-covered wastebasket beside his desk. "Drop it in there."

On his way out, Geoff said, "If you hear anything you think could be of help, would you call me?"

"Sure thing. Oh, I almost forgot. Some peckerwood named Tom Darnell showed up outside of court yesterday evening ranting and raving about wanting his momma's carriage back right now. You know anything about that?"

"Indeed I do. He won't be getting it anytime soon. Thanks for telling me."

Robertson watched him to his car, then closed his front door and went back to whatever Saturday afternoon football game he'd been watching.

Geoff called Amos from his car and said, "Merry Abbott might be in real danger from Whitehead." He repeated the salient facts of his interview with Marks. "Time to check his alibi very closely. He looks to have the best motive for killing Lackland."

"Better warn her not to work alone out at the farm," Amos said. "Better yet, I'll tell Peggy Caldwell to go with her when she's out there. Peggy could use a hobby. Ida says her heart's never really been in gardening, although she gives it a go every year. We got an email for you from your office, by the way. They're fast, and on Saturday. Impressive."

"Hey, old buddy, crime never sleeps and neither does the Georgia Bureau of Investigation. Want to take a run over to talk to Imogene Darnell?"

"Sure thing. Pick me up."

Sandy stopped Geoff in the moment he walked into the hall of the police station and handed him a sheet of paper. "Your office emailed this. I printed it off for you."

"What's it say?"

Sandy blushed. "I would never read your emails, Agent Wheeler."

As they closed the door to the police station behind them, Amos whispered, "Sure she would. You're just lucky she decided you could have it."

Geoff shook his head, laughing, and followed Amos out the door. He read as they drove out of Mossy Creek toward Bigelow. "Well, well, well. I think I know why Whitehead backed off."

"You gonna tell me or keep it a deep, dark secret?" Amos asked as they turned onto the highway. He sped up. Even the sheriff wouldn't dare stop Amos's car for speeding.

"Hiram had extensive soil and water tests done after he bought the land. Apparently he didn't confine his activities to his own land, but had the surveyor move over the border into the governor's parcel and take samples there. Lackland's soil and water are fine. The streams run off straight down his side of the hill. The other side, however . . . "

"The governor's side?" Amos asked and passed an eighteen-wheeler before swinging back into his own lane.

Geoff nodded. "The other side once hosted some hard-scrabble diamond mining in the early twentieth century. Know what you use to clean diamond dust? Arsenic and Cyanide."

Amos slammed on his brakes, pulled over onto the shoulder and stopped. "Sweet Mother. The ground water's contaminated?"

"Not the ground water so much," Geoff said. "The topsoil itself, down the hill where there were tailings. Acres of it. And not badly contaminated, just enough so you wouldn't want to drill wells for private homes into it."

"Could it affect Mossy Creek? Can it be fixed?"

"I don't have the whole report, just a summary. And a snide note from one of my colleagues about not asking for miracles on the weekend. Mossy Creek is not involved. Any ground water flows the other direction, away from town and away from Lackland's property. The soil problem can be fixed, but it will cost a bundle to remove the topsoil and replace it, which would entail cutting down trees, and test anywhere they want to drill a well. Bringing water from Mossy Creek or Bigelow would cost an arm and a leg. Have to build the lines and a new water tower."

"Those reports are a matter of public record," Amos said.

"Only if the public is looking for them, and they wouldn't be, would they? Not if Whitehead and his buddies don't mention them in their real estate prospectus. He's not above burying them or removing them entirely if he gets the chance."

"Now that, my friend," Amos said as he started the car and pulled onto the road, "Is a dandy motive for murder."

Imogene Darnell lived in a big old farmhouse that had once been white and needed to be scraped and repainted. The old paint was peeling like the bark of a birch tree.

A large barn that looked as though it had once been used for cattle stood behind the house. If it had ever been painted, the paint had long since flaked away leaving unpainted gray clapboards. The whole structure canted slightly towards the pastures in back of the house.

"Hard to tell how much acreage she has," Amos said as they bumped into the rutted circular driveway and stopped at the sagging front porch. "Probably not nearly enough left to support a cattle operation, but it could have been a thriving farm once upon a time."

The house might be in bad shape, but the foundation plantings of old English boxwood, azaleas and roses were meticulously trimmed. Jonquils were already blooming, and the azaleas were in bud. Interspersed with the jonquils were grape hyacinth and sprouting iris that would bloom in another month. This was a woman who loved her garden.

"Wonder whether son Tom ever helps her," Amos said. "Nah."

"She's no spring chicken," Geoff said. "But she looks as though she's worked hard all her life. Probably outlive us all."

The steps to the porch sagged under their weight, but the porch felt secure enough. When Geoff twisted the old-fashioned doorbell, he heard it snarl inside the house. Even a deaf person should be able to hear that sound.

He thought she might be off with Tom doing her shopping,

but after a long minute, he saw her tall, gaunt figure moving toward them through the etched oval of glass in the old front door.

She peered at them, then held the door open wide with a welcoming smile. "Why, if it's not Amos Royden and Agent Wheeler." She stepped aside. "Y'all come right on in." She led them into the front parlor that was probably only used for company. The furniture dated from the fifties, but was immaculately clean, and the room smelled of lemon furniture polish. A dried fan of magnolia leaves stood in a brass vase on the hearth. "Now, y'all sit right down. I'll just go get us some sweet tea."

"Please, ma'am," Amos said, "Don't go to any trouble."

"It's no trouble. I was about to have a glass myself. It's all made." She strode out of the room, and a moment later they heard the clink of ice in glasses.

When she came back in carrying a big wooden tray with glasses, pitcher, and a dish of lemons, Geoff jumped up to take it from her and sit it on the coffee table in front of the sofa.

"Why, thank you, Agent Wheeler." She poured and handed round the glasses. "Now, what can I do for y'all on a Saturday afternoon?"

"We wanted to ask you about your carriage," Amos said. "Your son seems extremely anxious to get it back."

Her face darkened. "Huh. I am flat tired of making excuses for that boy. What's he done now?"

The boy in question was probably in his forties. "Nothing illegal," Amos said. "How'd it wind up in Mr. Lackland's shop?"

She leaned forward and put her large, arthritic hands on her knees. Unlike most of the women of Geoff's acquaintance, she was actually wearing what his mother would call a housedress instead of jeans or slacks. She wasn't wearing stockings, however, and wore flip-flops on her bony feet. "Hiram was helping me clear out the barn. I'm going to have a big yard sale when we get it all done." She sighed. "Or I was planning to. Now I don't have anyone to help. Hiram knew how much things you find in a barn would sell for. He'd been around barns and rich people a long time. I don't want to be selling any treasures for fifty cents if I can help it."

"How'd he come to be doing that, ma'am?" Amos asked.

"First pickin's." We looked at her blankly and she continued. "My son is bound and determined he's going to get me out of this house and into a retirement community. I tell him if he'll just wait a few years, I'll be dead and gone for good, but he's anxious." She looked at the room with its faded cabbage rose wallpaper. "I tell him I intend to die here just like his father and his grandparents before him did. It's hard to keep the place up on the little money I get, so I put an ad in the *Mossy Creek Gazette* for a yard sale. Just some junk I didn't need any longer. Hiram came to see what I had. He was such a nice man, I told him my old barn was packed with things I needed to get rid of but couldn't find the time or the energy to go through. He offered to help."

"That's where the carriage was?"

"Tell the truth, I'd forgotten it was there," she said and ran her hand down her cheek. "Been in my family forever. We got to talking, and he said he could refurbish it so I could sell it, maybe get as much as two thousand dollars net out of it." She beamed at them. "With two thousand dollars I could pay part of the back taxes and keep a little bit to fix the porch steps. I never planned to tell Tom about it, but he went looking in the barn for whatever he could run off with, and saw it was missing. He dragged the whole story out of me." She drew a cavernous sigh.

"He was so mad, but I finally got him to see that having Hiram fix it up was a good thing. He let it go until he saw about Hiram being dead. He thinks he can find somebody else to fix it up cheap enough to sell and keep the money himself to make a down payment on one of those tiny little apartments in that retirement community." She lifted her head and Geoff could see tears in her eyes. "I won't let him have it. It's mine and the money's mine too."

"Of course it is," Amos said. "Mrs. Darnell, has he . . . threatened you in any way?"

She gave a sharp bark of laughter. "I could still spank his bottom if he tried and he knows it." She looked away and touched her cheek again.

Geoff and Amos exchanged looks. Geoff thought that whatever she said, at some point the bastard had slapped her. Although no bruise remained, her memory of it did. Geoff knew

Amos agreed. Tom was going to pay. If not for murdering Hiram, then for domestic violence. She might not be a pushover, but she was probably over seventy, and her son was a man in his prime.

"He threatened you, didn't he?" Amos asked gently.

When she turned to look at him, her eyes brimmed with tears that threatened to spill over. "He said if I didn't do what he said, he wouldn't take me to the grocery or church or the funeral ladies or the garden club or anywhere. He knows I can't drive anymore. The other ladies are real good about toting me, but I hate to keep asking them."

She was obviously *embarrassed* to ask them, to have to admit that her rotten son was for all practical purposes keeping her a prisoner in her own house.

"Mrs. Darnell, you let me know if he so much as hollers at you," Amos said. "Here's my card with my cell phone number on it. I'm *serious* now."

She took the card in trembling fingers. "But I'm not in Mossy Creek."

"You let me worry about that. Now, may I have your son's address? I think it's time I introduced myself."

She sucked in a breath and her eyes widened. "You mustn't talk to him about any of this. Please, promise you won't."

"Ma'am, we can't promise," Geoff said. "We have to talk to everyone. I promise we won't mention we've talked to you, though."

"He didn't do anything to Mr. Lackland," she said, twisting her liver-spotted hands in her lap. "He'd never hurt a living soul. He yells sometimes, and he drinks a little when he's upset, but he's never raised a hand to Charlene that I know about."

Geoff noted she didn't say he'd never raised a hand to *her*. This was one of the times he wished he wasn't hamstrung by the law. He'd like to take Tom Darnell out into the woods and beat the crap out of him.

Actually, arresting him for murder might be equally satisfying. They just had to prove he'd commit murder for a couple of thousand bucks. Geoff had seen murders committed for *five* bucks, so killing a man over two thousand didn't seem much of a reach.

Mrs. Darnell waved to them as they drove away, and stood

in her open door until they reached the road.

"I hate him," Geoff said quietly.

"Me too," Amos said. "Want to go haul his ass in and keep him until Monday morning just for fun?"

"Great idea, but I'd rather leave him loose until we can prove he's our killer. Then we can keep him much, much longer."

Chapter 27

Sunday morning
Merry

"Want a job?" I asked Peggy on Sunday morning before I drove out to the farm to feed and clean stalls.

"What sort of job? I am not overly fond of manure."

"Just think how great your garden will be this spring with all that well-rotted manure dug in."

"Only if you do the digging. Assuming you're still here, that is."

All four cats sat in the kitchen doorway like a jury in a jury box. Dashiell's tail lashed. He had a suspicion that whatever we were talking about would take Peggy's lap away from him, and he didn't like it.

"It's your fault I have two lessons lined up this afternoon and four others to be scheduled during the week. Plus driving Heinzie and finishing the upholstery on the vis-à-vis. I'd pay you the same hourly wages I'm paying Jacob."

"You don't have to pay me. I enjoy being out there."

"The Bible says the laborer is worthy of his hire. Or *her* hire. Besides, if I don't hire you, I won't ever be able to fire you if you piss me off."

"What about if you piss *me* off?" Peggy said.

"Never happen. I am a joy to work for." I smiled at her blandly. "And you can't keep feeding me breakfast and making me sandwiches to take to the farm and half the time feeding me dinner too. I'd like to stop being a parasite."

"We're still living on funeral baked meats," Peggy said. "Just like Hamlet's mother and step-father."

"How about a steak tonight?"

She shook her head. "I've got my usual Sunday dinner with my daughter and her family. Would you like to come? Marilee keeps hinting how much she wants to meet you, and my granddaughter wants to see the horses."

"Thank them for me, but I'm going to go groom horses and get ready for my lessons this afternoon. Can I put off meeting your family until next Sunday? They can come applaud you while you drive Heinzie through the streets of Mossy Creek."

"In the meantime, what happens if Whitehead shows up again?"

"I'll shoot him."

"Good idea. We can talk about the job tomorrow. I'll come out after lunch today and help with the lessons, then we can pick up a pizza on the way home. Deal?"

"Deal." I put my breakfast dishes in the dishwasher, scratched each cat behind the ears, and went to the farm.

This time I left the barn padlocked, and didn't bother to lock Don Qui in his stall to eat. All the horses needed to be groomed, and the smaller Meadowbrook readied for my lessons. Horse people have to work on weekends. That's when people with weekday jobs are available.

I'd be using Golden Boy, the Halflinger, and I wanted Peggy to drive him before my first student arrived, so I could get an idea of how well he obeyed a driver who actually *drove* him and didn't fall on her face in the dirt.

After I ate my sandwiches, I decided to walk over to Jacob's trailer. I knew he wasn't there, but I hadn't seen it close up, and had no idea how he got down his side of the mountain.

The trailer wasn't new, but he and Hiram had removed the rust and repainted it, and the outside looked neat. Jacob had drawn all the curtains, so I couldn't see inside. I did, however, find a newly-graveled parking area beside his front door and a rutted track that led down through the trees and presumably wound up on the same road Hiram's driveway led to. The parking area might have been graveled at the same time as Hiram's driveway, but Jacob's road had not.

Hiram's used tractor was parked over by his trailer, so I went back to inspect it and the attachments. The tractor lacked either a roll bar or air-conditioned driver's cab. It did, however, possess a front loader, so that I could load manure from the pile to be spread in a month or so, a drag to keep the arena neat, a bush hog for the pastures, and the auger he and Hiram must have used to dig the post holes for the fences.

Nothing was new, but it looked clean and serviceable enough. I climbed onto the tractor, set the throttle and turned it the key. It started instantly. I was definitely coming to appreciate Jacob. Now if I could manage to endure his attitude and his alcoholism . . .

Looking back over the pasture, I could see the dressage arena and both the stable and the barn. At some point there had been a structure here. Parts of an old foundation showed back of the trailer, although the cellar, if there had been one, had long since been filled in. Whoever had built the house had chosen well. Jacob's trailer had a perfect view of the whole place, and yet was far enough away to offer privacy.

If I planned to stay and run this place, I couldn't keep living in Peggy's basement and commuting. I'd need to build some kind of dwelling, and although I wasn't certain I wanted to be so close to Jacob Yoder, the old house's location seemed perfect. If I could sell my townhouse in Lexington—big *if* given the current real estate market—maybe I could afford to build one of those fancy pre-fab log houses. Maybe even get a dog that could go with me when I went to shows. Whitehead wouldn't have walked in on me if I'd had a yappy little terrier.

*

My first lesson was with the veterinarian's wife, Casey Blackshear. Dr. Blackshear offered to make me copies of everything he'd done for Hiram.

"I keep a computer file on my patients," he said. "So I know when shots and Coggins tests are due. At the moment, we're up to date until the end of May."

"I'll give you a call to schedule," Casey said. She rolled her wheelchair over to the side of the arena where Peggy waited with Golden Boy put to the small Meadowbrook.

Good thing Dr. Blackshear came with her to lift her into the cart. The Meadowbrook was cumbersome with its rear entry, but he managed. I stood in the center of the ring and coached while Peggy sat beside Casey in case of trouble, but Golden Boy was as good as Peggy said he was.

After the lesson, I went over to talk to Casey. "You know, there's a big group of, I don't know the politically correct term these days . . . "

Casey laughed. "Try physically challenged."

"Okay. There's an international group of physically challenged drivers with carriages specifically designed for wheelchairs. If you're interested, I could look into the costs of one of the carriages for you."

"I am *so* interested!" Casey said. "I can't ride a horse and I love them to pieces. Driving would be perfect."

"You can even show if you want to travel a bit. In the meantime, if you're game to learn with a bigger horse like the Friesian, I think getting you in and out the larger cart might be easier."

After settling her in their van, Dr. Blackshear squeezed my shoulder. "Let me know about the cost of a handicapped carriage. I think driving would make a world of difference to Casey. She's always looking for new challenges."

"That will be all over town before nightfall," Peggy said as they drove away. "You're going to have more lessons than you can handle."

"No, more lessons than *you* can handle. Come on, time to drive Heinzie to the vis-à-vis.

The rest of the afternoon and my next lesson passed in a blur, and by the time I fell into bed after stuffing myself with pizza, I thought I'd fall asleep instantly. Instead, I worried. I didn't see that we were one bit closer to finding out who killed my father. My father. When had I called him my father last?

Chapter 28

Monday morning
Merry

I am blessedly free from ESP, but something warned me to get my tail out to the farm on Monday morning. Jacob had not fed the horses, and Don Qui was telling me about it at the top of his lungs.

After taking care of the chores, fuming all the time, I strode over to Jacob's trailer. His truck was there. The hood was cold, so he'd been home a while. I banged on his door. No answer. Either he was passed out inside, so hung over that he was hiding from me, or his tootsie had followed him home and taken him back to Bigelow in her car to drink some more. I tried the door of the trailer, but it was locked, and although in books anyone can pick a door lock with a hairpin, I didn't have hairpins or the expertise Jacob had gained in the Joint.

My first lesson arrived before Peggy did. I had groomed Golden Boy and put him to the Meadowbrook, so I was ready. Eleanor Abercrombie didn't want to drive alone, however, even in the dressage arena. I called Peggy on her cell. Quiet weather equaled cell reception on the mountain.

"Five minutes away. Where's Jacob?" she asked.

"Bastard's not here. Probably hungover at his ladyfriend's house. I am *so* going to kill him when he shows up."

Life would be much simpler if I could climb up onto the Meadowbrook beside Eleanor, pick up the reins, and drive off. I could take the chance of sitting beside Peggy. She knew what she was doing and wouldn't expect me to take the reins. My disaster with Golden Boy had proved to me I wasn't a bit closer to laying my demons.

When Jacob had not showed up by nightfall, I called Geoff Wheeler to ask him for his girlfriend's telephone number.

"I'll call her," he said. He called back to say that whatever-her-name-was hadn't seen Jacob since Sunday afternoon when he left her place to drive back to the farm.

"His truck's here, but he isn't," I said. "Do you believe her?

Maybe he decided to run for the hills and didn't want to do it in a truck you could identify. Are there any car rental places in Bigelow? She could have followed him home to pack and leave his truck, then driven him back to Bigelow to rent a car or even catch the bus to Atlanta."

"One of the sheriff's people can check the car rentals and the bus terminal," Geoff said. "That should make him feel a part of the investigation." I could hear the sneer in his voice over the phone line. "If Yoder doesn't show up by tomorrow, as his employer you can report him missing, and Amos and I can break into his trailer."

"Don't you need a warrant?"

"As his landlord you can give us permission. He could be passed out in there or worse. Want me to come break in now?"

"You know how an empty house feels empty?" I asked. "Jacob's trailer feels that way, empty. He's not inside."

After I hung up, I sat on a bale of hay and took off my left paddock boot and sock very carefully. My foot still hurt.

My little toe was black and blue from the Meadowbrook but the swelling in my instep had gone down, revealing a perfect semi-circular bruise the size and shape of Don Qui's left front hoof. He hadn't broken the skin, but I'd have that bruise for a while. I hated to think how much damage he might have done if I'd been wearing Nikes instead of paddock boots.

I'd given up locking the damn animal in his stall to eat, but I'd have to lock him in tomorrow morning, if I could persuade Peggy to drive Heinzie down to the driveway.

Hopefully, Jacob would be back by then, but I didn't think so. He was gone for good. Something had happened over the weekend to spook him so badly that he left his truck. It was a wreck, but it was drivable. As a parolee, he wasn't supposed to leave his job or the area without permission. Either he'd rented, borrowed, or stolen a car, caught the Greyhound from Bigelow, or hitchhiked, unless someone from his old life helped him.

I didn't know why he'd killed Hiram, but there was no reason for him to run if he wasn't guilty. He must have thought that Geoff was closing in on him.

Geoff would have to catch him. I didn't even know how to start.

To add to my troubles, I realized as I led Golden Boy back

to the pasture that he was limping. I put the others out, tied him on the wash rack, and found that he had a swollen suspensory below his left knee. Not yet a bowed tendon, but if I left it untreated, it could easily bow. If that happened, he'd be laid up for six weeks to six months.

If, however, I could ice the leg down every couple of hours all night, I should be able to get the swelling and heat down by morning. Ordinarily, that would have been Jacob's job, but no Jacob meant it had become mine.

The small refrigerator in the clients' lounge had an icemaker that wouldn't put out nearly the amount of ice I'd need, but would give me a good start.

Golden Boy cooperated when I stuck his leg into the ice bandage, but he wasn't happy about it. After his first treatment, I noted the time, and called Peggy to tell her I'd be spending the night in the barn.

"I'll sleep on the hay between horse blankets," I said. "I've done it plenty of times before."

"I have an old cot from when Ben and Marilee used to go camping together. You're welcome to borrow it."

"You didn't camp?"

"Huh. My idea of roughing it is the Great Western or the Marriott. Mosquitoes find me really tasty, but they used to bite Ben and Marilee and fall off dead."

"A cot would be great," I said. I could set it up in the clients' lounge close to the bathroom. "I'll come get it and pick up some of the leftover funeral meats and buy a couple of bags of ice for my cooler."

"The cot's in the attic. I'll bring it down while you fix up an ice chest and some sandwiches."

"You sure you don't want me to come with you?" Peggy asked an hour later as she helped me load my truck. "You'll be all alone out there."

"The night is clear, so I'm bound to have cell phone reception. I'll keep my pistol with me. Nobody but you knows I'll be there. I can't ice Golden Boy's leg every two hours unless I stay out there."

"I could kill Jacob for taking off like that."

"You and me both. That sort of thing was supposed to be his job."

*

I was actually looking forward to spending my first night in the stable, even on a cot in an empty clients' lounge. Hiram had mounted one dawn-to-dusk floodlight that lit the parking area and hung another that lit the walkway from one to the other from the peak of the stable, so I didn't need the flashlight I had with me to find my way.

In the spillover from the lights, I could see the other four equines at the pasture gate watching me silently, keeping tabs on their friend. When I turned on the lights in the stable, Golden Boy stuck his head over the stall door and nickered to me softly. I filled his water bucket and gave him a flake of hay, then walked him to the wash rack. He still limped, but not badly.

"Poor baby," I said and ran my hand down his leg to the pastern. I could feel the slight swelling and warmth in the suspensory. He endured the ice pack for ten minutes while I talked nonsense to him. I gave him Bute, an equine analgesic to keep him comfortable, and left him munching hay in his stall, while I bedded down in the clients' lounge with flashlight, pistol and ice chest. I repeated the treatment every two hours, although he wasn't thrilled to be waked up.

*

Some idiot had set an alarm clock, something I rarely do. I struggled up from the depths of a naughty dream and felt around for the thing so I could kill it, but I couldn't find it. My watch said five a.m. I could sleep for another hour, damn it.

Another second and I recognized the sound. Smoke alarm! I rolled out of bed and into my shoes, grabbed my flashlight and went to cut it off, praying that it was a false alarm.

The doorknob wasn't hot, and the door wasn't warm. I cracked it and got a face full of oily smoke that stung my eyes and made me cough.

As I stared into the smoke, one of the three bales of hay near the front entrance burst into flames. It sat pressed against the other two, and all three leaned against the wooden front of Heinzie's stall.

Every decent barn keeps big fire extinguishers close and ready, but I didn't have a clue where I'd seen Hiram's. I yanked my shirt up over my mouth and nose, raced to the wash rack, turned the hose on pulled it to the front of the stable with me.

I ran the hose on the burning bale of hay, grabbed the manure rake and pulled it out into the aisle to get it away from the stall front and the other bales before they caught.

The fire sizzled and popped when the water hit it. As it subsided, the smoke increased. I had to force my burning eyes open.

I shot myself in the face with the water, so I could wipe my eyes. Then I went back to dousing the bale.

The flame seemed to be out, but I know hay. It can smolder inside for hours, then suddenly burst into fire again all by itself. I laid the hose on top of the other two bales, dragged over the manure cart, forked the charred hay into it and trundled it outside onto the gravel in front of the stable. If it burned up the manure cart, I could live with it. On the gravel, it wouldn't burn anything else.

Then I dragged the other two bales away from the wall of Heinzie's stall.

The wood of the stall front was charred black. Close to flaming. Too close.

Instead of fanning the flame as it had done before, the breeze through the front began clearing away the smoke, blowing it toward the back of the stable.

Where Golden Boy was trapped in his stall unable to get away from it.

The clay floor of the stable had turned into a mud slick from the water I'd run on the hay. I turned too fast and slid shoulder first into the side of Don Qui's stall. My shoulder felt as though someone had struck it with a baseball bat, but I slid on.

Horses can't vomit, but they can cough. Golden Boy was doing his best to expel the smoke from his lungs. His eyes streamed the way I felt certain mine did.

As I walked him out, I wiped his eyes with my wet work shirt, then we both stood under the stars and gulped huge quantities of chill spring air until neither of us felt the need to cough.

Desperately afraid of fire, the other horses crowded as close to Golden Boy and me as they could get without jumping the pasture fence.

After I settled him again, I went hunting and finally dug out two fire extinguishers from behind a pile of blankets in the tack room, and another two under the sink in the clients' lounge. I'd have to speak to Jacob about *that* if he came back. Then I called Geoff Wheeler's cell phone.

"What time is it?" he grumbled.

"Six. Somebody just tried to burn the stable down with me in it."

I heard him take a single breath. When he spoke again he sounded wide-awake. "I'll be there in twenty minutes."

While I waited I spread a bale of wood shavings on the mud in the aisle, brushed my teeth and downed two diet sodas. My throat felt raw, and the face I saw in the mirror through my bloodshot eyes was streaked with smut. My wet hair drooped in lank tendrils around my face, my shirt and bra were soaked and felt like Golden Boy's ice pack on my boobs. I stank of smoke.

Nothing stops chores, however. I had just finished putting feed and water in the horses' stalls when Geoff charged around the corner of the barn, grabbed me by the shoulder and spun me to face him. "You look like hell. You okay?"

"Thank you, Agent Wheeler."

"Here." He handed me a giant latte and a couple of sausage biscuits.

"Thank you, and this time I mean it." He started to sit on one of the two bales of hay remaining in the aisle. "Don't! You'll get your rear end wet."

"Don't you people believe in chairs?"

"Come on, we can sit on my cot."

When we were settled side by side, he said, "You sure this wasn't an accident?"

"Hay baled damp and packed tight can spontaneously combust, but that hay isn't fresh or damp." I sucked down half the large latte in one gulp and wolfed down one of my sausage biscuits. "I take back whatever nasty things I've said about you."

"Do I want to know?"

I shook my head but kept eating.

"When you get through stuffing your face, tell me what happened."

I finished my first sausage biscuit and told him. "Whoever did it must have seen my truck parked out front and known I was around someplace. From here you can't see headlights coming up the drive, and apparently with the door to the lounge closed, you can't hear tires on gravel either."

"Or they parked down the hill and walked up. What about Yoder? Did he know you were spending the night?"

I shook my head. "He left before I decided to stay. I don't think he's come back."

"You wouldn't have heard him walking across the pasture."

"The last thing he wants or *says* he wants, at any rate, is for this place to go under."

"I didn't smell kerosene or gasoline when I walked in, so they didn't use an accelerant," Geoff said. "Good thing. If they'd blocked both ends of the aisle with the fire, you'd have had to break that window over there and crawl out. Assuming you woke up before you died of smoke inhalation."

Golden Boy would have died. I'd never have been able to reach him.

Until then I'd been chugging right along the way I always do in a disaster, but that hit me. I hunched over and my teeth started chattering.

"Shoot," he whispered. He set my second wrapped biscuit and the latte on the floor beside him and dragged my sleeping bag up around my shoulders. "You're freezing. This place got a shower?"

I nodded and pointed toward the bathroom in the corner. "You got any dry clothes?"

I pointed to my duffel. "I wasn't planning to go home until later." I shook off his hand. "I'm fine." *Chatter, chatter.*

"The heck you are." He pulled me to my feet. "Don't kick over the latte. You can finish breakfast after you're warm and dry." He hoisted my duffel and shoved me toward the bathroom. "Stand under that shower until you're pruney. In the meantime, I'm checking that hay."

Twenty minutes later my eyes were still red, but I was warm and clean and well-fed. My teeth no longer chattered. I joined Geoff at the front of the barn.

"Do you smoke?" he asked.

"Certainly not. Nobody smokes in a stable. And before you ask, Peggy doesn't. Jacob chews tobacco."

He held out a small plastic bag. He was wearing Latex gloves.

"What's that?" I asked.

"The granddaddy of all arson tricks. So old it has a beard. Take a matchbook, close it, but leave the center match outside. Light that match, set it down, walk or run away. The match burns down to the matchbook and ignites the whole book. That, in turn, ignites whatever it's sitting on."

"Who'd know that?"

"Most of the known world. All teenaged boys. Doesn't work unless it's close to something that will go up readily and has plenty of air circulation."

"Doesn't it burn itself up?"

"You'd be surprised how often it doesn't burn up. My guess would be this one fell down behind the hay after it caught fire and put itself out. No air."

"Where did it come from?"

"This is the place where the detective says it's from Sadie's pool hall and has Sadie's fingerprints all over it. No such luck. Too charred for prints, and you could probably pick up this brand of matchbook in most of the mom and pop grocery stores in the eastern United States. What good would it do to burn your stable down?" he asked.

"Assuming I wasn't inside burning to death, no stable, no business."

"And if you were?"

"My daughter would sell this place in a heartbeat once she inherited."

"That would make Whitehead very happy."

"As well as a number of other people, like maybe the governor."

"He doesn't do things like that."

"Of course he doesn't. He has Whitehead do them for him," I said. I tugged one of the two remaining bales into the aisle. Hoisting it into the hay cart was going to take some doing since the hay strings that held it together had burned.

"Who else have you teed off?" he asked.

"Nobody."

"I doubt that." He brought over the hay cart and hefted as much as he could hold into it. "The tuna casserole was loaded with Ipecac and a powerful laxative. You and Peggy would have been very unhappy if you'd eaten it."

"But not dead," I said as I picked up a quarter of the remaining bale.

"Probably not. But in the emergency room or the hospital at least overnight."

"Leaving nobody to guard Peggy's place but the cats. Somebody looking for whatever they didn't find in Hiram's apartment the night I arrived."

"Be my guess. What are you hiding?"

We finished loading the first bale and started on the second. It threatened to topple off, but Geoff grabbed and steadied it. "Give me a break. If anybody hid anything, Hiram did it, and I haven't found it," I said.

I leaned my forehead against the bars of the stall. After a moment I pushed away and faced him. "Now they've gone too far. There was a horse in this stable last night that would have died of smoke inhalation or burned to death. You better get the SOB fast, because if I get to him first, I'm going to kill him."

Chapter 29

Monday evening, Tuesday
Merry

That evening I called Dick Fitzgibbons in Aiken to bring him up to date. "So, I no longer have a groom," I said. "With so few horses and all of them in pasture, I don't have a huge amount of work, but I'm teaching, and that takes time." I told him about Peggy. "I may have to cancel putting Heinzie to the vis-à-vis on Easter if Jacob doesn't show up to help drive. Peggy isn't comfortable doing it alone."

"How about I drive down on Saturday? I could bring Hiram's files, spend Saturday night, pass along my great wisdom in finding stable hands, drive with this Peggy on Sunday, and take you both out for dinner Sunday night."

"I can't ask you to do that." *Please God, let him come.*

"What else do I have going at the moment? I'll leave Saturday morning so we'll have a chance to practice Saturday afternoon and get everything loaded for the trip to Mossy Creek."

"You are a saint. Shall I make you a hotel reservation at the Hamilton House Inn?"

"I'll have my secretary handle it. I'll call if I have a problem. Otherwise, I'll see you Saturday."

I hung up feeling a hundred pounds lighter. If Jacob stayed gone, or if Geoff arrested him for Hiram's murder, I'd simply put an ad in the *Mossy Creek Gazette* and hire somebody else.

*

Geoff and Amos met me at Jacob's trailer at nine on Tuesday morning. The door was still locked, but trailer-flimsy. Amos had brought a small battering ram of the kind the SWAT teams use for drug busts, but waited for Geoff to give him the nod to go ahead. Geoff rolled his eyes, gave the door a good kick and sent it flying back against the wall.

"All right, be that way," Amos said and took the battering ram back to his cruiser.

"Stay out here, Merry," Geoff said. He clicked on a big

hand lantern and climbed the steps.

I've never known why those CSI types on television use flashlights instead of simply turning the lights on, but that's what both Amos and Geoff did. They even pulled their guns before they checked the trailer.

"I told you he was gone," I said from the threshold.

"Go away," Geoff said. "Don't you have manure to shovel or horses to groom?"

"As a matter of fact I do." I turned on my heel and marched off across the pasture. The long grass soaked my boots and jeans nearly to my knees before I got back to the barn. As usual Don Qui met me in the aisle. This morning I had actually locked his door to see how he opened it, but he'd beat me to it. I didn't even try to sucker him back into his stall, but I kept Heinzie inside since we planned to drive him after Peggy arrived. Don Qui hovered outside his door, but mercifully kept his mouth shut.

Peggy and I had Heinzie put to the large Meadowbrook when Geoff and Amos drove up. They hadn't come through the pastures, nor gotten their clothes sopping wet. Nooo, they had driven down Jacob's rutted drive, around by the road and up Hiram's driveway to the neat parking area outside the barn.

"Hard to tell if he's taken anything with him," Geoff told me. "Place is a mess. What kind of housekeeper was he?"

"How should I know? I've never been inside his trailer. He kept a neat stable, but that doesn't equate to housekeeping. *I* keep a neat stable. My house, on the other hand . . . "

"There's an old duffel bag in his closet, but it's full of dirty clothes. He may have taken a couple of suitcases."

"Razor and toothbrush in the bathroom," Geoff added. "He left in a hurry."

"He killed Hiram," I said flatly. "He lost his nerve and ran."

"What about his alibi?" Geoff asked.

"Assuming his girlfriend isn't lying, you said he could have driven out here, killed Hiram and driven back to Bigelow. Or even killed Hiram before he left to see his tootsie on Friday evening."

"Motive?"

"Maybe they argued about my visit. If Hiram had promised him a share in this place, then reneged . . . He hit Hiram when his back was turned, then tried to make it look like an accident. Case closed." I turned away so they couldn't see that I was on the verge of tears. More and more I believed my visit caused Hiram's death. I just didn't know how, but that didn't make me feel any less guilty.

"Evidence?"

"That's *your* problem. Now, I have a horse and driver to coach."

The rest of the day was busy, but uneventful. Peggy drove Heinzie and the Meadowbrook down to the road and back three times with Don Qui tagging along.

"We'll have to take him with us Sunday," Peggy said as we rinsed Heinzie off.

"We will look like idiots."

"Everyone will think it's cute and that we planned it that way."

"No, they will think *I* am an idiot who can't separate a Friesian from a donkey. I do have a reputation to protect, you know."

"We'll worry about it tomorrow."

"By the time Dick Fitzgibbons arrives on Saturday, the decision had better be made."

I had finally persuaded Peggy to let me stay in the stable with Don Qui on Thursday morning, while she drove Heinzie down to the road and back a couple of times. She still refused to try the vis-à-vis alone on those curves. I didn't try to force her. Dick was an expert driver, and Heinzie was his horse. With him along, they'd do fine on Easter, with or without Don Qui.

On top of driving Heinzie, Peggy's friend Louise Sawyer had asked to bring her pair of Bouviers out mid-morning, even though we didn't have sheep or goats for them to herd.

"She likes to let them run free when she can," Peggy said. "They're lovely dogs now that they have a job to do."

"Will they herd the horses? If they try, they may get kicked."

"Not if Louise tells them not to. They're very obedient."

When they climbed out of the back seat, I could see they were actually larger than Don Qui. The giant, blue-gray pair romped off joyfully toward the back of the pasture the minute their mistress, Louise, let them off their leads. After five minutes or so, she blew a whistle. Both dogs stopped as though they'd hit the end of a leash, turned and galloped back to her as fast as they'd left and sat at her feet with their stubby little tails wiggling their entire bodies. She gave them a treat each and scratched behind their pointed little ears.

Louise released them again. This time they investigated the stable with their noses to the ground and their sterns in the air.

"I'd love to learn to drive," Louise said. "Could the dogs be trained to ride with me?"

"Sure, although from the size of them, you'd need fair-sized carriage and probably at least a Morgan to pull it with. Or you might train them to run alongside. They're too tall to trot under the carriage like Dalmatians, but they seem to have plenty of stamina."

"More than I do, unfortunately," Louise said. "Although I've dropped ten pounds since we started herding classes. A carriage would be the perfect compromise."

The larger of the two dogs trotted out of the stable and headed for the back of the barn, then veered left around the corner.

"Uh-oh, he's headed for the manure pile," I said. His buddy trotted after him.

Louise whistled. The dogs ignored her. I have always requested that my clients leave their pet dogs at home when they come for lessons. If I had a dollar for every time I have heard someone say, "But he never does that at home," I wouldn't need to work again. Louise clapped, and called, "Come back here, you imps."

The dogs had disappeared around the corner. "Oh, dear, they'll be filthy. I am so sorry," Louise said. "I can't understand why . . ."

We followed. They'd stink up the back of Louise's van on the way home, but that was *her* problem.

As we rounded the barn, we could see both dogs digging madly into the manure and growling as they went.

"Digging out a rat," I said. "They can smell him in there even if we can't." I walked over to them. "Drop it."

The magic words. They sat back on their haunches and looked up at me expectantly, obviously proud of what they were doing. They'd dug a considerable hole in the pile, but it would be easy enough to fill in with the front loader. "Come on," I said and turned away.

The larger dog barked once, but neither of them made a move to obey. "Call your dogs," I said to Louise, who stood at the edge of the pile. She obviously didn't want to wade in manure and shavings.

She clapped and called. They both barked this time, but didn't move.

I reached over to hook my hand in the collar of the nearest dog to start him moving. I was prepared to give way if he snapped at me, but he didn't. Instead, he braced his full weight against me and yanked me off my feet. I landed on my stomach with my hand still hooked in his collar.

"Oh, my God," I whispered, and scrambled back.

"He bit you?" Louise asked. "I can't believe . . . "

"Get their leashes and shut them in a stall," I said as I stood up. "Call Amos Royden. Tell him the dogs just found Jacob Yoder."

Chapter 30

Tuesday
Geoff

This time Geoff had a real crime scene to investigate, although the sheriff tried to take the case from him. "It's not in Mossy Creek proper," he said. "So it's my jurisdiction and not Royden's." He stared down at Yoder's body, still face down where Merry Abbott had discovered him. The back of his head was a pulpy mess. Flies were already landing in droves.

"We settled this already over Lackland. Same place, different body," Geoff answered. "This isn't the primary crime scene. He wasn't killed where he fell. Not enough blood."

"You don't think the killer asked him politely to step into the center of the manure pile so he could beat his head in?"

Geoff ignored the sarcasm. "I'll be grateful for your assistance, Sheriff. I don't have any techies up here."

"Techies? Who the hell has techies? I need to process evidence, I send it down to you folks."

Geoff spread his hands. "See? Works out fine. I'm just cutting out the middle man. I'll take pictures and collect evidence, then send it down to my office in Atlanta."

"Had to be that Abbott woman did it," the sheriff grumped. "Didn't have none of this mess 'til she showed up. Nice peaceful county. Don't know what Governor Bigelow's gonna say about this. Ought to arrest her right this minute."

He should have known Sheriff Campbell would go for the easiest solution. "We don't even know precisely how or when the man was killed. I'd hold off on arresting anyone."

"Sure as shootin' didn't dig hisself into the manure pile and suffocate."

Geoff had to keep his temper, but it wasn't easy. Sheriff Campbell might be a good enough lawman to keep the governor's county quiet, but this was beyond him. "Probably flattish and broad-surfaced with a sharp edge."

"Like a manure shovel?" asked a young woman deputy. Both men turned to look at the object in her gloved hands. "I found it in the wash rack. Looks like it's been scrubbed recently."

"See? I told you that woman done it," the sheriff said.

"Sheriff, the man weighed one-seventy or one-eighty. The killer had to move the body, dig a hole big enough to shove him into, and cover the whole thing up."

"Woman's big and strong." He sounded sulky.

"Why would she kill him?"

"Easy. He saw her kill her father and tried to blackmail her."

"Sheriff," said another deputy. "Medical examiner's office called. Can we bring them the body now?"

"Heck, why not? Dig it out and carry it to town." The sheriff ran his hand over his bald head and turned to Geoff. "I'm leaving this in your hands. You better make an arrest soon or I'm calling the governor to personally to kick your butt off this case and tell Amos Royden to git the hell out of my territory." He stomped to his squad car.

Geoff found the three women sitting in the stable on fresh bales of hay brought in from the storage shed behind the stable. The dogs lay asleep at Louise's feet, but the moment Geoff walked arrived, they stared at him in silent reproach. He had taken their toy away from them. He loved dogs, but occasionally their priorities disturbed him.

"When can I leave?" Louise asked. "I have to take them to Blackshear's to have them scrubbed and their teeth cleaned. Then I need the inside of my van detailed before I take them home." She shuddered. "I don't want to think about any of this."

"Neither does anyone else, Ms Sawyer." He scratched the ears of the nearest dog. "However, in a sense they're heroes. We might not have found Mr. Yoder's body for quite a while buried under that manure pile. The dogs could pick up the scent. I doubt humans could."

"How long has he been there?" Merry asked. He didn't think she'd been this shaken over her father's death, but then she hadn't been working around a corpse for a couple of days without realizing it. "I can't believe I actually dumped fresh manure on top . . . I may be sick." She clapped one hand over her mouth and the other across her stomach.

"Put your head between your knees," he said. "As to how

long he's been dead, we won't know for certain until the medical examiner tells us. My guess is Sunday evening after you and Peggy left, although it could have happened early Monday morning before you arrived."

"So he didn't run away," Peggy said. "In a weird way, that's a comfort."

"Not to him," Merry whispered. "Sheriff wanted to arrest me, didn't he?"

"Yes."

"Why didn't he?"

"No evidence and a good alibi. You'd hardly have let those dogs roam loose if you knew you had a dead body around."

"I might not have thought they could smell it." She gave a convulsive shudder.

"You ever fox hunt?" he asked.

She frowned up at him. "Of course."

"Then you know how well dogs can smell." He said to Louise, "Mrs. Sawyer, you and your dogs can go. Call Sandi and make an appointment to come by the station tomorrow to give Mutt your statement."

"Shouldn't I stay with them?" she asked and gestured toward Peggy and Merry.

"We'll be fine," Peggy said. "Go on, Louise."

"I'm so sorry," Merry said.

"It's not *your* fault. I still want to drive after this is over with."

The dogs fell in behind her as she left the stable for her van. Geoff called, "Please don't talk to anyone about this, Mrs. Sawyer."

"I intend to tell my husband, but no one else. I promise."

He watched her out of sight down the driveway. She drove very slowly as though still shaky.

"I may have to buy you a couple of cheap chairs from Wal-Mart in self defense," Geoff said. He moved a bale of hay into the aisle and sat down across from the two women.

Before he spoke, the pretty young deputy stuck her head in the stable door. "Agent Wheeler, I think you maybe need to see this."

"Stay," he said to the two women, and followed her outside and around to the parking area at the front door of the barn.

"This gravel doesn't take tire tracks," she said, "but sometime since it rained on Friday a vehicle drove over the edge and onto the grass for a couple of feet."

He squatted to look at the tracks. "Tires look worn," he said. "Mrs. Sawyer's tires are nearly new."

"Tread doesn't match either Mrs. Abbott's or Mrs. Caldwell's vehicle, or the big diesel truck."

"Check Yoder's truck over by his trailer. He may have driven up here."

"Already did, sir," she said and flashed him a broad smile. His treads are worn, but they're a different pattern."

If she was looking to make points, she was doing an excellent job.

"Take a cast, then get on the net and see if you can identify make, model and year."

"Yes *sir*. Right away, sir."

"Mrs. Abbott has taught some lessons since Friday afternoon. I'll get a list of her students. We'll have to check their cars as well."

"Of course, sir." She looked crestfallen. She was undoubtedly hoping he'd tell her that she'd identified the killer's vehicle and caught him red-handed. Police work was not that easy. She'd learn soon enough that it was generally a matter of checking and rechecking and half the time finding nothing usable.

He found the two women sitting where he'd left them. They had leaned their heads against the stall behind them with their eyes closed. For the first time, Peggy looked her age, and there were dark circles under Merry's eyes.

He sat. "Either of you kill him? You could have done it together and alibied each other."

Both women sat up. "Why would you ask a dumb question like that?" Merry snapped. "No, we did not kill him. I *needed* him."

"Even if you found out he killed your father?"

"If I'd found that out, I'd have called you and told you to haul his sorry butt out of here. If he did, it was voluntary manslaughter, not first-degree murder. He got mad and snapped. There can't have been any long range planning involved."

"At his age and with his record, that wouldn't have made

much difference. Any sentence would have been a life sentence."

"When he disappeared, I felt certain he'd done it," Peggy said. "But now . . . "

He waited.

"He was sneaky and not too smart. He knew something or found out something, tried to make a buck out of it, and whoever he tried killed him."

"You agree?" he asked Merry.

"What could he have known? If he didn't kill my father, he wasn't here when it happened."

"You didn't go into his trailer at all?"

"I stood in the door and watched you and Amos. That's the closest I ever came to going inside."

"We already have your prints. Yours too, Mrs. Caldwell. We'll have to check against the ones we find in the trailer."

"Check away," Peggy said. "You think somebody killed him in his trailer and dragged him all the way over here to bury him?"

He hesitated. He wasn't in the habit of offering information, but this time he thought he might be justified. "We're pretty certain his trailer was searched."

"His door was locked when I tried it."

"So was your apartment. The killer borrows keys. We found Jacob's wiped clean in the ignition of his truck."

"What were they looking for?" Peggy asked.

"If it was the same person who turned over our stuff, they were looking for information." Merry leaned back and closed her eyes. "I feel like that guy in Lil' Abner that has a black cloud over his head. Everything I touch turns to crap."

"Go home," Geoff said. "Take a hot bath, have a drink, eat something, go to bed."

She laughed. "Thank you for the advice, Mother Wheeler, but I still have horses to feed this evening."

"Then do it now and leave. We'll be here a good bit longer."

"Come on, Merry, I'll help," Peggy said and pulled herself to her feet.

Geoff offered Merry a hand. She took it and let him pull her up. He felt for a moment as though she'd lean against his chest and let him wrap his arms around her. At the last second, however, she stepped back, squared her shoulders and walked out of the stable.

Peggy glared at him. "You two need to get your act together."

He gave her a 'whatever do you mean' raised eyebrow.

She sniffed and went after Merry.

Was it that obvious that he was attracted to Merry? He was fairly certain she was attracted to him as well. Having to arrest her for murder wouldn't be the best next step in building a relationship. He'd better clear her and find the real killer before he was forced to do just that.

He wound up calling the inn from his car and ordering a couple of steak sandwiches, then eating them in his room in front of the television set with the sound off. The local eleven o'clock news carried a short story on the discovery of a body in Bigelow County, but that was all. Tomorrow's stories would be more extensive. Merry would probably be met with half a dozen news vans when she went out to feed the horses in the morning. Hiram's death had been put down to accident and hadn't roused the newshounds. This one would. He decided to be there first.

She would find soon enough that the big wheelbarrow she used to carry fresh manure from stable to manure pile was missing. It was on its way to the crime lab in Atlanta. When she found it had been used to transport Jacob's body from the murder site in front of the barn around back to the dump site, he didn't think she'd want it back. It had been hosed out, but there were still traces of blood in the crevices around the edge. DNA would confirm what he knew in his gut. The blood belonged to Jacob.

Once the medical examiner confirmed what he suspected, that Yoder had been killed and buried Sunday evening, he'd have to start checking alibis all over again. He didn't much care whether Tom Darnell or Ken Whitehead was guilty. Had to be one or the other.

So long as Merry was safe. Peggy too, of course. They alibied one another from two in the afternoon Sunday until Monday morning. Merry might have had barely enough time to kill Jacob when she went out to the barn Monday morning, but not enough to bury him and clean up her mess before Peggy arrived. He could think of no way they could be in this together.

They'd known one another a week. Hardly time to make an alliance to commit murder.

Sheriff Campbell might believe Merry was Superwoman. Geoff didn't. He hoped she'd turned off the ringer on her cell and landline phones tonight. Reporters were capable of calling at two in the morning. He'd already told the front desk at the Hamilton Inn not to put calls through to him. Merry and Amos both had his cell phone number. Anyone else could wait until morning.

He woke at one a.m., still dressed with a crick in his neck and the television flickering. He brushed his teeth, stripped, slid under the covers and slept again instantly.

His last thought before sleep took hold was that tomorrow would be a bitch anyway you looked at it.

Chapter 31

Wednesday, Thursday, Friday
Merry

I'm used to handling local reporters who cover the horse shows I manage, but they generally want human-interest stuff, not crime interviews from one of the suspects. I had to shoo two TV trucks and three reporters' cars out of my way so I could drive up the hill to the farm. They had enough sense not to follow me onto my property. It would be up to the cops to move them out of the public road. Geoff could speak to them if he wanted to, but Peggy and I wouldn't even give them a 'no comment.' With luck they'd give up by lunchtime and move over to bug the sheriff and Amos Royden.

When I talked to her at Hiram's viewing, I hadn't given Katie Bell from the *Mossy Creek Gazette* anything but salient facts about Hiram's life that she could have gotten off Google, and I wasn't about to add anything now.

Peggy had cancelled the two driving lessons scheduled for the afternoon. Ida called to ask if we were still planning to drive in Mossy Creek on Sunday afternoon.

"Up to you," I told Peggy.

She nodded and said into the phone, "We'll be there." After she hung up, she asked, "This Fitzgibbons guy is definitely coming to help me drive, right?"

"To the best of my knowledge. It's obvious we can't drive Heinzie to the road again until the reporters leave, so we'll work him to the vis-à-vis in the arena. I'll shut Don Qui in his stall and let him yell his head off."

Over his objections, I fastened his door securely. No way he could open it. He brayed and kicked while we harnessed Heinzie, but when I followed Peggy out to the arena, he was still confined to his stall.

Heinzie didn't seem to miss him much, which was good. That meant we could load up Heinzie and the vis-à-vis, leave Don Qui locked securely in his stall, and do our Easter duty in Mossy Creek.

Don Qui kept up a bray that would have gone an ocean lighthouse one better. After twenty minutes, however, he went silent.

"Finally," I said. "He must be worn out."

She stopped Heinzie in the middle of the arena beside me and pointed toward the in-gate with her whip. "I don't think so." And in he trotted.

"No way!" I ran into the stable and stopped at his stall. The latch was in the upright position instead of pointing down, and the sliding door was open enough for his fat little body to squeeze through. I had closed and latched it tight, but he was out, and I still had no idea how he'd done it.

He was furious, of course. He tried to stomp my other foot. This time I narrowly avoided having a matching semi-circular bruise on the instep of my right foot to match my left.

When I led Heinzie back to the pasture, Don Qui trotted beside him, then wheeled and kicked the gate again.

I prayed we wouldn't have reporters and TV trucks rolling down the streets of Mossy Creek on Sunday if we were forced to take Don Qui along. He'd probably bite or kick or generally misbehave and be caught on camera and flashed over the news.

We ate sandwiches sitting on the hay bales. "Geoff has a point," I said as I tried to find a position that didn't poke me with hay. "We need chairs even if we have to make do with canvas jobs until the estate's settled."

We had decided to lacquer the vis-à-vis and put the newly upholstered seats back in while the weather stayed warm and dry, so we hauled it out to the far corner of the parking area onto a big tarpaulin and sprayed it black. We finished tacking and stapling the new seat covers and screwed them back in as well.

"The old girl doesn't look bad at all," Peggy said, as we cleaned up our mess and rolled the carriage back into the barn. "The red upholstery and the black lacquer look spiffy."

"Still got a lot of work to do before it goes to its new owner, whoever that might be," I said. "You know, if we're going to have a black and red carriage and a black horse, we need to fancy Heinzie up some. I could braid his mane in a French braid with red yarn, and we could put red rosettes on his hames."

Hiram had taught Peggy about harness, so she didn't ask me

to define hames. Farmers know what they are, but most non-driving people don't.

There are two basic types of carriage harness. One uses a breast strap that goes across the horse's chest. The other, frequently seen in draft hitches or pairs pulling larger carriages, uses a big leather horse collar that fits over the horse's head and lies against his neck and shoulders. The harness itself is attached to hinged metal pieces that fit into the grooves of the horse collar and buckle at top and bottom. The metal pieces are called hames. Anyone who has watched the Budweiser Clydesdale hitch has seen the big horse collars fitted with shining silver hames that rise like wings high above the horse's neck and end in big silver balls that are often decorated with streaming ribbons or fat rosettes.

Heinzie's harness was much less elaborate, but its hames did end with a pair of steel balls that stuck up over his shoulders. Perfect for ribbons.

"Can you do that?" Peggy asked.

"Piece of cake. I'm sure Hiram has a braiding kit with everything I need somewhere."

"I haven't seen anything like that," Peggy said dubiously. "Would he have red yarn and ribbons?"

"Probably ten colors of yarn, gel to comb the mane smooth, braid hooks, little bitty rubber bands . . . A complete grooming kit and buckets as well, so he wouldn't have to pack and repack every time he went to a show."

"I don't remember seeing anything like that in his truck."

"I'm sure it's all in the trailer tack room. Up to now we haven't needed anything from it. You sweep the trailer bed. I'll check out the tack room."

When I opened the tack room at the front of the gooseneck, I felt a tremendous jolt. Here was the essence of Hiram, my professional horseman father, in a way almost as palpable as the scent of his aftershave.

The trailer tack room was as excessively neat as the stable and his workshop. Much neater than his apartment in Peggy's basement.

Trailer tack rooms run the gamut from landfill filth to laboratory cleanliness. Hiram kept *his* immaculate. A film of dust coated everything, but he'd organized and labeled every hook.

He'd stacked clean water buckets and feed tubs in one corner beside a square feed container built to keep out moisture and vermin. He'd hung perfectly coiled lead, lunge and long lines on hooks beside oiled halters and bits of harness and buckles handy for emergency repairs on harness and carriages. A polished brass whip rack held lunge and buggy whips, each carefully coiled around its personal whip roller.

I opened the lid of the plastic step stool sitting against the gooseneck and found woolen horse coolers and fly sheets folded and interleaved with blocks of cedar to prevent moth damage.

No braiding kit, however. It must be tucked away in the gooseneck, which was taller than my head and deep in shadows this late in the spring afternoon.

When I came back five minutes later with a hand lantern and flashed it into the recess, I could see several grooming boxes, and in the very back, a couple of metal boxes the size of computer printers.

The first box I opened held brushes, curry combs and other normal grooming supplies. The second held the braiding stuff.

I had to climb into the gooseneck to grab the two metal boxes. The first held a horseman's pharmacopoeia of drugs, ointments, liniments and fly sprays.

The second felt heavier and was locked. It didn't make any sound when I shook it. I dragged it out, set it on the floor and perched on the top step while I juggled keys on Hiram's key ring to find one small enough to fit.

I thought I was out of luck, but finally a key that looked small enough to fit a woman's jewelry box clicked in the lock.

When I opened it I realized I'd found Hiram's records. His logbooks for the last two years lay on top of a hanging file of manila folders.

I opened the current log. Suddenly he spoke to me as clearly as though I heard his voice. He might not have noted my birthdays, but he wrote down the date when each horse was wormed, or given a rhinopneumonitis or strangles shot, and when the next would be due. Between us, Peggy and I horsed the box into my truck and my apartment while we repeated "no comment" endlessly to the media.

The twenty copies of Hiram's death certificate had arrived,

so the first minute I had free, I could start transferring Hiram's assets to my name, and beat my American Express bill. Since we knew we'd be trapped at home once we got there, we'd made a side trip to Bigelow and loaded up on Chinese take out. No Chinese restaurant yet, in Mossy Creek.

We decided to eat in my apartment for a change, although Peggy said the cats were annoyed. She'd been away more than she'd been home lately.

"I've been taking horrible advantage of you," I said as I opened one of the little paper boxes and found egg rolls.

"I haven't done one thing I didn't want to do," she said as she opened the Moo Shu pork and searched for the pancakes and black bean sauce. "I don't know why, but I have the feeling we're nearly finished."

"It's finding Hiram's log books," I said, and divided a box of shrimp fried rice between our two plates. "I'm certain it must all be there, if we have the sense to understand it."

"When are you going to tell Geoff you have the box?" She concentrated on unwrapping her chopsticks to avoid looking at me.

"After dinner."

"He'll be furious that you moved the box, and he's going to ask why it's taken this long to find it."

"It never occurred to me that Hiram would put paperwork and bills into the trailer where they could mildew. Stuff in that trailer nose is entirely too hard to get ahold of, and it was never part of the crime scene. Geoff never asked for a search warrant for the trailer. He wouldn't have gotten one anyway. I suppose I could have given him permission to search the trailer, but why would I? Why would he? What was Hiram thinking?"

"That Jacob Yoder or someone else would come looking."

*

When I called Geoff at the Hamilton Inn, they refused to put me through, so I used his cell phone. After I told him what I'd found, he started to yell at me, then he went very, very quiet. Uh-oh. I was in deep doo-doo. "I'll be there in ten minutes," he said. "Don't touch anything."

"I already have."

When he walked, no, stalked in, I handed him a cold beer with one hand and a sheaf of papers with the other. "The ground water on the governor's side of the hill stinks."

"I know."

"So does Ken Whitehead. Hiram made a note in his log book that he'd sent copies of the reports to Ken with a cover letter telling him politely to back off, or he'd go public." I sat on the sofa and pulled my legs up. "Those are Hiram's copies. Did he kill Hiram to shut him up?"

"Possibly."

"And Jacob?"

"Possibly."

"Why?"

"Maybe blackmail," he said. "What else have you found, and don't hide anything. I am not feeling charitable toward you at the moment."

"There's the box, here are the log books for this year and last. Knock yourself out. Don't you dare remove a single piece of paper. I intend to watch you."

Actually, I fell asleep on the sofa again. I was exhausted, but I also felt the release of tension as though by delivering the box to Geoff I had delegated the responsibility of finding Hiram's killer to him.

When I woke, he was gone and I was snuggled under the quilt off the bed. Falling asleep on the man was getting to be a habit. I probably slept with my mouth open and snored. Not the best advertisement for a possible hookup when this was over.

At which point he'd go back to Atlanta and I'd never see nor hear from him again. Nuts. Long distance relationships never worked out.

What the heck, this one was never going to get off the ground.

He did leave me a note and a slip of paper marking a page in Hiram's log book.

Lackland bought carriage with provenance from Darnell for two thousand dollars. See notation. Tom Darnell lying.

Suddenly I was wide awake. I settled down to read the log book and check the paperwork in the box.

All the information I needed about Hiram's operation was right here. I now knew who the two Dutch warmbloods belonged to and could discuss their future with their owner. I had copies of board bills, vet bills, feed bills, bank statements, brokerage statements—everything for the last two years.

I read Hiram's notation of his purchase of the carriage with proof of provenance, but neither the original sales slip nor the provenance was in the box. Odd. Everything else was.

One of the bank statements listed a charge for a safety deposit box. Probably where Hiram had stashed his most important papers, possibly including that sales slip and provenance.

Why on earth would he consider a puny two thousand dollar sales slip and an old provenance valuable enough to put in a safe deposit box?

*

Friday no media waited for us. We could drive Heinzie down to the road and maybe some distance along it. Saturday Dick would arrive and he and Peggy could practice driving the vis-à-vis on the road as they would do on Easter.

While I watched Don Qui. "The only thing I can figure," I said, "is that he throws his body against the stall door until he jars the latch loose, then somehow gets his nose or his hoof into whatever space he's created and shoves until he has room to squeeze through."

"An animal that smart deserves to get loose," Peggy said. "He's not really doing any damage."

"We *cannot* take him to Mossy Creek. We just can't. I'm going to put a halter and lead line on him and physically hold him inside his stall this morning."

"He'll kill you."

"Then I'll shut the front and back doors of the stable and let him run free inside."

"He'll destroy everything."

"I swear you're on his side," I said.

"Maybe. I like him."

"I don't dislike him, although he seems to have taken a major dislike to me. He's driving me nuts is all. Okay, you win. I'll shut him in his stall as usual. If he gets out, so be it."

Chapter 32

Friday
Geoff

Friday morning, the Bigelow County medical examiner's office called Geoff before he'd even taken his shower. "Agent Wheeler?" said a young female voice. "You asked us to call as soon as the autopsy results were in."

"Blunt force trauma, right?" He held the phone against his shoulder while he poured coffee from the coffee maker on his bureau and took it back across the room.

"The blows to the head would have killed him, but maybe not right away. Somebody made sure. After the killer shoved him face down in the manure, he put a forty-five slug into his skull, right in the middle of the blood."

Geoff sat down hard on the edge of his bed. "You find the bullet?"

"Uh-huh. I'm amazed that it didn't go straight through his forehead and into the manure pile, but it was old ammunition that hasn't been used in thirty years. Maybe the powder was unstable."

He'd barely finished shaving when Amos called. Geoff brought him up to speed on the autopsy report. "You know anyone with an old forty-five hanging around?"

"Not off hand," Amos said, "Everybody around here has guns. I called to tell you that Whitehead has a solid alibi. He was in Atlanta all weekend."

"If he's telling the truth, he didn't shoot Jacob personally."

"Think he hired somebody to do it?" Amos asked.

"He's smarter than that. Beat somebody up, maybe. Put himself in a killer's power? I don't think so."

"I'll have Sandy check gun permits in his name."

"Unlikely Whitehead would keep old bullets."

"Tom Darnell would. He doesn't have any permits, but that doesn't mean he doesn't have any guns."

"Give me twenty minutes to grab a sweet roll and I'll pick you up. I assume you want to go with me to talk to Darnell,"

Geoff said.

The two men found Tom Darnell in his office. When he looked up from his desk and saw them, his face flamed, and his shoulders tightened. "What do you want?" he whispered. "You can't just walk in here . . . "

"Sure we can," Geoff said. "Any place private we can talk?"

"Or we could take you back to Mossy Creek," Amos said with a smile.

"You can't arrest me. I didn't do anything."

"Who said anything about arrest?" Amos said, still smiling. "Couple of questions. Simple. Five minutes, tops."

"My boss . . . "

"Will understand you're helping us to fight crime," Geoff said. He didn't smile.

Darnell's eyes swept the office. The four other people went back to their computers and acted uninterested, but they were obviously dying to hear what was happening. He stood up. "We have a break room down the hall."

"Perfect."

The Darnell that led them down the acid green hall was not the cocky, argumentative Darnell from the funeral. He was scared.

The small break room was set with three beat-up Formica tables, a dozen chairs, and three vending machines, one drinks, one candy, one snacks. At nine-thirty in the morning it was empty.

The three men sat at the table closest to the machines.

"Why don't you people leave me alone?" Darnell straightened his shoulders tried to sound truculent. It didn't work.

"We'd like to borrow your forty-five," Amos said.

"I don't have a forty-five. I don't keep guns in the house. Darlene would kill me. Not with the kids." He started to add something, then stopped and caught his breath.

"So you keep it out at your mother's house."

He shook his head. "She . . . no."

Geoff sat back. "Easy for you to borrow and put back without her knowing."

"I didn't! It was my daddy's gun from Korea. I haven't seen it since Daddy died. She probably sold it."

"You ever buy ammunition for it?"

"I told you, no. "

Amos and Geoff looked at one another. Amos nodded almost imperceptibly.

"When did the pair of you drive out to Lackland's? Sunday night? Monday morning before work?"

"You're crazy. I didn't drive her anyplace except church on Sunday morning. Why would I drive her out to Lackland's place? He's dead and that lawyer says Momma can't get her carriage 'til the will is probated."

"Who else might have driven her?"

"Nobody! She lives too far out of the way for those funeral ladies. Most of the time I have to tote her." He dug a cigarette out of a beat up pack and lit it from a book of matches.

Amos grabbed his wrist and took the matchbook from him, careful to touch only the edges of the book.

"Hey! Give that back. We can smoke in here. It's the only place we *can* smoke."

"Not at the moment," Amos said. He raised an eyebrow at Geoff who shrugged.

"Could be," Geoff said. "Your mother smoke?"

Tom laughed. It turned into a cough. After he recovered, he said, "Made my daddy smoke in the yard. She'd kill me if she knew *I* smoked."

"So why are you so anxious to get that carriage back?" Amos asked.

"It's no secret. She knows I want to move her into that retirement home. Got to have money for that. She can't stay out at the home place alone any longer. I'm spending a fortune on gas, not to mention time waiting on her hand and foot. Nobody else will put up with her temper. Lord knows what else she's got in that old barn. The minute I move her out I'm having one hell of an estate sale."

"How does she feel about that?" Geoff asked.

The smile Darnell gave him made his skin crawl. "The old bitch wants to die at the home place. I wish to God she would."

Amos said. "If anybody in that family has a temper, it's you, not your mother."

Abruptly Darnell stood, went to the drink machine, fed in quarters until he got a Coke. When he came back and popped the lid, his hands were shaking. "When I was little and did something she didn't like, she used to make me cut my own switch so she could switch my legs."

"Yeah," Geoff said. "You learn real fast not to pick the thin ones. They hurt worse."

Darnell looked up at him gratefully. "I think my daddy died to get away from her. With strangers like y'all, butter wouldn't melt in her mouth, but when she gets mad, she goes flat crazy."

"You said she didn't drive. Could she have borrowed your car?"

"Listen, she *can't* drive. She's not touching my keys and I've got hers. I'm the only one drives her car. Got to keep the battery charged, don't I? If she ever lets me sell the thing, it's got to run."

The two men froze. "She has a car?"

"Probably get a thousand dollars for it. It's twelve years old, not but thirty-five thousand miles on it."

"Where does she keep it?"

"In the barn of course, along with a hundred years of junk. That's why I never thought that old carriage was worth anything." He made a sound. "Now she swears it's worth twenty thousand bucks to one of those fools put on Civil War uniforms and act like they're fighting."

Amos leaned forward. "Why does she think it's worth that kind of money? I've seen it. It's a mess."

Tom took a deep breath and said as though he were explaining the ABC's to a very small child, "It's a family heirloom is why. One of Momma's great-uncles was a doctor. Bought it from another doctor along with a journal proving it's the carriage Dr. Mudd drove when he went to set John Wilkes Booth's leg after he shot Lincoln. Don't know why that would make it so damned valuable. It's still just an old carriage. She says Lackland took the journal when he took the carriage to restore. She's got to have 'em both back to sell the thing."

*

Back in Geoff's car and headed for Imogene Darnell's farm, Geoff said, "Some of those re-enactors are rich doctors who like to act like they're running a field hospital. With proof Dr. Mudd drove that carriage it might well be worth twenty-thousand."

"If Hiram Lackland bought the carriage and the journal from

Mrs. Darnell outright for a couple of thousand bucks . . . "

"If she thought he tricked her . . . "

"And if she really can drive and had another set of keys . . . How would she find out how much it was worth?"

"If she has her husband's gun, why not shoot him? Why hit him with that carriage shaft and lay him out like that?" Amos asked. "Would she have the strength?"

"Adrenaline does great things. I doubt she went out there to kill him, but Darnell says she's got a temper. Maybe she hit him and wanted to cover it up, so she tried to make it look like an accident."

"If we're right, she damn near succeeded, but my Lord, the woman's seventy if she's a day," Amos said.

"And could probably still work the average field hand under the table. You see that garden of hers? I never even considered her, but now . . . "

They pulled into her driveway and walked up on the porch. Someone had stapled an orange sheet of paper to her front door. It was headed, "Notice of Tax Sale."

"Says here if she doesn't pay her delinquent taxes before the end of the month, the county's going to put the place up for auction," Amos said.

"Now, that's a motive for murder," Geoff said. He twisted the bell several times and listened to the squawk inside. The two men waited, but no one came. After five minutes, he said, "She's not going to answer. Let's check out that car. If she drove it to Lackland's place, we ought to be able to find pea gravel in the tire treads."

"If we're lucky, the tread will match that cast we took from the grass."

The barn was unlocked, but the two halves of the wide door were pulled shut. "We don't have a warrant," Amos said.

"If the car's there, we can always go get one," Geoff said.

Amos nodded and swung the nearest panel open far enough to shine his light through, then pulled it the rest of the way.

"Whew!" Geoff said. "No wonder Tom Darnell forgot about that carriage! This place is stuffed to the rafters with junk."

"Except in the middle," Amos said. An oblong empty space in the center was large enough to hold a big car. He turned his light onto the dirt floor. "Tire tracks."

"And an oil slick about where the oil pan on an old car would be."

The two men looked at one another. Geoff said, "No telling how long she's been gone or where, but we better take a run out to Merry's farm in case she's gone out there to try to get her carriage back."

"You think Sheriff Campbell would arrest me if I used my siren in his jurisdiction?"

Chapter 33

Friday
Merry

Peggy and I were nearly ready to start down the drive with Heinzie when I heard a car chugging up the hill toward us. A moment later a big old maroon Mercury gunned into view over the brow of the hill, nearly sideswiped Heinzie and the carriage and came to rest in a cloud of dust beside my truck.

"Who's that?" I asked.

Peggy shrugged. "No idea."

The door opened and Imogene Darnell stepped out looking frazzled. She wore an unflattering flowered housedress several sizes too big, as though she'd dropped weight since she bought it. Her pink hair had escaped from her bun, and she wore flip-flops on her bare feet.

"She said she couldn't drive," I said.

"Her son said she can't see. He took her car keys."

"Obviously she has a second set." I stepped forward with a smile. "Morning, Ms Darnell. Can I help you?"

"You can give me my twenty-thousand dollars right this minute."

I blinked. "I beg your pardon."

"I want the twenty thousand dollars you're going to get for my carriage, and I want it now."

"Hiram already paid you two thousand dollars . . . "

"When we did his uncle's funeral a while back, one of those Confederate reenactment folks told me Hiram was selling it for twenty thousand dollars. You'll get your money back and come out even when you sell it, but I need that money right this minute."

I've never actually seen anyone wring his hands, but she did. One definitely held an ignition key.

"Why on earth would you need twenty thousand dollars in such a hurry?" Peggy asked.

"County sent me a notice they're gonna take my house for back taxes if I don't pay up right now. They've given me all the extensions they're going to. I'll wind up in one of those retirement homes with no room to swing a cat just like Tom wants."

"Surely your son can help," Peggy said. "The County won't ask for it all at once."

"Help? He's been trying to get me out for years. He'll buy the place for a nickel on the courthouse steps and throw me out on the road, you see if he doesn't."

"But you signed the bill of sale for the carriage and the journal," I said reasonably.

"No!" She screamed. "Hiram tricked me! Then he stood right here and said he'd give me ten per cent finder's fee out of the goodness of his heart after he sold it, but not before. Ten per cent! Another piddly two thousand dollars. I'm not a fool to settle for that when that carriage was mine and he stole it."

"When did he offer you ten per cent?" I asked softly. I glanced at Peggy. She sat in the cart holding the reins. I could see the dawn of the same idea I had in her eyes.

Imogene looked confused. "Why . . . I ran into him in town one day."

"So you've never been out here before," I said. "Why did you say he stood right *here?*"

"I have never been near this place." She drew herself up. She was as tall as I am, and her short-sleeved dress revealed not flabby old lady arms, but the biceps of a woman who has worked the land all her life. A woman who knew how to wield a hammer or a shovel or a hacksaw. Who knew how to knock a jack loose or tip a heavy wheel onto an unconscious man.

She backed away from me. One of her flip flops caught for a second against the rough gravel, and she stumbled before she caught herself. Nobody has any business wearing those things around a barn.

But I could see why she didn't have on regular shoes. The instep of her right foot was badly bruised and swollen. Around the edge of the swollen area ran a neat semi-circular dark line.

Just like mine.

"You've been here before all right," I said and pointed to her foot. "I'd know Don Qui's hoof print anywhere. When did he stomp you? It's too fresh to be from when you came out here to see my father. Just about right for last Sunday evening when you came to see Jacob Yoder. Did he know you killed my father? Was he blackmailing you?"

"I don't know what you're talking about. How could I get out here?"

"Duh. You drove yourself."

She smirked. "Tom will swear I never drive. My car's been in my barn for weeks. This is an emergency."

I thought of the tire track where someone with old tires had run off onto the grass beside the parking lot. From what I could tell, nothing about Imogene's car was new. "So how often do these so-called emergencies occur?"

"Don't you make fun of me. Mr. Straley at the funeral home said you got your death certificates. You go right on down to the bank and bring me my money."

"Why on earth would I do that?"

"Because if you don't, I'll shoot that woman and burn this place to the ground."

The gun must have been on the driver's seat. One second she leaned into her car, the next she held the biggest pistol I've ever seen pointed straight at us.

"This is my husband's army forty-five," she said. "It's old, but it shoots straight and makes big holes. I don't miss, not at this distance. I brought down a bear in the front yard a while back with one shot."

Peggy must have jerked the reins because Heinzie woke up, snorted and took a step forward.

"Don't you move!"

Peggy froze. So did I. I held up my hands in a gesture of surrender. "You don't have to shoot anybody."

"I will if I have to. I'm not losing my house at my age."

"Hiram didn't have to offer you a red cent more than he paid for your carriage, but he did and you killed him anyway?" I never expected her to admit anything. What evidence did I have except a bruise, a car key, and a gut feeling?

"I never meant to hurt a living soul, but when he wouldn't give me my money and turned his back on me like I couldn't do a thing about it, I got so mad I hit him. I couldn't leave him like that, could I? He'd have told."

She sounded completely rational, as though arranging his body and crushing his throat was the most natural thing in the world.

"And Jacob? What could he have told?" Peggy asked.

Her mouth snapped shut for a second and her eyes hardened, then she said, "He swore he knew where Hiram kept my family's journal and the bill of sale. If I'd give him five hundred dollars he'd hand them to me." Her voice had risen.

"Without the bill of sale you could have taken the carriage back," I said. "With the journal, you could have sold the carriage directly."

She nodded. "Hiram called on that Friday before the storm to see if he could come help me clear out the barn some more on Saturday with *her*." She waved the gun at Peggy. "Looking to steal something *else*. Told me his daughter was coming down to join him and he wouldn't have much time for a while. He'd have told you about the carriage the minute you showed up. I had to have the money or the journal and bill of sale before he got the chance to brag how he'd put one over on the little old lady."

So I *had* been the trigger that killed my father.

"But why would you drive out here in the storm?" Peggy asked. "He should have been home."

"He wasn't, though, was he?" Imogene tossed her head. "Drove by your house real early Saturday. No truck. I like to have run off the road getting up here in all that mud. He was here, all right. Spent the night here. Glad to see me until I told him what I wanted."

I've never believed that old saw about killers needing to confess, but she was running her mouth pretty good. She was also making me sick to my stomach.

She was *proud* of herself. Must have been hard not to tell someone how clever she was.

She'd already said she didn't leave witnesses. That meant Peggy and me. There had to be some way to get out of this without getting either of us shot. At the moment, the best plan was to keep her talking.

"Do you have any idea how hard it is for a woman in my distressed circumstances to come up with five hundred dollars?" She whined. "I had to pawn my daddy's guns. I got to get 'em back before they sell 'em."

So there *was* evidence she could drive. The pawnbroker

would remember her and the date he gave her the money. Couldn't be that many pawnbrokers in Bigelow. Probably none in Mossy Creek.

She must have taken the money back after she killed Yoder.

"Couldn't you use that five hundred dollars to pay the taxes?" Peggy said in a small voice. Good thing she could think straight. I sure couldn't.

"And let go of my daddy's guns?" Her voice rose. Obviously she had no more intention of letting go of those guns than she did of her house. "That Yoder knew I could drive. He saw me on the road coming back from here and recognized me at the funeral."

"Was that the night you cut my spokes?" I asked.

She waved the hand not holding the gun. "Brought my pruning saw. Didn't take five minutes. Nobody saw or heard me."

"You could have killed somebody!" Peggy snapped. She must have yanked on the reins, because Heinzie gave out an exasperated whinny.

"Just wanted her gone from here so I could look better. Didn't hurt anybody, did I?"

"Seems like you do a fair amount of driving for a woman who can't see," Peggy said.

She drew herself up. "That's what Tom thinks. I see fine as long as I don't get a bunch of cars driving at me with their headlights on."

That was a scary thought, but not as scary as that gun in her hand.

"Yoder told me to get my tail out here and pay him if I wanted the journal. Fine way to talk to a lady."

"Very rude," Peggy said. I didn't dare look at her. The whole thing had taken on a nightmare quality, but the gun was real enough.

Maybe she was a crack shot, maybe not, but I didn't want to test her marksmanship, and I didn't think Peggy did either.

"Did Jacob tell you where to find the journal?" I asked.

"He laughed at me! He thought Tom killed Hiram. That boy couldn't kill a spider in the bathtub. He swore they were in a lockbox in Mossy Creek where nobody could get to them except you once you got the death certificates. I didn't believe him. Not then."

"So you waited until you knew I had them."

"Saw Mr. Straley send 'em. I didn't dare come out while those reporters were hanging around this place and your house." The hand holding the gun steadied. "Then yesterday I got that notice. We've wasted enough time. Bank's open by now."

"Must have been hard work burying a grown man."

"I had all night to do it and the manure was soft. My car was back in the garage before morning." She laughed. "Y'all think I'm fit for nothing but making deviled eggs for the funeral ladies." She giggled. "How'd y'all like my tuna casserole?"

I stuck my arm out in back of me to keep Peggy from flying out of that carriage straight at her and getting a bullet instead. "You nearly killed my cat!" she shouted.

"Expected y'all to eat it and wind up in the emergency room so I could hunt in your house. This worked out even better." She made an exasperated sound. "Couldn't start those computers and didn't find the journal."

"So you smashed them?" Peggy was losing it. I turned and shook my head at her.

"Cool it," I mouthed. She glared at me, but she subsided.

"Why on earth did you try to burn down the stable?" I was genuinely curious. It hadn't made much sense at the time and less now.

She looked downright smug. "Didn't think there'd be a soul since Yoder was gone, and I could search all I wanted."

Gone was right.

"I didn't believe Yoder. Wanted to search the stable, then I saw your car. At first I was real mad, but I thought if I started a fire, you'd run rescue the journal . . . "

"I didn't know it existed."

"I didn't know that, did I?" She snapped. "I parked down the road where you couldn't see my car and walked back. I watched you drag that bale of hay out . . . "

I had wondered if I were being watched. I shivered. This woman was crazier than Cooter Brown.

"All you did was go get that dumb horse. Figured I might as well go home. I *thought* I had plenty of time. I could wait." She actually stomped her foot the one without the bruise. "I deserve that money." This came out as a whine, but the change in her voice was only momentary. A second later she was back to angry. "I worked hard all my life. Who does Tom think digs the garden and keeps the house neat?"

"I'm sure it's not easy," I said.

"Don't think you can get 'round me. You." She pointed the gun in my direction. "Go get me my twenty thousand dollars. I'm not asking for more than what I'm due. We'll be waiting when you get back."

"Ms Darnell, I truly can't take any money out of Hiram's accounts, and I definitely don't have that kind of cash. Mr. Robertson says they won't let me transfer the money in his account to my name until the will is admitted to probate." Sounded reasonable. Not true, but reasonable.

"You're lying." She pressed both hands around the gun. "I've seem those TV shows where they hold the bank manager's family hostage while he goes and gets a bunch of money."

It never worked on TV and wouldn't work now, but it might get Peggy killed. "I'm not lying. Do you think I'd risk Peggy's life or mine if I could give you what you want? Maybe I could arrange a loan, but that'll take a few days."

"I can't *wait* a few days."

"Why don't you take the journal instead?" Peggy said in a very small voice. Both of us stared at her. She still sat in the carriage like Queen Victoria, while Heinzie wriggled. He could definitely feel the tension in Peggy's hands and sense something wrong. He whinnied in obvious distress.

"You said if you had the bill of sale and the journal you could make the deal yourself," Peggy said. "Merry can open his lockbox with his death certificate so long as there's a bank officer there to inventory the money and stocks. She can bring the journal and the original bill of sale back here. Those Confederate people may not give you quite so much since the carriage isn't restored . . . "

"On the other hand," I jumped in eagerly, "They may actually prefer it in the original condition and give you more."

She thought about it. "The minute I let you go, you'll call Amos Royden."

Damn straight I would.

"And leave Peggy as a hostage? I don't *think* so. Once you

have the journal and bill of sale, you don't have any reason to hurt us."

As if. Surely she wouldn't believe we were that dumb. On the other hand, she'd backed herself into a corner by coming here. Either she let me go, or she forfeited any chance of getting the money to pay her taxes.

We were trapped in a corner with her. I would not leave Peggy. There was nothing to prevent Imogene from blowing her away the minute I drove out, then waiting for me to come back so she could blow me away as well. In her view, nobody would suspect her. Everyone thought she was sitting peacefully at home with no car keys.

But my own pistol still lay in the center console of my truck. Once I was in my car, I should be able to sneak it out. I might not be able to kill a bear, but I was damn sure mad enough to kill *her*.

"All right," she said. "Go on right this minute. If you tell anybody, if I so much as hear a car start up the drive in the next hour, that's not enough time, and I'll know it's not you. I swear I'll shoot first and ask questions later. I don't have much to lose."

"I can't leave."

"What?"

"You nearly hit the horse and carriage when you drove in. I can't possibly get my truck past without backing him out of the way."

"So back him." She waved the gun at Peggy.

"I don't know how," Peggy said. "We were practicing going *down* the driveway, but I can't back him up." *Thank you, Peggy. You pick up fast.*

"Then *you* do it," Imogene said to me. She sounded exasperated. "I am losing my temper. Maybe I should shoot the horse."

"No!" Peggy and I shouted together.

"You shoot the horse, you really will block the driveway," I said. "He can't back up if he's dead."

"You," she waved the gun at Peggy. "Get down from there. You," she pointed at me. "Back him up and go to the bank."

"Stay where you are," I whispered to Peggy as I walked over to her. "Look behind her."

Don Qui poked his nose around the barn. That whinny must have alerted Don Qui that all was not well with Heinzie. He'd finally worked his way out of his stall and come to find him.

He had already stomped Imogene the way he stomped me, so he was predisposed not to like her. And she stood between him and Heinzie.

I put my hand on Heinzie's halter. "Back!" I shouted as loud as I could. Instead of backing him, however, I pulled him forward toward the driveway.

Don Qui thought Heinzie was about to desert him again, and that woman stood between him and his beloved.

He galloped toward her, and at the last minute twisted and let fly with both hind hooves.

She shot forward like she'd been fired from a cannon. The gun fired, but her shot went wide. The pistol flew out of her hand and landed in the shrubbery.

Closer to her than my truck was to me.

Her ignition key flew even farther. She landed on her face in the gravel.

Heinzie woke up.

I jumped into the Meadowbrook. "Go!" I shouted to Peggy.

"*You* have to drive. I can't handle this!"

I could see Imogene scrabbling around searching for the gun. We had to get away *now*.

Peggy shoved the reins at me.

"I can't. I haven't driven . . ."

"Damnation, Merry, drive or die! I'll kill us as surely as her bullets."

She had a point.

"Trot on!" I shouted. Obligingly Heinzie trotted off down the road toward the highway. I heard the patter of tiny hooves behind me. Don Qui was following, bound and determined not to let Heinzie out of his sight.

We'd never beat that lunatic woman at a trot. I grabbed the whip from Peggy, flicked the reins against Heinzie's rump, popped him on the shoulder and shouted "yah" at the top of my lungs.

Startled, Heinzie lifted his head and took off. Dick Fitzgibbons swore Heinzie was lazy. He was wrong.

I could no longer hear Don Qui's hooves over the noise we

were making, but I felt certain he was galloping down the driveway after us.

"Come back here!" Imogene howled.

"No way, witch!" Peggy yelled back at her.

"Hold on tight and swing your weight to keep us on the road." I flicked the reins. "Move, dammit!"

I hadn't touched reins in twenty years and all of a sudden I was hurtling down the side of a mountain with a crazy woman behind me.

Peggy clutched the wooden fender over the wheel for dear life. Just like my mother. This time, if I screwed up, I'd send all of us crashing down the side of the hill.

The wheels slid toward the edge of the road. A moment later something whined by my ear and I heard a pop.

"She found the gun!" Peggy screamed.

"Get down," I shouted.

Heinzie bounded around the right hand curve, where Imogene couldn't see us. The left wheel scraped hard against the shrubs and trees. A branch lashed my forehead. It stung like hell. Blood dripped down over my eyebrow and into my eye.

I took the reins in my right hand to dash the blood out of my eye and saw we were heading straight for the edge of the cliff.

I hauled on the left rein, and Heinzie whipped us around the curve with one wheel in the air.

"When we get down to the road, I'll swing left and stop. Jump out and yank loose the traces and tugs on your side. I'll get the left."

"We can't stop!"

"We can't outrun her in the carriage on pavement. Once we pull Heinzie free, we can ride him double."

"What? I can't . . . "

"Yes, you can. She can't drive a car down a deer path. Heinzie can take us into the trees out of sight. Left! Now!"

The carriage hit a rock, and for a moment we went airborne. We hit hard enough to jar my kidneys into my skull, but Heinzie didn't miss a step.

I could see the break in the trees between the two big boulders where the driveway met the pavement.

I stood on the brake and prayed.

Heinzie slid down the last dozen feet on his haunches, then

swung left onto the road. The carriage rocked but stayed upright.

Don Qui slid into the back of the carriage and brayed in rage.

"Whoa, horse! Out! Now!"

Peggy leapt out, yanked the trace and tug on her side loose. I looped the reins around my forearm, something no one in their right mind should ever do unless they want one less arm, yanked the harness loose, and dragged the cart back far enough to free Heinzie. "Listen," Peggy whispered. "She's coming."

A car growled and squealed behind us.

"Climb on in front of the saddle," I said.

"How would you suggest I do that?"

"Put your left foot in my hands, grab hold of the hames and swing yourself over his back. Then grab my shirt and pull me up."

"I can't."

"You damn well *will!*"

I doubted Heinzie had ever felt a human being on his back, much less two. I prayed he was too tired to buck.

The growl of the car grew louder, coming faster than I thought she could.

"You take Heinzie," she whimpered. "I'll hide in the trees with Don Qui."

"Foot, dammit!" She stepped into my hands. I tossed her up so hard she nearly went all the way over Heinzie's back to land head first on the pavement.

I scrambled onto the nearest boulder and swung onto Heinzie's back and clamped my legs around him.

"I'll never stay on," Peggy cried.

"Grab the balls on the hames." I kicked Heinzie off with the extra rein length dragging behind us, praying that Don Qui wouldn't get tangled in it and yank me off onto the road.

"We have to call Amos." Peggy's voice bumped up and down with Heinzie's trot.

Ahead of us the highway veered to the right. If we could put that curve between us and Imogene, we could plunge off down the mountain at the first break in the trees and call Amos from cover.

I peered back over my shoulder. Don Qui was managing to

keep up.

Imogene's elderly sedan roared like a 747 on final approach. At the road, she'd have to stop, get out of her car, pull the Meadowbrook out of her way and climb back into her car before she could chase us again. The light cart wouldn't hold her up for long, but with luck, by the time she had the road clear, we'd be out of sight down a deer trail.

Imogene must have been doing fifty when she saw the cart and stood on her brakes.

Too late. She crashed it dead center.

It exploded into kindling. One of the wheels flew a dozen feet into the air straight at us. Wood shards rained down around us.

The wheel hit the ground, bounced, rolled past Heinzie and into the trees.

That did it for Heinzie. He spun away. Peggy keened and clutched the hames.

I hauled hard on the reins to stop him and watched in horror as Imogene's car went airborne, sailed across the road and crashed down the mountainside on the other side.

Maybe Imogene screamed. Peggy and I sure did. Don Qui let out a bray of triumph.

The screech of tearing metal and the snapping brush seemed to go on forever.

Then silence.

Imogene couldn't chase us any longer. At least not in her car.

I slid off, handed Peggy the reins and ran back toward the spot Imogene went over. "Take Heinzie. Call Amos," I said over my shoulder.

"She's got a gun! Stay here."

I didn't think Imogene was in any condition to shoot, but I ducked behind a tree just in case. I risked a look back. Peggy had her cell phone in one hand and Heinzie's bridle in the other. She was leaning against his shoulder as they walked side by side. Hard to tell at this distance, but I think they were both shaking.

Don Qui, on the other hand, was munching clover on the shoulder of the road.

I kept the trees between me and Imogene's path of

destruction. Her car hung twenty feet down the hill with its nose accordion pleated around a pine and its rear end hiked in the air. Its tires spun, and smoke drifted lazily from under the hood.

I couldn't see Imogene behind the remains of her air bag, but all four doors stayed closed. No way she could have climbed out that fast and ducked out of sight. She must still be inside.

Alive? Conscious? Still armed?

Still murderous?

Cars seldom burn in real accidents the way they do in movies, but that smoke under the hood scared me. Did I dare work my way down to the car and take the chance that Imogene was hunkered down in the front seat waiting to shoot me?

"Amos is already on his way," Peggy called. "Come back here!"

"I've got to get her out."

"No, you do not! Get back here or I'll come down and get you."

"You have to hold Heinzie." I slid down in the underbrush, while I prayed any snakes in the area had been scared away.

I dropped low behind the car and peered over the trunk. I couldn't see Imogene.

When I touched it, the car rocked. The pine tree against the hood was the only thing holding it. If it gave way, the car would slither all the way to the bottom of the valley and possibly cartwheel.

The car rocked a couple of inches and slid forward. I thought I heard a groan. "Can you open your door?" I asked.

Behind me I heard sirens. Car doors slammed. Man, that was fast.

"Merry, get back up here!" Geoff's voice. "Now."

"The car's going to catch fire. I can reach her."

Branches whipped behind me. A moment later someone grabbed the back of my collar and yanked.

"Hey!" An arm clamped around my waist. I recognized Geoff's scent even as he hauled me summarily up the hill like a sack of potatoes. My feet scrabbled for purchase in the damp leaves. "Let me go."

"Then climb."

"All right!" He released me and I twisted to look up at him.

"She has a gun."

"Great." He shoved me past him. Amos slid down beside us. "Gun," Geoff said.

Amos rolled his eyes. Both men unholstered their guns.

When I reached the road, I ran to Peggy and Heinzie and wrapped my arms around both of them. Heinzie whuffled against my neck. He was so foamed with sweat he looked like a black and white pinto.

"He's still blowing," Peggy said.

His sides heaved with exertion. "Poor baby. Good boy."

"The Meadowbrook's toast."

We moved Heinzie to the shoulder as an ambulance pulled up. For a horse with issues, he had performed magnificently. If Dick Fitzgibbons was willing to sell him, I intended to buy him. And Don Qui, of course.

Somehow, possibly from sideswiping the same bushes I had, he'd managed to peel a four-inch swath of skin and hair off his left shoulder and split his ear. Blood dripped down onto his shoulder. "Good boy," I said over and over as I stroked his sweaty neck. "You saved our lives up there. If you hadn't kicked her, we'd never have gotten away." He ignored me and kept right on eating.

Peggy turned me to face her. "No, Merideth Lackland Abbott, *you* saved us. You drove that horse like a Roman chariot racer. Don't you ever, ever again say that you can't drive. You *did* drive and you *will* drive."

"This was different."

"Different, schmifferent! You drove that horse brilliantly."

"I could have killed us."

"But you didn't."

"It was Heinzie, not me."

"Bull hockey. Heinzie trusted you, even if you didn't. It is time you cut out all this nonsense. You have a driving barn to run, horses to train and a career to forge."

"The last time . . . "

"I do not care what happened the last time."

I considered telling her about my inglorious attempt to drive Golden Boy, but that could wait. Instead, I said, "I refuse to drive marathons."

"Fine. Drive dressage. Teach *me* to drive marathons. Teach

Ida, teach Louise, teach the entire Garden Club and Sandi and Mutt and Geoff Wheeler. Teach Eula Mae, for pity's sake. She's over a hundred, but she drove mules in her younger days. Get yourself up in the box and show them how it's done."

"What if I hurt someone again?"

"Go take some classes with the experts and get your nerve and your skill back. Merry, you are not seventeen and mad at your father any longer. You are a grown woman. He gave you back your life. Don't you dare turn your back on him."

Chapter 34

Easter Sunday
Merry

The weather Easter Sunday was perfect for riding in a carriage around Mossy Creek.

Hank Blackshear had wanted to keep Don Qui overnight at the clinic to be certain he wouldn't tear the stitches in his ear loose, but I wanted him in his own stall across from Heinzie. It was the least I could do. The Bible says something like, "Greater love hath no man than this, that a man lay down his life for his friend." Don Qui would have done just that for Heinzie. Peggy and I simply received collateral benefits.

I wouldn't separate them again. Dick agreed to let me have the pair for much less than he'd paid for Heinzie. After all, he couldn't show Heinzie with Don Qui perpetually in tow, and I didn't *want* to show him, simply use him to teach.

Since we'd duded Heinzie up with red ribbons and rosettes in his mane, we had to do something to dude up Don Qui. He was already annoyed about the stitches in his ear, but we managed to wind red ribbons through his halter and attach a single rosette to his tail without getting stomped, kicked, or butted, then attached a lunge line to his halter to keep him with us, although I didn't think he would leave Heinzie for an earthquake.

The Mossy Creek children loved all over him. I held my breath, but he accepted the attention with dignity.

As the rides were about to start, I hugged Peggy. "You'll do fine."

"No, I won't," she said. "Get up on that box and take the reins. Dick's here to keep you out of trouble."

After I settled down, I even let Geoff sit on the box beside me while Peggy and Dick drank iced latte in the square. They had taken to one another as soon as they met. "How'd you get out to the farm so fast?" I asked Geoff.

"We were already on our way." He told me about his interview with Darnell.

"She seemed so nice at the funeral home," I said.

"Long practice. When we saw that tax notice, we realized she had even more motive than Tom did for getting that carriage back. We figured she might be headed to your place to try to get some money out of you. We were nearly too late."

"You got her out of her car before it burned," I said.

"Too close. Next time, leave the detecting to the professionals."

"What did *I* do? I didn't figure out she did it until I saw that bruise on her foot and realized she'd been to the hill recently."

"What would you have done if Don Qui hadn't taken her out?"

"Tried to reach my gun to shoot her."

I clucked to Heinzie and moved him around the corner of the square. Don Qui pattered along beside us.

"You're serious."

"Damn straight I'm serious. I wasn't about to leave Peggy alone with her."

We were now our last tour. Amos and Ida knew how to relax. The kids had been a handful.

I scratched at the stitches that closed the cut on my scalp. My bandaged hands in their heavy driving gloves were starting to burn. I pulled up beside Dick and Peggy to let Amos and Ida out. I'd already acquired appointments with several new students.

"Can you do Memorial Day?" Ida asked as she climbed down.

"The town'll pay you, of course," Amos said and dug Ida in the ribs.

She glared at him. "But not much."

"We'll see," I said. Of course we'd do it. I wasn't certain when *I* had become *we*, but from here on, Peggy was part of the equation.

Peggy and Dick took Heinzie, Don Qui, and the equipage back to the farm, fed and buttoned up for the night, then picked up cheeseburgers and fries for dinner.

Geoff and Amos came by for coffee.

"Imogene just confessed," Geoff said. "Against her lawyer's advice. Actually, she seems proud. Said that'll teach us to ignore old ladies." He grinned. "She gave me the finger and said, 'tell *that* to AARP.'"

"Yeah," Amos said. "She says she'd rather spend her remaining years in prison than in some nursing home where her son and his wife can visit her every Sunday. In prison she can keep them off her visitor's list."

"She's never been in a Georgia women's prison," Geoff said.

"Probably won't ever see the inside of one either," Amos said. "Her lawyer's already talking senile dementia, Alzheimer's, mini-strokes. Diminished capacity. She may wind up in a nursing home after all."

"Diminished my Aunt Fanny," Peggy said. "Why did she bury Jacob?"

"She figured the longer the body was buried before it was discovered, the harder it would be to figure the time of death. She must have thought the manure pile would speed up the process," Amos said.

"She was wrong," Geoff said. "She ought to watch more CSI."

"So what happens to Ken and the governor?" Peggy asked.

"If that water report ever sees the light of day, Ken and the governor will swear they weren't trying to suppress the report. Oh, no." Amos rolled his eyes. "They merely wanted to clean up their side of the site before they released it. No way did anyone threaten Hiram or offer him a bribe."

"And the state will go along with this?" Peggy asked.

"You bet."

"So the governor slides by again, and so does that snake Ken."

"Not so," Geoff said. "Either the governor and his cronies will have to clean up the water table and remove the polluted soil, which will cost a bundle. The one thing the Gov hates more than Mossy Creek is losing money on one of his real estate deals."

"Wait until all the Gov's buddies take their fancy riding crops to Ken's backside," Peggy said with a laugh.

The stitches on my forehead pulled. Since I'd driven Heinzie down that hill without gloves, my blistered fingers felt as though they'd been burned with a blowtorch. I had a big lump on my rear end from a massive penicillin shot and a feverish lump on my shoulder from a tetanus shot.

But I was alive. So were Peggy and Heinzie and Don Qui. "I would kill for a massive shot of morphine," I said. "The Tylenol definitely does not cut it."

"What you need is rest," Peggy said. "We'll get out of here and leave you alone."

"I'm sticking around for a couple of days," Dick said. "You're going to need help." He smiled at Peggy. A glowing smile.

Ooooo-kay, was something developing there? Since his wife died, Dick had squired rich, multi-tucked Palm Beach widows around, but nobody serious.

"I'll send you one of my guys until you hire somebody," Dick said. "I called Fergus Williams. He's bringing down his two year olds for you to train *here*. He knows you can't come up to his place after the show."

I had forgotten I had a show to manage in less than a week!

"I can handle things while you're gone," Peggy said. "If you trust me."

"I'd trust Benedict Arnold if he said he'd look after the horses while I'm away," I said. I could feel my eyes drooping.

I saw Peggy give Amos a look. He glanced at Geoff and said, "I'm going out to Ida's. You gonna come by and finish the reports before you leave tomorrow?"

I jerked awake. Of course he'd leave tomorrow. Geoff lived in Atlanta and worked all over the state. Still, I felt bereft. I thought we were making a connection. Apparently, he didn't agree. He followed the others. At the door he said, "You plan to stay here, run the place?"

"For now."

Suddenly, I was back in the full time responsibility business with a vengeance. Instead of running a house, tending to a husband and a child, I was tending to forty acres, and if not a mule, at least a donkey. And I felt good.

I didn't realize until I came to Mossy Creek how totally alone I had been for as long as I could remember. I didn't dare love anyone enough so they could hurt me. That included Allie, Vic, and my mother. I had tons of acquaintances. Friends? Not so much. Heck, I didn't even own a cat!

Geoff strode across to me. "Atlanta's not that far," he said.

"Try to stay out of trouble." Then he leaned down, took my face in his hands, kissed me soundly, executed a military turn that would have done a West Point cadet proud, and strode out.

Oh, well. The chances of my seeing Geoff again were slim. What were my chances of running into murder again?

Acknowledgements:

Thanks to Sam Garner, who trained my driving horse, Azora, known as Zoe the Tank, to drive, then trained me to drive her. Thanks also to Johanna Wilburn and her good-natured Welsh pony, Classic, who brought me back up to speed after a driving hiatus, and to Beverly Hollingsworth, my driving buddy. Thanks also to the Nashoba Carriage Driving Association and its members for telling me great stories and giving me excellent advice. Everything that I got right is thanks to them. Everything I got wrong is my own fault.

Finally, thanks to the Belles: Debra Dixon, the world's best editor, Sandra Chastain, Deborah Smith and Martha Shields. Finally, for Maureen Hardegree for keeping me up-to-date on the doings in Mossy Creek.

I had a great time writing *The Cart Before the Corpse*. I hope you have fun reading it.

Lots of love,

Carolyn McSparren

Other Cozy Mystery Series From Bell Bridge Books

Daphne Martin, Cake-Decorating Detective
By Gayle Trent

"I didn't poison Yodel Watson with a layer cake, even if she *was* the meanest gossip in Brea Ridge, Virginia."

In MURDER TAKES THE CAKE, cake decorator extraordinaire Daphne Martin has to clear her name – and her baking reputation. In the sequel, DEAD PAN, Daphne's confections are once again under suspicion when a neighbor dies after eating her cake at a party.

Coming soon: KILLER SWEET TOOTH. Daphne's peanut brittle is deadly, sure, but did it kill the local dentist?

Dixie Divas: Southern, Socialites, Sleuths
By Virginia Brown

When Trinket Truelove and her best friend, Bitsy, find Bitsy's ex-husband dead in a closet, Bitsy is the prime suspect. But the DIXIE DIVAS never let a friend down, and they're determined to find the real culprit. Armed with wit, sass, great designer shoes and margaritas, these Southern cougars are on the prowl with merriment and crime-solving on their to-do list.

Coming next: Book Two, DROP DEAD DIVAS and Book Three, DIXIE DIVA BLUES.